"It's time to look at things from a new perspective."

"A lot of time has passed," Rosie agreed coolly, "but my perspective remains the same. I lost my brother, my father and our baby in the space of a week, and you…" The anger turned to pain for an instant, but she tossed her head, seeming to shake it off. Being angry at him was apparently more comfortable than hurting. "You left me."

"You drove me away," Matt corrected.

"I had lost…three of the most important people in my life!" Her voice rose. "Did you expect me to be the same perky little debutante you married?"

"Of course not. I just wanted you to remember that I was there to offer support, comfort, a way back. But *you* didn't want to come back."

Dear Reader,

I'm a great lover of Christmas and all the warm and cozy rituals that surround it. This story incorporates them, but against a backdrop of old grief, the threat of danger and a husband and wife who loved each other more than anything until tragedy drove a wedge between them.

Even against those odds, love conquers all. And when this happens at Christmas, emotions are heightened and the joy is even greater.

Read all about it!

Happy holidays!

Muriel Jensen

The Man under the Mistletoe

Muriel Jensen

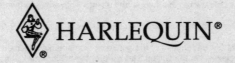

HARLEQUIN®

TORONTO • NEW YORK • LONDON
AMSTERDAM • PARIS • SYDNEY • HAMBURG
STOCKHOLM • ATHENS • TOKYO • MILAN • MADRID
PRAGUE • WARSAW • BUDAPEST • AUCKLAND

ISBN 0-373-71246-4

THE MAN UNDER THE MISTLETOE

In loving memory of my brother, Matthew Charbonneau, called home much too soon. I will always remember kitchen chairs lined up in a row as we played Rocky Jones, Space Ranger; Necco Wafers candies used for Holy Communion when we played Mass; and, when I was eight and he was twelve, flying down the Dean Street hill on the handlebars of his bike in complete confidence that he would get us safely to the bottom. Love you, Mattie.

Don't miss any of our special offers. Write to us at the following address for information on our newest releases.

Harlequin Reader Service
U.S.: 3010 Walden Ave., P.O. Box 1325, Buffalo, NY 14269
Canadian: P.O. Box 609, Fort Erie, Ont. L2A 5X3

PROLOGUE

ROSIE DEMARCO SAT opposite Jackie Whitcomb at a table for four in the Breakfast Barn's meeting room. The restaurant was the heartbeat of Maple Hill in western Massachusetts. In this first week of December, a waitress and two busboys were hanging paper snowflakes from the light fixtures.

Also at their table were Molly Bowers, a florist, and Adam Bello, who owned Bello Automobile Agency.

"So that's about it, Jackie." Rosie pushed away her half-empty plate and consulted her notes one more time. "Maple Hill's Industrial Growth Committee is officially reactivated, and all because Molly and Adam and I were at the same table at the fall festival dinner and got to talking about the health of business in this town. Molly has served on the committee before, but this is Adam's first time."

Adam smiled enthusiastically. He was young and personable. "We could use a little clean industry here to bring in jobs and give us more to depend on than tourism."

Jackie, Maple Hill's mayor and a descendant of

one of the town's founding families, was a lively red-head with a genuine devotion to the community. She spread her hands, her smile taking in everyone at the table. "That's great news. And you think Tolliver Textiles is willing to try us again?"

Rosie nodded. The company had been considering a move to Maple Hill from Boston two years ago, but circumstances had conspired to defeat the plan.

"I spoke to the new president of the company yesterday," Rosie told her. "They'd moved to a temporary space in an old mill on the Charles River when the last deal fell apart. He's anxious to get out of there, but we both agreed that the holiday season is a bad time to talk about it. Everyone is too busy. He's coming to Maple Hill right after the new year to talk to us in person."

"And we have a new location for him to consider," Molly said. She was a full-figured blonde in her mid-fifties who, not surprisingly, always smelled of flowers. "There won't be any environmental surprises like the last time when we discovered a heron rookery that was missed on the impact statement. I wish Dennis Sorrento could join us again, but he's had a few health problems and he's trying to scale back."

Dennis was a pharmacist who'd been an important part of the committee's first incarnation.

"That's too bad," Jackie replied. "But you sound as though you have a good handle on what you're doing, Rosie. Maple Hill has a reputation for sound business while maintaining its beautiful surroundings. Just keep that in mind."

Rosie nodded. "Haley's joined the committee, but she can't meet with us until January. She has her hands full with the special holiday-shopping edition. A good thing for the publisher of the *Maple Hill Mirror*, but not necessarily for the wife of a busy lawyer and the mother of a toddler."

Jackie rolled her eyes. "My niece is a wild child." Jackie was Haley Megrath's sister-in-law, and little Henrietta's aunt and godmother.

"I've seen her in action." Rosie reached into her purse for her wallet. "But my point was that with Haley on board, we'll be secure in the knowledge that our every move will be monitored." Haley was famous for taking on anything or anyone she considered a threat to Maple Hill financially, ecologically or in any way at all.

"Well." Jackie consulted the bill and took out her own wallet. "Your committee has my blessing. Keep me informed."

"We will." Rosie glanced at her watch, then smiled at her companions. "I've got to go back to my shop. Last fitting on my sister's wedding dress this afternoon."

As the group stood to go their separate ways, the lone occupant of a corner booth watched in angry disappointment and thought, *So Rosie chose to ignore my warning. Something will have to be done....*

CHAPTER ONE

ROSIE FLUFFED the tea-length hem of her younger sister's wedding dress and stepped back to get the full effect. One hand on the louvered door of the dressing room, she assessed the lace draped over Francie's impressive bosom, cinching her slender arms and tiny waist, fluttering around her ankles as she did a turn.

With Francie's blue hair and pierced eyebrow, she was hardly an ad for Vera Wang, but she did sparkle. And she looked happy.

"The alterations are perfect," Rosie said. "The dress is as beautiful on you as we knew it would be. What do you think of the muff?" A soft, faux-fur material, it matched the band of the hat she'd chosen. "Gives it all a Christmassy look, don't you think?"

Francie nodded at Rosie's reflection in the mirror. "I love it. Mom?"

Sonja Erickson, "Sonny" to friends and family, squeezed into a corner of the built-in bench, looked as though she had an appointment for cocktails at the Polo Lounge even though she was three thousand miles away in a tiny dressing room in snowy Maple Hill, Massachusetts.

The light blue gaze she cast over the dress revealed nothing. Then she sighed—a sign that she knew her opinion wouldn't be well received so she would keep it to herself. "It's very pretty," she said. "Very pretty."

Francie closed her eyes—a sign that after twenty-three years of dealing with her mother's criticism, she still let it get to her.

Rosie tried to distract Francie by reaching for the veiled hat she'd selected to go with the dress, but she was too late.

"It's the hair, isn't it?" Francie demanded, turning with a swoosh of taffeta to glare at her mother. "I told you it's staying blue. Deal with it, Mom!"

"I'm dealing," Sonny replied with a calm smile.

Rosie had always admired that her mother could do that—react to shrieks of anger and frustration like an amused goddess. She was the composite of a fifties upbringing that forbade expressing displeasure, and a talent for making everyone around her somehow pay for what she was feeling but couldn't show.

At last she heaved a long-suffering sigh. That meant all bets were off. Her mother would say what was on her mind.

"It's the eyebrow ring I'm worried about." She stood gracefully, still fashionable at fifty-seven in a classic suit. "What if your veil gets caught in it? Will there be blood everywhere? Will you need plastic surgery? What personal statement is worth ruining your wedding day?"

"It's not a statement of anything!" Francie screamed. Blue hair did not flatter a purple face. In the little room, the sound of Francie's voice ricocheting back and forth took on a physical force. "It's who I am, that's all. It's me!"

"Mom, Francie," Rosie pleaded quietly. "I have other customers…"

"You were *not* born with an eyebrow ring!" Sonny shouted back. "Believe me! I'd have noticed during my thirty-seven hours of labor!"

"Oh, God." Francie put both hands to her ears. "If you regret having me so much, why did you do it? You already had two beautiful overachievers!"

"I do *not* regret having you!" Sonny said heatedly. "But there are moments when I regret letting you live! I'll be in the car." She handed Rosie her Visa card.

Rosie pushed it back at her. "Mom, I told you. The dress is my gift to Francie."

Her mother took her hand and forced the card into it. "Don't be ridiculous. You know Happily Ever After will be out of business before spring. You're going to need the money."

That salvo delivered, she left the dressing room. Seconds later the bells over the front door tinkled. Her daughters knew she wasn't going far—she'd brought Francie to the shop, after all, and would be taking her home.

Rosie sank onto the bench.

"Why does she hate us?" Francie demanded.

"Try this." Rosie handed Francie a veiled bowler

hat. "She doesn't hate us. She just doesn't know how to love us."

Francie put on the hat, then tugged the veil carefully down to her chin.

Rosie knew she'd been right about the choice. A standard headpiece and veil would have accentuated Francie's nontraditional hair and piercing. The hat and muff worked *with* them.

Francie nodded at her reflection, her expression softening. She looked at Rosie in the mirror as she played with the veil. "I don't understand. What's so hard about it?"

"I've been working on that for a long time."

"I thought being willing to die for your children was supposed to be instinctive to all mothers."

"Oh, I think she'd die for us. She just finds it really hard to *live* with us."

Francie handed back the hat, then reached behind her to unzip the dress. Rosie stood to help her. "You and I," Francie said moodily, "are never going to make her happy. How do you stand it? She always makes me feel like the last kid picked for the baseball team."

Rosie held the dress with one hand and helped Francie step out of it with the other. "You have to get over the idea that you're responsible for her happiness." She eased the dress onto a hanger. "She's had a rough time, you know? She always looks as though she's got it together, so we expect her to behave that way. But inside, she's more at a loss than she'll let us believe."

Francie made a scornful noise as she slipped into jeans and a red, crushed-velvet sweater. "You're saying she wasn't like this before Jay and Daddy died? I don't remember. Seems like she's been on my case forever."

She watched as Rosie stuffed the skirt into the plastic cover, smoothed it neatly and pulled up the zipper, then asked, "Do you ever wonder about Dad?"

The confines of the tiny room made avoiding eye contact difficult. Besides, Rosie found it hard to lie to the sister to whom she'd explained menstruation, sex and geometry.

Still, she hedged. "About what, particularly?"

Francie shifted impatiently. "About not loving us enough to want to live."

God. Only her family could take an afternoon in a bridal shop and turn it into a Faulkner novel.

"And don't try to put a positive spin on it," Francie went on. "Even you can't do that. Dad was so devastated by Jay's death that he didn't want to live. I mean, think about it. What does that say about you and me, his daughters? Didn't it occur to him that I'd need him to walk me down the aisle one day? Or that you'd have babies who'd need a grandfa—" She stopped abruptly, looking horrified, then spread her arms in apology. "I'm sorry. I didn't think…"

Rosie snatched the dress off the hook and carried it out into the shop, needing to escape the words, knowing she couldn't.

The store smelled of a spicy-sweet carnation-and-vanilla potpourri and she breathed in a whiff of it to reestablish her equilibrium. *This is me,* she told herself firmly. Beautiful things, steady little business, cheerful, grateful clients. *Not the grim confusion my life has been for the past two years.*

"Don't be silly," she said, hanging the dress on a rack behind the counter as Francie joined her. "Women have miscarriages every day and don't expect other people to apologize every time a baby is mentioned. Now. Yes, it bothers me about Dad. He didn't have much time for us, but he adored our brother and there's nothing we can do about that now that they're both gone. So…try to have a little more sympathy for Mom. She played second fiddle to Jay, too. If you worry about Dad not caring enough to stay with us, imagine how *she* must feel."

Rosie reached to the shelves behind her for a hatbox.

"I feel sorry for Chase, too," Francie said, "living out here in the boonies with his grandmother and his aunts." She held the box steady while Rosie placed the hat into the tissue. Their eight-year-old nephew had already suffered more than his share of tragedy. His mother had run off with a group of musicians, and his father had died in a grizzly accident.

"Yeah, well, he's a brave little boy." Rosie put the lid on the box. "You want to take the dress and hat home, or do you want me to keep it for you?" The wedding was only a week away, but Francie's room in the family home still looked like a fourteen-year-old's.

"Keep it, please."

Rosie put the hatbox back on the shelf and slapped a label on it that read, Francie. "I worry about Chase, too," she said. "Fortunately, he has Jay's sunny nature."

"Did you find somebody to help you watch the shop so you can take care of him while Mom's in California with Aunt Ginger and Aunt Sukie?"

Rosie nodded. "It's all handled. I'll move from the guest house into the house while Mom's gone, and Sara will help me with the store if I need her." Sara Ross, a friend since high school, could be depended upon to step in whenever Rosie needed anything. "Now. What else do we need? Slip? Stockings?"

"Rosie?"

"Yeah."

"I have something else to tell you."

Rosie detected something worrisome in Francie's tone. For all her sister's pugnacious need to quarrel with their mother, she'd never argued much with Rosie. They'd been too busy commiserating with each other to fight.

"Francie," she said firmly, reaching into the storage under the counter to pull out a box of stockings, "you're going to be married in a week. It's no time to talk about death or miscarriage or—"

"I wasn't going to." Francie put a hand on Rosie's. Then she drew a breath, raised her eyes to heaven and blurted, "I asked Matt to give me away."

If anything could have made this day harder on Rosie's nerves than it already had been, the mention of her ex-husband was it. Especially as part of her sister's wedding party. Rosie was the maid of honor.

"I didn't ask him to take pictures," Francie continued. "I'm sure he'd do a better job than the photographer we hired, but I just want him to walk me down the aisle." Her fingernails were digging into Rosie's palm. "Please tell me you don't hate me. Please tell me you won't chicken out on me because Matt's coming. Please."

Francie was near tears. She had a theatrical turn to her nature and could call them up at will, but Rosie knew these were genuine. Francie had loved Matt from the day Rosie had brought him home to meet the family. With no father to give her away, she no doubt thought it logical to ask Matt. Their mother had offered to give her away as was often done in fatherless weddings, but despite her rejection of tradition in many aspects of her life, Francie had always been halfhearted about the idea.

Rosie smacked Francie's hand with the box of stockings. "I won't walk out, but I do hate you. When's he coming?"

"Friday. He's…" She avoided Rosie's eyes and added quickly, "He's staying with us."

Oh, good. There was nothing Rosie wanted less than to have the man who'd walked out on her in the darkest period of her life move right back in, even for a couple of days.

"He asked me if I'd asked you first. I told him I had

and that you said it was okay." Francie related the lie with no apparent evidence of guilt.

Rosie nodded. "I'm going to hurt you, Francie, before I kill you. He'd better be on his way home before I move into the house to stay with Chase."

Francie reached across the counter and hugged Rosie fiercely. "I'm sure he will be. He's going to China, you know."

Rosie was more puzzled than interested. "China?"

"He has a contract for a pictorial book. I guess he's giving up newspaper work for a while. He says he wants to travel." Francie glanced at the door. "I've got to go before Mom drives off." She hesitated one more moment to look into Rosie's eyes. "You're sure you're okay with this?"

How could she ever be okay with it? But she was the big sister. She had to be okay.

"Of course," she replied.

"Good. You going to be home for dinner tonight? Afterward, I'm making birdseed bags for the wedding."

"I'll be there."

"Okay. See you then. Thanks, Rosie."

Rosie stepped out into the sunshine to wave her mother and sister off as though the afternoon had been fun, rather than an exercise in anger management. All attempts to spend time together ended that way. She could hardly wait for dinner.

Her mother waved dutifully, the martyred little smile on her face; it was first cousin to the long-suffering sigh.

Rosie watched the dark blue Mercedes drive away and had the same thought that crossed her mind every day. She should move away, get her life together, find out who she was when she wasn't connected to the high-strung eccentrics who made up her life.

But that would leave Chase without an ally now that Francie would be out of the house, and though her mother loved Chase, Rosie knew from experience that that didn't necessarily mean she could help him develop into a well-rounded individual.

Rosie also hated the thought of leaving Maple Hill. Her father had been born here and inherited her grandfather's construction company. Though he'd worked for his *own* company in Boston for many years, the family had spent summers and the Christmas holidays at Bloombury Landing, their family home on the lake. In Maple Hill, in the foothills of the Berkshires, winter, and Christmas, particularly, were spectacular.

Maple Hill dated back to colonial days, and its main street still looked as though a minuteman with a musket might appear at any moment. Most of the buildings built around the town square dated back to that time, or had been rebuilt in keeping with that era's architecture. It was a lively little center of commerce in a picture-perfect setting.

Rosie loved it here. She loved the town's rich history, the press of tourists in the summer, the red and gold leaves of fall, the pristine snow in the winter. Add to that the warmth and comfort of old friendships, and it was a wonderful place to be.

She felt she belonged here. Her reasons were complicated, but primarily, she thought it was because her dreams had been born here. They had died here, too, yet somehow, strangely, that had only strengthened her bond. Right now she existed somewhere between hope and devastation, unable to believe in a future here, but also unable to give up on it.

And—she even hated to admit this to herself—she couldn't quite dispel the feeling that her mother clung to her. Not physically, of course, not with any apparent emotional dependency, but sometimes Rosie heard something in her voice, saw something in her eyes that recalled a long-ago past when things had been different.

Every time it happened, Rosie would chase the memory only to come to a dead end. Then she would tell herself she'd been imagining things, that she and her mother had never been that close. But that look in her mother's eyes said things Rosie felt, rather than remembered, and she couldn't quite dismiss it.

So she had to stay. At least for a while. At least until Gillian Howe of the Runway Boutique got serious about adding wedding dresses to her shop in Springfield just a few miles across the Connecticut River and bought Rosie out.

Then, with money in hand to plan the future, Rosie could think about whether it would be worth it to leave the place where she really wanted to be, to find the woman she really was.

"YO! MATT!"

The frantic sound of a woman's voice was followed by loud rapping on the darkroom door.

"We're developing!" Shorty shouted as he washed the contact sheet. "Don't come in, Jenny!"

Matt DeMarco looked over Shorty's shoulder as the faces of children at a local science fair began to materialize into the neat little squares of the contact sheet that represented every frame on the roll of film. He was fairly sure the *Sacramento Sentinel* was the only newspaper in the West that still developed film in a darkroom. Shorty and technology didn't get along.

"I need Matt!" Jenny shouted.

"Control yourself, woman!" Shorty hung the contact sheet by a clothespin to an overhead line. He pointed a pen to one particular shot, as usual picking out the best one on the roll. It wasn't showy or necessarily dramatic, but a ten-year-old boy's excitement in his science experiment shone from a pair of dark blue eyes. "That's it, Matt. Discovery. Pride. How do you always manage to find the definitive face?"

"I don't *find* it, Shorty. I just shoot what's there."

"Come, now. When you have a fifty-thousand-dollar advance in your pocket, there's no need to be modest."

"Ma-att! I need you! There's a fire at Hudson's Department Store! Top floor completely engulfed!"

"Too bad," Shorty said as Matt snatched his camera off the stainless-steel table. "I thought she just wanted you for a quickie in the news van."

Matt reached for film in an overhead cabinet and headed for the door. "Well, I can always dream," he said with a chuckle, opening the door to a small hallway.

"Come on, Matt, let's go!" Jenny Morrow grabbed Matt's arm and pulled him down a corridor to the back door and the newspaper's parking lot. Matt marveled at her energy. She was out-of-control enthusiasm and mouth.

She was also very beautiful, glossy brown hair flying as she ran toward her Honda.

Matt peeled off toward his Mustang, unlocking the door with the remote as he approached.

She finally realized he'd taken off in another direction and raced to follow. "Why don't I ever get to drive?" she asked, catching up with him. She climbed into the passenger seat as he got in behind the wheel.

The Mustang did zero to sixty in five seconds, shooting out of the parking lot like a thumbed rubber band. It wasn't as though the fire would be out before they got there, but he always wondered what he was missing while he was still on his way.

"You have a tendency to drive where other cars are parked." He braked at the corner and cast her a grinning glance before looking quickly left, then right.

"One time! I hit a parked car one time!"

"It was a police car."

She groaned. "The cop forgave me. Isn't it time you did?"

"It was embarrassing."

"Oh, get over yourself. It's time you trusted me." She put commands into her laptop even as she spoke to him and helped him watch for a break in the traffic. "We've been on stakeouts together, we've barfed at traffic accidents, we've lied our way out of tight spots, we've cried together…"

"When?"

"That story on the children's wing of the hospital. Remember? The little girl with—"

"Oh, yeah." He raised a hand to silence her. Somehow that little girl fighting lymphoma had reminded him of his own child, who'd never even lived to see the light of day. "I remember."

The road clear, he sped off, as much to escape the memory as to take advantage of the opening in traffic. "I'm an important photojournalist now." He faked an imperious air. "I have an image to protect."

Jenny made a scornful sound. "Well, unfortunately for you, my mother believes that. You're invited to dinner again next weekend."

Jenny's mother had designs on him for her daughter. She tried to be subtle about it and failed miserably. Matt and Jenny smiled at her matchmaking efforts, knowing that nothing more than friendship was possible between them. Matt was too reserved for Jenny, and her hyper behavior made him crazy.

He made the turn toward the department store. Smoke and flaming cinders filled the air. She pointed ahead. "There's the police barricade." He pulled over to park.

"Notice how I did that without hitting anything?" he said.

She punched him in the arm.

In the next block fire trucks and hoses were entangled in the street and a crowd of people had gathered to watch the flames. "Please offer your mom my apologies," he said, reaching for his camera, "But I can't go. I'm leaving tomorrow for my sister-in-law's wedding."

Jenny frowned at him. "You mean, the dragon's sister is getting married?"

"Who said she was a dragon?"

"Aren't exes always dragons?"

"I don't know. Rosie's the only ex I have, and she's more of a…" What? he wondered. What described a woman who'd withdrawn so completely he could no longer reach her? "A turtle, I think."

"You mean she moves slowly?"

"No." He shook his head to end the discussion. She didn't get it. But then, he'd been there, and he didn't get it completely, either. He pushed his door open. "Come on before they put the damn thing out."

CHAPTER TWO

"WHAT DO YOU THINK?" Rosie's mother did a turn in her deep pink mother-of-the-bride silk suit. "Imagine silver hoop earrings, a white poinsettia corsage with silver ribbon, and Ferragamo pumps and clutch."

Rosie opened her mouth to tell her she looked spectacular even without the accessories. But she was interrupted by her aunt Virginia, who'd arrived two days ago for the wedding. Known as Ginger to everyone, she'd earned her nickname because of her sharp opinions on everything.

"Very pretty," Ginger said, walking around her smaller, more curvaceous sister. Then she swatted Sonny's backside with sibling familiarity. "But I'm not sure you need two layers of fabric right there where you've always had more than the rest of us. You should have gone for a shorter jacket."

Sonny put both hands behind her and looked over her shoulder, checking her reflection in the mirror over the mantel. She had to walk some distance away before she could see herself.

"It looks beautiful," Rosie assured her, then said politely to her aunt, "We Erickson women are proud of our curves. And the heels will give her more height. She'll look perfect."

"They'll also give her more jiggle," Ginger declared. "You are wearing a shape enhancer, Sonny?"

"A what?"

"A girdle," Rosie translated, then made a point of looking at her watch. "You don't need one, Mom. And aren't you two meeting Camille Malone for dinner?"

The ormolu clock on the mantel chimed six as though in compliance with Rosie's need to get her mother and aunt out of the house—and out of her hair. She had every detail of the wedding under control except for those two.

"We are!" Ginger exclaimed, shooing her sister toward the stairs and the bedrooms. "Hurry up! Let's get changed."

"Relax." Sonny resisted the attempt to hurry her. "Camille won't be upset if we're a few minutes late."

"I want to try to charm her into writing her autobiography," Ginger said, hurrying around Sonny and starting up the stairs. "Old movie stars are hot stuff these days," she said.

"But she's led a very quiet personal life."

Ginger nodded greedily. "But I understand there's a scandal involving her oldest daughter's father."

"Jasper O'Hara?" Sonny asked, clearly puzzled.

Ginger continued up. "He wasn't the father," she said.

"What? How could you possibly know that? You've been here all of two days."

Ginger shrugged. "It's a gift. I know where the stories are and who wants to buy them. I met a woman on the train coming in who knew all about her. She was returning from Christmas shopping in New York. Seems Camille told a mutual friend of theirs in confidence and she told me."

"Some friend." Sonny chased her up the stairs. "You will not ask her about her…" Her voice faded as a door closed.

Oh, no. Camille's daughters, Paris Sanford and Prudence Hale, were Rosie's friends. Rosie knew there were shocking facts about Paris's father that Camille wouldn't want to discuss. Rosie trusted her mother to talk her aunt out of promoting the book idea.

Of course, talking Ginger out of anything was a major undertaking. She's been married at seventeen, divorced at nineteen, married again at twenty-one, divorced five years later—and then married a third time at the age of thirty. She was now divorced again.

The four Chamberlain sisters, of whom Ginger was the eldest, had grown up in Beverly Hills, daughters of a prominent heart surgeon and a gifted cellist. Ginger was now a literary agent in New York City, while the second eldest, Sonny, had given up her plans to study law when she'd married Hal Erickson in her senior year at Princeton. Sukie, or Susan, had been sickly most of her life but thanks to a doting husband, lived comfortably in Palm Springs; Sonny and Ginger planned to visit her together right after the wedding. The youngest sister, Charlotte, had had a brilliant career in music, before dying in a tragic traffic accident when she was only twenty-five.

Rosie still found it difficult to equate the motivated and single-minded mother she knew with the dewy-eyed college senior who'd thrown in her lot to support the brash and ambitious son of a longtime Maple Hill family.

Hal Erickson had built a large, successful construction company in Boston. When his father passed away, he sold his business and took over the helm of his father's Berkshire Construction in Maple Hill. He'd maintained the company's reputation for quality work, got involved in bringing business to the community. He'd been serving his second term on the town's Industrial Growth Committee, and Rosie had been in the middle of her first term, when Jay had the accident. The projects under way at the time were stalled by his death, and Tolliver Textiles had backed out of the deal. The committee had been dormant until its resurrection at the fall festival dinner. She was convinced that if she was staying here, she had to take a hand in strengthening business.

But someone wasn't happy about the plan, according to a message left on her answering machine several days ago. She hadn't recognized the voice and caller ID had been blocked, so she'd just erased the vaguely threatening request that she let the textile plant remain in Boston.

It was impossible to please everyone, but she thought once she had Tolliver Textiles firmly interested in moving to Maple Hill, she'd ask Haley Megrath of the *Maple Hill Mirror* to report on the process of making the project happen from the Environmental Impact Statement on the parcel of land in question, to the construction of the building so that fears were allayed.

Frankly, she was grateful for the challenging project, even though real work wouldn't begin until the new year.

She didn't know how long it took other people to recover from loss, but she suspected she wasn't even halfway there. She kept going because she didn't know what else to do. And she had the feeling that if she stopped or gave up, her mother and sister might flounder with her.

And then there was her nephew, Chase; all he really had was the three of them. She had to keep going.

Rosie went back to the gift cataloging she'd been doing before her mother had modeled the pink suit. A corner of the large living room had been turned into a receiving area and temporary storage. Francie and Derek Page, her fiancé, had opened gifts as they'd arrived, and left the cards in the item or attached to it as Rosie had advised. Now she was being a helpful big sister and making Francie a list for thank-you notes.

"You're sure your services don't include writing the notes?" Francie had said, looking forlornly at the sea of gifts.

Rosie had shaken her head. "Hey, you're the blushing bride. That's your job."

"I'll pay you."

"There's not enough money in the world." When she'd married Matt six years ago, their treasure trove of gifts had looked a lot like this. And she'd written thank-yous in her spare time from Thanksgiving to Christmas.

Matt. She didn't want to think about him, though when he arrived, she'd be forced to. Until then she was going to pretend, just as she'd been pretending for the past year, that he'd never come into her life.

"Aunt Rosie!" Chase raced in, arms wide like the wings of an airplane. "Look! I'm a navy Tomcat!"

"Really." She glanced up from her notes. "You look just like my nephew."

"Is he fast and maneuverable?"

She smiled at his vocabulary. Obviously he was smart, just like his father. "Yes, I believe he is," she replied. "But no one else in our family is an airplane."

"You're forgetting Uncle Matt," he said, circling her again, apparently in a holding pattern.

"Uncle Matt's an airplane?"

"He says he's a cargo bus," Chase said between bursts of jet-engine noises. "'Cause he carries around a lot of stuff inside."

She stared at Chase in surprise as he landed and taxied toward her. She guessed Matt hadn't been talking about freight. "When did he say *that?*"

"Just now. He's parking the car. He said to tell you he was here in case you wanted to hide or something." Chase frowned. "Does he mean like hide-and-seek?"

Rosie was caught somewhere between rage and

horror. Matt was here! After two years of struggling with her bereavement, she was going to have to confront the only other person who'd gone as deeply into hell as she had. Only, he'd surfaced again within months, and hadn't been able to wait for her to resurface, too. And then he'd left.

He wasn't supposed to be here until tomorrow. But…today, tomorrow—what difference did it make? Thanks to Francie, she couldn't avoid him. Sooner or later she had to look into the face that she'd once loved so much but that now would only remind her of the darkest part of her nightmare.

There was a firm knock on the door. Her heart leaped against her breastbone, then sank again, thudding dully. She wanted to take a moment, draw a breath, prepare herself, but Chase was already running to the front door. He had to use both hands to pull it open.

Matthew Antonio DeMarco stood in the oak-framed doorway. He was big, though in her painful memories she'd made him smaller. Long, jeans-clad legs, broad shoulders in a gray tweed jacket over a blue sweater. Dark hair unruly.

Even from across the room, she found it hard to look into his face. But after he affectionately ruffled Chase's hair, his dark eyes sought her. He found her, though she tried to disappear into the spread of gifts. She would have sworn she heard the sound of their eyes meeting—metal on metal—like swords clashing.

"I told her you were here!" Chase said, taking Matt

by the wrist and pulling him into the room. "But she didn't hide. Maybe she doesn't want to play, but *I* do! Want me to go hide and see if you can find me? Huh?"

Matt had always been one of Chase's favorite people. Eighteen months did not seem to have dimmed that affection.

Matt gave him a very adult, guy-to-guy look. "Let's find something to do after I put my stuff away, okay?"

"Okay. Grandma says you're gonna stay in Aunt Rosie's old room."

"Old room?" Matt asked.

Chase nodded. "She lives in the guest house now. But she's moving in here to take care of me when Grandma goes away. Want me to go put the light on for you and check under the bed for monsters?"

That was a duty Matt had done for Chase when he and Rosie had baby-sat their nephew years ago. But Chase prided himself on his bravery now that he was eight.

Matt laughed. "Yes, please," he said.

"Want me to take your bag?" Chase reached for it.

Matt held on to it. "It's pretty heavy. But thanks, anyway."

"Full of all that old stuff you carry around?" Rosie asked. She hated that the first words out of her mouth were snide. She'd wanted to appear cool and remote, not reveal that he could affect her from the moment he arrived.

Chase, already on his way upstairs, hadn't heard her. Matt nodded simply, his eyes turbulent.

Then he smiled politely, like a visiting stranger.

"Hello, Rosie," he said. "Sorry I'm early, but connecting flights from Hartford come in only on Monday and Thursday. I didn't remember that." He walked farther into the room and stopped to look around him. Her mother had redone the living room since he'd left. The formal wallpaper and dark wood he probably remembered had been replaced by soft yellow walls, crisp white woodwork, and floral and ivy patterns in the upholstery and draperies. She'd put away Rosie's father's collection of sailboat models and had her own trinkets set about—Montovani statuary, crystal bowls filled with flowers, a Victorian lady fabric doll Aunt Sukie had made.

"It's sunnier in here," he observed.

"Yes, it is," she had to agree. "Redecorating gave Mom something…something to do." Her mother had insisted, furthermore, on doing the redecorating herself rather than hiring the work out.

Rosie had volunteered to help, grateful for something to do to keep her hands and her mind occupied.

Francie had stayed away as much as possible after their father's and their brother's deaths and Matt's defection. She said the house was like a mausoleum and no amount of paint was going to change it.

Matt focused his attention on her as she replied, and now she pulled herself together. If he was going to be here for a couple of days, she had to find a way to cope.

MATT KNEW that gesture, that drawing up of her leggy height, the aligning of her shoulders, the tossing of her long dark hair and The Look. It was a superior angle of her chin, an imperious expression in her bright blue eyes. She was suppressing emotion in favor of appearing controlled. He hated that she could do that so well.

As she stood there, all graceful, slightly disheveled femininity, old anguish tightening her mouth, anger at him in every line of her body, he wanted to drop to his knees and scream his frustration to the world.

But he'd done that two years ago and it hadn't moved her. And that had been a valuable lesson to him. As much as he loved her, as hard as it was to walk away from all they'd been to each other, she'd dug a hole for herself he wasn't going to be able to pull her out of. He'd had to save himself, or he wouldn't be around to try again to save her. And just before her father's suicide, Matt had stumbled upon information about shady dealings on Hal's part that could have hurt her further. He'd had to get away.

She looked as remote today as she had then, but he had to believe that the intervening year and a half had had some kind of effect on her.

"How's the business doing?" he asked, looking for a topic that didn't relate to family or their relationship. That was difficult. Everything had been so tightly bound together in those days.

"Oh, you know," she said, dropping a pad of paper on what appeared to be a crystal bowl in a nest of tissue. "Sometimes really good, sometimes not so good. Mom's convinced I'm going to be bankrupt by spring.

But I think I just have to have faith in love and romance and the business it's going to bring me."

That remark hung between them like a foot of sizzling fuse. She shifted uncomfortably, obviously wishing she'd chosen her words more carefully. He was tempted to tell her it would have been good if she'd had a little faith in their love and its ability to heal, but instead he smiled politely again, extinguishing the fuse—at least for now.

"Where's Mom?" he asked.

"She and Aunt Ginger are having dinner with Camille Malone tonight. You remember her?" At his nod, she went on. "They just left. Have you had dinner?"

"No, I haven't. Is the Breakfast Barn still in business?"

"Yes. And it's brisk."

"Then I'll put my bag upstairs and go get myself something to eat. Has Chase eaten?"

She shook her head. "Not yet."

"Shall I take him with me?"

She nodded. "I'm sure he'd love that."

He debated the wisdom of inviting her along. It would be foolish to think they could easily pick up the threads of their relationship as it had been before her brother died, before she'd found her father with a .30-caliber hole in his temple, and before the shock of that had caused her to lose their baby. Her rejection of his offer would hurt and pile up behind all the other times since then when he'd tried to touch her, hold her, make her turn to him, only to have her push him away.

But that was part of the reason he was here. He loved Francie like his own sister, and he'd come because she'd asked him. But this was the opportunity he'd been waiting for, a way to walk in under cover of some other mission and assess Rosie's emotional situation and whether he could fit into her life again.

"Want to join us?" he asked intrepidly.

He saw the civility dissolve and the anger come forward in her eyes. "Now, what do you think?"

"I think a lot of time has passed," he said reasonably, "and it's time to look at things from a new perspective."

"A lot of time has passed," she agreed coolly, "but my perspective remains the same. I lost my brother, my father and our baby in the space of a week, and you…" The anger turned to pain for an instant, but she tossed her head, seeming to shake it off. Being angry at him was apparently more comfortable than hurting. "You *left* me."

"You drove me away," he corrected.

"I had lost…three of the most important people in my life!" Her voice rose. "Did you expect me to be the same perky little debutante you married?"

He had to focus on keeping his voice down. "Of course not. I just wanted you to remember that I was there to offer support, comfort, a way back. But you didn't want to come back." He remembered clearly the helplessness that he'd felt then, and that had lived with him ever since. "I know how much you loved Jay and your dad. And I loved our baby as much as you did and would have been happy to be the second most important person in your life. I'd have even dealt with being in line behind your father and Jay if you'd given me some sign you knew I was there."

"You wanted…sex!" She whispered the last word like an accusation.

"I didn't want sex," he said, having a little difficulty keeping his voice calm. "I wanted to make love to you, to remind you that in spite of all the people you'd lost, we were still alive. And that was almost six months after…after that hellish week, and you hadn't touched me or let me touch you in all that time. I was desperate to get through to you, to make sure you knew we could go on if you wanted to."

Her response to that effort had made it clear she didn't want to go on. He smiled grimly and added, "Instead, you slapped me, hard, and told me you never wanted to see me again. I didn't leave you, Rosie. You sent me away."

She looked puzzled, almost as though she couldn't quite remember that.

Chase ran down the stairs, his skinny, lively little body cutting right through the tension. "Aren't you coming up to unpack, Uncle Matt?" he asked breathlessly. "I put the lights on, and Grandma put towels and stuff for you in the bathroom."

"Great." Matt struggled to redirect his attention. He'd known that returning to Bloombury Landing would be hard. He had to pace himself and his emotions. And he was sure it wasn't easy for Rosie, either. "Want to come to dinner with me, Chase?"

"Yeah!" Chase danced along beside him as he headed for the stairs. "Can Aunt Rosie come?"

"She…" He hesitated over an excuse.

"I have to fix something on Grandma's suit for the wedding," she said with a smile for the boy. When her gaze bounced off Matt, it revealed a complex mixture of resentment, suspicion and simple annoyance—a variation of The Look. "You go with Uncle Matt and have a good time."

"Want us to bring something back for you?" Matt pushed, wanting her to know he wouldn't be put off by her efforts to hold him completely at bay.

"No, thank you." Her reply was icy as she picked up her notepad again and looked away.

"Okay." He handed Chase his briefcase and picked up his brown leather bag. "You lead the way, sport. We'll wash our hands and be off. Are chicken wings still your favorite?"

"Yeah! Only now I like the hot ones, just like you! And they don't make me puke anymore!"

Matt followed him upstairs, remembering the time he and Rosie had been baby-sitting Chase and he'd allowed the boy to sample his buffalo wings. When he'd liked them, Matt had bought the boy his own order. Matt had insisted that it was the large banana shake that followed the wings that had made Chase sick most of the night, but Rosie had still blamed him.

Matt walked into Rosie's old room with some trepidation. After they were married, they'd shared this room whenever they stayed over, and there were memories connected to it he was reluctant to explore.

But it was time. He'd tried not to think about her for the past eighteen months, and he'd been successful only a very small part of the time. So he'd pushed away all the good memories and let himself recall only how difficult those six months before he'd left had been. He'd remembered her as stiff and angry and inaccessible.

This room, though, brought back all the delicious times before that when what ultimately happened to them would have seemed unimaginable.

"Nobody stays here now," Chase said, "but Grandma had all the windows open all day so it wouldn't smell funny."

In the old days, he remembered, Rosie's fragrance had been everywhere. A friend who worked in a cosmetics company in Boston had developed a personal fragrance for her and had started, of course, with roses. She'd added a list of spices Matt could never quite remember, but the end product pinpointed her personality to perfection—a soft sweetness with a surprising bite.

Rosie must have been away from this room long enough that it no longer smelled of her, but her stamp lingered all the same. The walls were a terra cotta color, the woodwork a creamy beige. The bed, dresser and desk were light oak, and there were plants in colorful pots everywhere, standing on the hardwood floor, on surfaces, hanging near the curtainless bay window that looked out on to the lake.

A window seat was upholstered in a shell-and-sea-birds pattern in shades of white and gold, and matched a wallpaper border that ran around the room near the ceiling. They'd made love on that window seat one night when they'd stayed up late to watch a meteor shower.

"Grandma put some hangers in here for you." Chase slid open one side of a wardrobe and pointed to the odd assortment of hangers on the rod. "Those fluffy ones are from her closet." He pointed to a padded white silk hanger. "And the wooden ones are from my dad's old closet."

Matt, opening his suitcase on the bed, turned to the boy, wondering if it hurt him to think about his father. But Chase simply smiled and pointed to two plastic hangers. "Those are from my room."

Chase had been only six at the time, and two years was probably like an eternity in the life of a child. He seemed remarkably well adjusted for a boy who'd endured such tragedy and was now growing up in the same house with Sonny.

He was sure Sonny was a good woman. Though she didn't relate to her daughters very well, Francie's free spirit particularly, he had no doubt she loved them. And she'd always been kind and welcoming to him since the first time Rosie had brought him home. But she was the stiff and slightly superior product of a privileged background and a life he guessed had turned out to be less than she'd hoped for.

She had appeared to have everything—beautiful home, handsome and successful children, an intelligent and successful husband loved by everyone. But there was always a certain disappointment in her eyes and in her manner, and everyone who loved her seemed willing to assume the blame for it.

That had always intrigued him. He's been an only child in the most dysfunctional family this side of a Jerry Springer marathon. His father had been addicted to drugs, his mother an alcoholic, and by the time he'd been taken away by the state at fourteen and put in foster care, his father was in prison for armed robbery. His mother died of liver failure not long afterward.

But he'd never felt responsible for his parents' lives the way the Erickson offspring felt responsible for their parents. Maybe it was because he hadn't loved his. He'd wanted to, but neither had been sober or conscious long enough for him to really get to know them well enough to love them. Their bodies had been present, but no mind or heart for him to connect with.

He'd grown up strong and self-sufficient, and mercifully philosophical about coping with the life he'd been given. But he'd been lonely. Sometimes very lonely. Then he'd met Rosie at a party and everything had changed. Life was no longer simply acceptable, but happy, fun, filled with hope. He'd moved to Maple Hill and gone to work for the *Mirror*.

And then he'd lost it all again. He didn't think he was to blame, but he *had* kept secrets from Rosie. When her emotional distance had made it impossible even to talk to her, he'd taken his secrets and left.

The move had seemed like the noble thing to do at

the time, but he'd wondered since if it had really been cowardice.

That was something he intended to find out while he was here.

Matt hung up the few things he'd brought, put socks and underwear in the highboy, then put a pair of dress shoes and his bag in the bottom of the closet.

"What's in here?" Chase asked, handing him the briefcase he'd carried up.

"My laptop," he replied, "and some stories I'm working on." He took the briefcase and placed it beside the bag.

"But that's work."

"Yes. I thought if I needed something to do…"

"But it's Aunt Francie's wedding. Grandma says she's going to work everybody like slaves until it's over." The boy grinned happily. "Then she's going away for a while and Aunt Rosie's going to move in and stay with me until Grandma comes back. We're gonna go to the movies and have pizza and take long walks around the lake. And sometimes she's going to take me to the new arcade."

"Sounds like fun." Long walks around the lake had once been his and Rosie's specialty. They'd identified all the flora and fauna around the lake, had loved spotting any new ones. "But right now I guess it's just you and me."

"That's cool, too," Chase said with enough enthusiasm to convince Matt that he meant it.

At the Breakfast Barn, they found a booth near a window. Rita Robidoux, a redheaded, middle-aged woman who always knew what was happening in Maple Hill and why, brought them menus and glasses of water.

"Well, will you look who's here!" she exclaimed, grinning broadly at Matt. "Prue and Gideon Hale just got back together, you know. And now you just appear like a miracle. Goes to show you love's catching. Where's Rosie?"

"Hi, Rita." Matt smiled into her welcoming face. "That's great about Prue and Gideon. I read that she had a fashion show in Boston. But unfortunately, unlike them, Rosie and I are still separated. I'm just here for Francie's wedding."

Rita nodded skeptically over her order pad as though she knew better. "Yeah, that's how it starts. Gideon came through on his way to Alaska and, well, you see how that turned out."

"That's them, Rita. This is Rosie and me." He shook his head. "So, what's the special?"

"Sirloin tips over noodles, comes with soup or salad and a roll. Or chicken-fried steak. Same deal."

Matt consulted Chase.

Chase handed Rita his menu. "Hot buffalo wings, please, with blue-cheese dipping sauce, and…" He paused and turned to Matt. "It comes with celery, but I don't like that. I usually get a side of coleslaw, but that's extra."

"And a side of coleslaw for my friend," Matt told Rita. "Same for me, except that I like the celery."

She wrote quickly. "Okay. And to drink?"

"Coffee, please. Chase?"

"Banana shake."

"Wait a minute." Matt stopped Rita's hand before she could write that down. He leaned toward Chase and asked quietly, "Are you sure?"

Chase beamed. "I have hot wings all the time and I never get sick. I'm eight now, you know."

Matt noticed the careful wording. "But does Grandma let you have a banana shake with them?"

"Grandma doesn't come here. I come with Aunt Rosie." His beam dimmed. "She *never* lets me have a banana shake. But I'd really like to have one now."

"What if you get sick?"

Chase shrugged his bony shoulders. "Then I'll still have had my two favorite things together."

That was logical and rather profound; he was willing to pay for what he wanted. Matt found it hard to argue with such a sane philosophy.

"Okay. Banana shake," he told Rita.

"Okay," Rita said. "Be back with your drinks in a minute."

"How's school?" Matt asked. Rita returned almost immediately with the coffeepot and filled his cup. "Are you in third grade now?"

"Yes." Chase made a face. "Multiplication tables. Yuck. But art is fun. I made Grandma a bill holder out of paper plates, and I glued a picture of me and my dad on it. She misses him a lot."

Matt looked into his nephew's open face and saw the sadness there. "You miss him, too?"

Chase nodded as he opened out his paper napkin. "Yeah. But Grandma doesn't like to talk about him. Aunt Rosie does, though. Did you know that she used to ride on the handlebars of his bicycle when they were little? You're not supposed to do that, but sometimes they did it anyway 'cause they were late for dinner and only Dad had a bike. Aunt Rosie almost drowned when she borrowed the bike and tried to ride it into the lake."

Matt smiled. He'd heard that story. Water levels had been way down and a precocious seven-year-old Rosie had thought that meant the whole lake was knee deep. "Yeah, your dad told me," he said.

Chase looked pensive for a moment. "Sometimes I miss him a lot, but then it's okay 'cause I loved him very much and he really loved me. Aunt Rosie says not everybody gets that, so you have to be happy that you had it."

"That's right." Matt wondered if that meant she'd come to terms with the losses in her own life or if she was just giving her nephew advice that she knew would help him cope.

Chase's banana shake arrived with a large dollop of whipped cream on top, a little, round slice of banana sticking in it. The boy suddenly lost interest in the conversation.

ROSIE WAS PERCHED on a stool at a small bar in the kitchen, watching the news on a tiny television, when they came home. There was a bowl of cereal in front of her and a cup of tea. She slipped off the stool to give Chase a hug.

"Did you have a good time, Chaseter?" she asked.

"We had dinner," he replied, sending Matt a look that asked him to honor the male code of silence about the banana shake. "Then we went to the store 'cause Uncle Matt forgot his toothbrush." He held up the battery-operated toothbrush with a Nemo figure on the top that he'd exclaimed over and Matt had felt compelled to buy. "And look what I got!"

She admired it, then handed it back. "Cool. You should get to your homework, Chase."

He rolled his eyes and blew air noisily. "But Uncle Matt's only here for two days and I have to go to school tomorrow, then it's the wedding, and then—"

"His room is right across from yours. I'm sure he'll be happy to look in on you and say good night."

"Maybe he could tuck me in tonight instead of you." Chase turned to Matt hopefully.

Matt nodded. "Of course. I'll be in my room working on a story. Just come and get me."

Rosie looked just a little injured, but smiled at Chase when he hurried off. The smile vanished, though, when she turned off the television with the remote and confronted Matt. "You let him have a banana shake, didn't you? I saw that guy look pass between you."

What the innocent Chase didn't know, Matt thought, was that women had long ago broken every code men had developed to keep things to themselves.

"Yes, I did," he replied calmly. "If he gets sick during the night, you'll be back in the guest house and I'll be right across the hall from him. So I don't see that you have anything to worry about."

"Except the very fact that you let him do something you're pretty sure *will* make him sick," she said judiciously.

"He made the choice," Matt argued calmly, "and understood that was a possibility. He said he didn't care because then he'd have had his two favorite things together."

"As the adult…" she countered, drawing closer to him. She did it only in anger, but it revved his pulse, anyway "…you're supposed to help him understand that he should do what's best for him."

"Considering he's an orphan living with a bunch of women who love him very much but are all a little eccentric and overprotective, I thought the momentary pleasure of having hot buffalo wings and a banana shake together was better for him than ordering something sensible."

"You always have made decisions the easy way," she accused.

He was in little doubt what she meant. When she tried to turn away from him to go back to her cereal, he caught her wrist to hold her there. He saw anger flare in her eyes, but he thought he caught a glimpse of something else for an instant. Then it was gone.

"If I made decisions the easy way," he said, holding on to her when she tried to pull free, "I'd have made an excuse when Francie called and asked me to come. But I'm here. I knew you'd take every opportunity to blame everything that happened on me, but I came, anyway."

"I hate you, Matthew DeMarco," she said feelingly.

She looked and sounded completely sincere. But he knew her. He heard that subtle, sad little sound under the harsh declaration, felt the energy in her body drawing her to him even as she tried to pull away.

"No," he corrected. "I don't think you do."

She yanked away from him and stormed off.

He knew her. That didn't mean he understood her.

CHAPTER THREE

IN THE FRONT ROOM of her shop, surrounded by the male members of the wedding party, Rosie studied the fit of their tuxes. Though Derek and his brother had been carefully measured for them, and Matt had assured her in a fax that his measurements for the tux he wore at their wedding remained the same, she wanted to be sure there were no last-minute surprises.

Despite the animosity between them, she could appreciate how wonderful Matt looked in his tux. Not only did he have the ideal broad-shouldered and lean-hipped frame, but his rugged good looks were lent an urbane maturity she didn't remember in him.

On the job, he'd always been rough and ready, no subject too mighty or intimidating to tackle, no detail too small to track down. At home, he'd worn old jeans and sweatshirts while he worked on the house, the lawn, the car. That was what had appealed to her about him in the beginning—he'd been an intellectual with the body of a quarterback.

Francie's groom, Derek, on the other hand, was tall and very slender, and the tux gave a sort of polish to his thin-faced, bespectacled self. His brother, Corin, an inch shorter, more thickly built and five years married, was so cheerful and funny that he'd have looked good no matter what he wore.

"Everyone comfortable?" Rosie asked, walking around them, checking length of sleeves, leg, and smoothness across the shoulder.

"No," Derek complained, pulling on the small bow tie at his neck. "I wanted to get married on the beach in shorts and sandals."

"It's December in western Massachusetts," she reminded him, pulling his arm down to see if she could adjust the tie. "There's no beach and there's snow on the ground. You'd freeze to death."

He tipped his head backward while she worked. "I was thinking in terms of Florida or Hawaii. But Francie thought getting married somewhere else might upset your mother."

"I couldn't have flown to Hawaii, anyway." Corin did a turn in the three-way mirror. "I have a mortgage and pediatrician bills." His many reflections grinned at his brother. "I'm sure you wouldn't have wanted to get married without me."

"True. Ah, that's better." Derek breathed a little easier as Rosie loosened his tie. "I'm sure this is best, all in all. I just hate the fuss, you know?"

"Women are about fuss," Corin said as Rosie drew him forward to stand beside Derek. "You'd better just resign yourself to that now. And once you have children, there's no going back, fusswise."

Rosie tuned out the children remark, refusing to let her brain hold on to it, and did one last walk around the men to make sure everything was perfect. But she was aware of Matt shifting his weight, and when she walked around them to stand back and take in their appearance one last time, she noted the grim line of his jaw, his unfocused gaze.

When she stood in front of him, he refocused on her, and for one split second they looked into each other's eyes. She saw his pain and knew that he saw hers, though she tried not to feel it. But, however unwittingly, they shared the moment.

Then Corin went on about teething and sleeplessness and the moment was gone.

"You all look very handsome," Rosie said finally. "And contrary to what usually happens, your tuxes seem to be perfect fits. Take them with you, but please don't let them get rumpled."

"What time's the rehearsal dinner tonight?" Corin asked. "Katie's excited about a night out without the kids."

"Seven o'clock," Derek replied. "Yankee Inn. Same place we're having the reception, just in a smaller room."

"Right. Okay."

Corin and Derek went back into two of the three dressing rooms. As Matt headed toward the third, Rosie noticed what appeared to be a small split in the seam of one of the sleeves. She stopped him with a hand on his arm. She was so into her wedding-planner mode that she forgot for a moment what touching him might do to her.

As she explored the split seam to see if it went through to the lining, she felt the hard ridge of his shoulder, the warmth through the fabric of the flesh and blood that covered it. She saw the broad expanse of his back, the wiry dark hair at his nape, the shirt's starched, white collar pressing into his neck.

Though he didn't move a muscle, she was suddenly aware of the tension in him. For a moment she couldn't breathe, couldn't think, couldn't speak. Finally, impatient with herself, she dropped her hand from his arm and said a little sharply, "The collar looks tight. It's cutting into your neck."

"Formal clothes are always uncomfortable," he replied quietly, turning to her, her change of mood noted in his eyes. "It's not as though I'll be in the tux that long."

"Still, it doesn't have to be uncomfortable. I'll have a larger one overnighted to the house from Boston. You told me your measurements hadn't changed."

He shrugged. "I've been working out a little, but all my regular clothes fit."

"Yes, well, so many fabrics have stretch and give today that you probably wouldn't have noticed. Just leave the tux in the dressing room so I can fix that small tear." She paused. "Uh, do you remember where the Yankee Inn is?"

"Of course."

"Francie will expect to see you there."

"I'll be there. Want me to drive?"

"I'll be working late, so I'll leave from here. But you can drive Mom, Aunt Ginger and Chase."

He accepted that for the dubious honor it was. "I don't suppose you're going to want to dance with me once we get there."

"No, I won't." She thought she sounded firm, though she was still a little unsettled by his nearness, and surprised that he'd even suggest they dance. "Please save us both the embarrassment of doing anything to make it look as though we've remained friends."

"Then please don't touch me anymore," he said with the same firmness. "And how is it going to look to the wedding guests if we're at war throughout the day tomorrow?"

"We won't be at war," she argued. "We just won't be…in contact."

It wasn't until Derek cleared his throat that she realized he and his brother were standing nearby and had probably heard most of what she and Matt had said.

"Just wanted to say thanks," Derek said quickly, doing his best to pretend they hadn't heard anything. "Anything I can do to take some of the burden off you?"

Rosie was momentarily distracted from Matt by Derek's sweetness. Francie was a lucky girl. "I think everything's under control. Just hang up the tux, and be ready on time tomorrow."

"You got it. See you tonight." Derek and Corin left, and silence fell over the shop.

Matt eased out of the jacket and handed it to her. "I know this isn't the time for it, but I want to sort through what happened between us and try to figure out where we lost each other."

"There's no going back," she said. But she took the jacket from him and clutched it to her. He wondered if the small gesture spoke of what she truly felt but wouldn't allow herself to say.

"I don't want to go back," he assured her. "Believe it or not, there's as much pain there for me as there is for you. But if we put effort into it, maybe there's a way ahead."

He saw the smallest flare of hope in her eyes. Or maybe he wanted to see hope so much that what he saw was merely the reflection of his own hope.

"*You* left *me*," she said. Her free arm closed over the one holding the jacket. She was creating the creases she'd warned against.

"You no longer *wanted* me," he said, feeling a little crazy that she didn't remember it that way. He strained for patience. "You have to stop blaming me for what was ultimately your fault. You hated me, but for what? I didn't do anything. Unless it was just that I was still alive and our daughter and all the other men you loved were dead."

She looked stricken but didn't seem to know how to respond.

"It doesn't get us anywhere to go over that old ground," he finally added. "Let's just agree to talk about it after the wedding."

She met his gaze, then seemed to realize what she was doing to the jacket. She held it in front of her and shook it out in disgust. "I don't want to," she said finally. "Thanks for driving the family to the dinner. I have to go fix this. Excuse me."

He'd been with her long enough to know that when argument turned to polite dismissal, there was little point in continuing. She'd frozen up, turned off. He went into the claustrophobic little room, changed into his own clothes, hung up the slacks, placed all the other accessories on the bench and left the shop.

THE REHEARSAL DINNER was an exercise in charm and good manners. The Yankee Inn had been decorated for the holidays with chunky garlands wound with lights, huge Christmas trees in the lobby and the banquet room, and festive table linens.

All the guests did their best to be amenable. Even the outspoken Aunt Ginger engaged Corin's wife, Kate, in pleasant conversation. Sonny captivated Derek's parents with stories about Francie and the amusing things she and her siblings had done as children.

Francie tried to listen, but Rosie seemed determined to distract her with a brochure featuring all the highlights she could expect to see on her honeymoon in Bermuda. Rosie wore a simple purple suit, her hair loose and full, the sight of it almost more than Matt could bear. She tossed it a lot, and he knew that to mean she was acting. This good cheer was all for Francie's benefit.

The only tense moment of the evening came when Derek's mother asked if Matt's presence at the wedding meant they were together again.

"No," Rosie replied politely. "Matt and Francie have always had a great affection for each other, and with our father gone, he was the logical choice to walk her down the aisle."

Mrs. Page frowned. "Isn't that awkward for you?"

"Not at all," Rosie lied, then tucked her arm in his to prove her point, and walked him onto the dance floor.

He hesitated before taking her into his arms. "I thought you didn't want to dance with me."

She placed her hand firmly on his shoulder. "I don't, but I didn't know where else to take you. I want everything to be perfect for Francie."

"So you keep saying, but what about how things should be for you?"

She seemed surprised that he'd asked such a question. He had to forestall what he was sure would be her response.

"If you say, why should I care because I left you," he warned, "I swear I'll kiss you senseless right here in front of God and everybody."

She took his hand and forced him into a dance attitude. "Then I'd say dancing is the lesser of two evils."

Taking her into his arms was so easy. Her hand on the shoulder of his sports jacket, her fragrant hair skimming his nose, her slender body in his arms. Everything was dearly familiar.

Painful as hell, but dearly familiar.

She did, however, hold herself rather stiffly tonight, when she used to lean into him trustingly, comfortably. She'd always been warm and invitingly physical, even in a crowd, touching him, bumping against him, whispering things to him, her lips and her cheek touching his. He wanted that back with a desperation he struggled not to show.

But he'd been the one to admit there was no going back. They couldn't recapture even the best parts of the old days. They had to find a new way to connect, another method of communication.

He splayed his left hand between her shoulder blades and applied enough pressure to bring their bodies into contact.

"Matthew…" she warned under her breath.

"Relax, Roseanne. It's just a dance. That's all life is. That's all love is."

"I'm not…" She tried to wedge some distance between them, but he thought the effort a little half-hearted, so he held on to her.

He lowered his head until his cheek rested against the side of her temple. "You're still a warm and vital woman. The three most important people in your life may have died, but you didn't. Just let yourself be alive for the space of this dance."

"I…don't want to dance," she complained, but she'd stopped pulling away.

"You led me to the dance floor," he reminded her.

She said in a breathless whisper, "There was nowhere else to go."

He held her closer. "That's right. Until the music stops, just pretend you belong right here."

To his amazement, she did. "Embraceable You" played on, mellow and torchy, and when it was finally over, she drew out of his arms with seeming reluctance. Her eyes brimmed with unshed tears, and all he knew for sure was that she considered him responsible for those tears. That was fine with him, he thought, watching her hurry off the dance floor toward the ladies' room. He'd become familiar with assuming the blame.

FRANCIE AND DEREK'S wedding was as perfectly organized and executed as any major military or political event Matt had ever covered as a journalist. He knew it was a testament to Rosie's expertise that every detail was perfect, right down to the red ornament at every place setting. FRANCIE AND DEREK and the date, had been hand-printed on it in gold leaf.

Matt overheard several women at a table behind where he sat with Chase speculate over why it was, when Rosie could probably be an event planner in Hollywood if she wanted to, that she felt tied to Maple Hill.

"She lost everything here," one of them said. "Her brother, her father, her baby, her marriage. And contrary to popular opinion, you don't run when that happens, you stay and spend the rest of your life trying to figure out what went wrong."

"I think she stays because her mother needs her,"

another guessed. "Sonny Erickson comes on like she knows and understands everything, but I'll bet she's hollow inside since the tragedies. If it wasn't for Rosie, she'd fall apart."

"I think she'll leave now that her sister's moving away next year." That came from a younger voice. "Francie's brilliant, but a little wild. Rosie's been a steadying influence."

"Rosie was just waiting for Matt to come and take her away," a fourth voice said with authority. "She never stopped loving him. Have you seen how she watches him now? There's *greed* in her eyes! I'll lay you odds—"

"Shh!" One of the other women, probably recognizing the back of his head, stopped her abruptly. Matt heard mad whispering, a giggle, a groan of regret. Ordinarily he might have been annoyed at being the object of gossip, but he was happy to hear that last opinion.

"Aunt Francie looks beautiful!" Chase said, scarfing down his third piece of cake with ice cream. "Even with her blue hair."

"Yes, she does."

"And so does Aunt Rosie."

She certainly did. The raspberry-colored dress clinging to her breasts and waist, and yards and yards of filmy stuff flying out around her, lent color to her complexion and drama to her very presence. Everything was going so well that she'd stopped being the wedding planner and reverted to her role as maid of honor.

He had a sudden flash of memory of when *she'd* been the bride and the sparkle in her eyes had been all for him. That had been an eternity ago.

"Hey, handsome." Sara Ross, Rosie's old high-school friend, sat down between Matt and Chase, looking very glamorous in a plum-colored suit and a broad-brimmed hat in the same color. She patted Chase's hand. "Or should I say, you two handsome men?" Chase preened. "You guys look so cool," she went on. "And I hear you're on your way to China with a hefty advance in your bank account, Matt."

Matt reached for the carafe in the middle of the table to pour coffee into her cup. He remembered her as a smart but plain young woman, not at all the curvaceous beauty she was today. He didn't even remember that she'd been blond. He had to stop himself from staring. "I am," he replied finally. "And what have you been up to? Whatever it is, it agrees with you."

"I'm working for a law firm here," she replied, placing a pink linen napkin on her lap. "And I'm going back to school next term to get a law degree."

"I'm impressed." As he recalled, she'd worked for the city, the hospital, and clerked in several stores. She'd even done a stint in the army, though there was nothing remotely military about her appearance. "Ambition is very appealing in a woman."

Her cocoa-brown eyes widened.

"To whom, exactly?" She heaved a big sigh as she picked up her fork. "I had a life of domestic bliss planned," she said in a jocular tone, "but that doesn't seem to be working out, so I'm making new plans. Smarts and money are my focus now." She winked at him and picked up her fork. "Well, tell me what you've been up to. If Rosie knows, she isn't talking."

They spent half an hour catching up, then Corin and his wife joined them, and by the time they noticed that the crowd was thinning and Francie and Derek were ready to leave for their honeymoon, it was midafternoon.

Everyone collected coats and gathered outside where Francie threw her bouquet. It was caught, ironically, by Sara. The small crowd pressed the bride and groom toward a waiting limousine, but Francie broke free to throw her arms around Matt's neck. "Thanks for coming," she said. Her smile was blinding. Then she grew serious and said for his ears only, "Make this work, Matthew. Get her back." Then she kissed him noisily on the cheek and got into the car.

They drove off to cheers and applause and birdseed thrown after them. Matt looked for Rosie, but she'd avoided him all day.

"You think I could have one more piece of cake?" Chase asked him, following him back inside.

"No." He did head for the buffet table. "Did you have anything at all substantial today? Ham? Cheese? Deviled eggs?"

Chase made a face. "I thought there'd be hamburgers or hot wings."

"It's a wedding. They have classier stuff." He studied the array of food. "How about some vegetables and dip?"

"How about more cake?"

"No."

Chase looked betrayed. "You sound like Aunt Rosie."

"That's because we love you and want you to be healthy."

Matt finally talked Chase into eating a spring roll by telling him it came with hot sauce. Chase felt honor-bound to try it.

By the time he'd finished two of them and a few carrot sticks, the Yankee Inn's banquet hall was empty of guests and the waitstaff was beginning to clean up.

Sonny appeared, changed out of her elegant pink suit and wearing casual slacks and a faux fur-trimmed black parka. She was still very chic. As Matt stood, she wrapped him in a fragrant embrace.

"A cab's picking up Ginger and me to take us to the airport. You'll be long gone when I return, so I just wanted you to know how good it was to see you again and…" Her smile seemed to falter and that deep sadness he'd often seen in her came to the fore. "And…how much I wish things had turned out differently for you and Rosie."

"So do I." He returned her hug. "I haven't given up yet, though she's not doing much to inspire hope."

"I think you should kidnap her," she said, "and take her to China."

"I'll give that some thought."

Ginger shouted from the doorway that the cab had arrived. Rosie, still wearing the raspberry gown, had pulled her coat on over her shoulders and hurried toward them from the other direction. She and Matt and Chase followed Sonny and Ginger to the cab.

It was almost four and the sun was already low on the horizon. Snow-covered rooftops and church steeples were pink in its glow.

There were hugs all around.

"Do think about what I said," Sonny murmured to Matt as she followed her sister into the cab. She held the door open when the cabbie would have closed it. "I'll be home the night before the community Christmas dinner," she shouted at Rosie. "If anybody needs me for anything, you can give them Aunt Sukie's number. You know Carol Walford. Everything's a crisis!"

"Okay, Mom. Don't worry."

"What's that all about?" Matt asked.

"Mom's giving the welcoming speech at the Revolutionary Dames' annual Christmas dinner on the tenth. Carol Walford is the chair, and Mom swears she wears starched underwear. You can imagine how stiff she is if *Mom* thinks she is." The cabbie closed the door. "I heard her tell you to think about something. What was that?"

"She wants Uncle Matt to kidnap you and take you to China," Chase reported, looking from one to the other.

Rosie gasped indignantly.

Matt brought his fist down playfully on top of Chase's head.

He should have let him have another piece of cake,

then he'd have been too engrossed in it to overhear their conversation. "Just a little joke, Rosie," he said placatingly.

Rosie turned to wave as the cab drove away with the snick of tire chains in the rutted snow. Quiet settled over the parking lot, now empty of cars. The staff still inside were parked in the employee lot in back.

"Like carting me off somewhere would solve anything," she said while she continued to wave. "You and I just aren't…"

Matt heard only part of her assurance that nothing in the world could bridge the chasm between them. His attention was caught by the glint of a slanting ray of setting sun on metal or glass. It had an eerie familiarity. He'd been a soldier during Desert Storm, and he'd covered a year of battles in Yugoslavia before he decided that he missed home too much and gave up being a foreign correspondent.

His brain processed what he saw more quickly than it reeled out the accompanying thoughts. He'd already pushed Chase to the ground when a bullet smashed into the ground between him and Rosie.

Rosie turned at the strange sound, and Matt lunged toward her to knock her to the ground as a second shot rang out.

Something slammed into his upper arm, burning like a branding iron, and knocked him to his knees.

He heard Rosie scream, saw her white and horrified face as she knelt beside him, and thought with perverse satisfaction that he finally had her attention.

CHAPTER FOUR

ROSIE COULDN'T SEEM TO get enough air. Shock, disbelief and horror at the sight of blood spreading on the sleeve of Matt's jacket took control of her body. How could this keep *happening* to her? The bloodstain brought back the memory of the red on the side of her father's face, streaming to his shoulder, the stuff dried on the sleeve of his shirt, congealed on the arm of the chair, in a little pool at his feet, her own backward tumble off the porch.

With that came the wrench of pain in her stomach and the certainty that something awful had happened to the baby she carried. Then there was blood on her legs, on her tennis shoes.

She remembered hearing herself scream and that sound came back to her with all the shrill clarity of the moment she'd made it.

She had a weirdly disassociated sense of having lost the past two years. Every small step she'd made in the recovery of her good sense, in her willingness to go on, in collecting her shredded hopes and dreams and trying to start over was being wiped out.

"Rosie," Matt said, his voice surprisingly strong. "Rosie!" He shook her, then swore, the action probably hurting his wound. "Rosie, come on."

She came back to the present, on her knees facing Matt. She had hold of his arms and he held hers, his fingers biting into her flesh. She'd lost the jacket she'd thrown over her shoulders to come outside and was aware of being cold as she yanked the decorative handkerchief out of Matt's pocket and reached inside his coat to press it to the wound. Nausea rose to the back of her throat. She prayed she wouldn't be sick.

"Chase," Matt said, "put Aunt Rosie's coat back on her shoulders."

Chase, his eyes enormous and terrified, scrambled to his feet.

"Never mind the coat," Rosie told the boy. "Run inside and get my purse. The cell phone's in it. Call nine one one and tell them where we are, and that Uncle Matt's been shot."

"Okay." The boy began to run off, but Matt stopped him.

"Get the coat first," he said calmly, "then call nine one one."

As the boy came back to do his uncle's bidding, Rosie snapped at Matt, "You're bleeding, you idiot."

"And you're freezing, angel voice," he returned. "Stop yelling, okay? I'm starting to get a headache."

The coat had fallen right beside her and Chase picked it up. He placed it on her shoulders, then took off at a run for the inn.

"You okay?" Matt asked, his eyes roaming her face as she held the handkerchief firmly to the wound.

"Of course I'm okay," she retorted. She didn't know why she felt so testy. "I didn't get shot. I swear to God, hunters get more careless every year. Farmers and ranchers have to put red blankets on their cows and horses so they're not mistaken for deer or elk! Pretty soon we're all going to have to wear—"

"It wasn't a hunter."

She'd been rambling and his statement stopped her short.

"How do you know?" she challenged.

"Because somebody aimed at me. Unless he's seen deer wearing tuxedos…"

"How do you know someone aimed at you?"

"Before the first shot, I saw sunlight wink off metal or glass. And I am shot, aren't I?"

She put her free hand to his forehead, certain he was hallucinating. "Matt, don't be ridiculous." She whipped the coat off her shoulder and put it around him. He was starting to look pale and there was blood everywhere. "Who'd want to kill you? And I was standing just a few feet…from…you."

Her denial that he'd been shot lost impetus as she remembered that moment. She'd heard Chase's gasp of surprise and turned to find that Matt had pushed him to the snow. She'd opened her mouth to ask him what he was doing, but he'd been coming toward her, his eyes on something in the trees across the road. Then she'd heard the loud pop, watched his body take the impact that drove him to his knees.

Her brain was muddled with lingering shock and the upsetting sensation of having his warm lifeblood oozing onto her fingers. She was having difficulty thinking this through. But if he'd thought there was a gun out there, and he'd been running toward her—

"You mean…the barrel of the gun was aimed at me?" she asked.

Before he could reply, Chase came running outside followed by Jackie Whitcomb, who, as well as being the mayor, was the owner of the inn. She was carrying a blanket.

"The ambulance is coming right away," Chase said, kneeling beside Matt. "You're not gonna die, are you?"

"No," Matt replied. "I think the bullet just nicked me."

Rosie doubted that. This was a lot of blood for a simple nick, but she knew Matt was trying to allay Chase's fears.

"Good Lord!" Jackie exclaimed, handing Rosie the coat and wrapping the blanket around Matt's shoulders. "Can you stand? Let's try to get you out of the cold."

They had him on his feet and, supporting his weight, they'd taken several steps toward the inn when the sound of a siren split the air.

"Here comes the ambulance!" Chase said.

Rosie pushed him gently toward the sidewalk. "Go flag them down, Chase, so they don't go in around the back."

Rosie and Jackie, Matt between them, reversed directions down the snowy path. The siren grew louder, then stopped.

They were intercepted by Chase who ran ahead of two EMTs, one carrying a bag, the other pushing a gurney. The one with the bag was tall and fair, the other short and sturdily built.

"Hi, Rosie." The tall one was Randy Sanford, her friend Paris's husband. He looked inside Matt's jacket, removing the large cotton square Rosie had pressed into the wound. "Not too deep," he said after a moment. "Okay, let's get you on the gurney."

The other technician, Randy's friend Chilly Childress, had opened it out and helped him ease Matt onto it. Rosie's reality teetered dangerously. Matt, whom she would never forgive for having abandoned her when she'd needed him so much, still represented for her the happiest period of her life. For the first time since then, she had a clear memory of how cold and distant she'd been. She wanted to remember why, but found she couldn't and Matt was now supine on a gurney, being lifted into the back of an ambulance, wincing and pale.

While Randy climbed into the back with the gurney, Chilly opened the passenger-side door of the ambulance, beckoning her. "Want to ride with us?" he asked.

She hesitated. She wanted Matt to be all right, but she didn't want to be where people were struggling for life and possibly dying. She'd had all she could take of that.

"Your husband's going to be fine," he assured her,

still holding the door. "But we have to get him to the hospital."

Her husband.

"Go," Jackie said, her hands on Chase's shoulders. "I'll take care of Chase."

"No, I want to come," Chase protested, trying to follow Rosie.

"You stay with Jackie, sweetie," Rosie said as she ran back to give Chase a hug. "I'll call and tell you what's happening, and the minute I'm home again, I'll come and get you."

"He's not going to die?"

"No."

"You're sure. 'Cause…lots of our family does that."

"Well, see there. He isn't our family. He's a De-Marco, not an Erickson."

"But you're a DeMarco, and he's *your* family and you're *my* family, so—"

"I promise you," Rosie said firmly, holding both his hands, "that he is not going to die, and I'm going to bring him home, and whenever that is—tomorrow or the next day—we're all going to have hot buffalo wings together. Okay?"

Chase finally bowed to pressure. "Okay. But I'm gonna be really mad if you're wrong."

"Go," Jackie encouraged Rosie. "And don't worry. Matt will be fine."

MATT FELT as though he was in hell—or, at least as if his arm was. Though he doubted seriously that Christmas was celebrated there. There were cardboard cutouts of Santa, elves, and puppies in Santa hats all over the windows and walls. A glittering, three-dimensional paper star hung from a light fixture in the middle of the ER.

The EMT had been right; it was just a flesh wound. He'd been bandaged, given an antibiotic and pain medication.

"You're going to have to rest this arm for a couple of days," the doctor said, then turned to Rosie. "The bullet scraped some muscle, so he's going to be pretty uncomfortable. This dressing will have to be changed a couple of times a day."

Rosie didn't look thrilled at that notion. Of course, she wasn't thrilled that he was here at all. But he'd seen that horrified expression in her eyes when she saw he'd been shot, and remembered that she'd worn it two years ago after she'd found her father on the porch and lost their baby. He guessed it was the blood that had upset her.

The doctor continued with his instructions. Rosie nodded, looking stoic and controlled.

The doctor studied her closely. "Are you all right?"

"Yes." She nodded.

He turned to Matt. "She should have a brandy when you get home."

"I'll see to it." Matt slipped off the table to his feet, feeling the pain in his arm reverberate all the way into his head. Okay. He was going to have to move more carefully.

The doctor caught his wince, shook one of the pills

he'd given him into the palm of his good hand and went to the sink for a paper cup of water.

"That'll take effect in about half an hour, but it might require the second dose before you feel any real relief. But no brandy for you, okay?"

"Right."

"Couple of days and you should be almost as good as new. Of course, if you have a problem, see your family doctor."

"Yes."

"Okay. There's been a police officer waiting patiently outside. You feel up to talking to him?"

"Sure."

The doctor walked away.

"You don't have a family doctor," Rosie reminded Matt.

"Yes, I do," he replied. "Dr. Norman Bashevis."

She gave him The Look. "I meant a doctor who isn't three thousand miles away," she said.

"I'm not going to have a problem."

"And how can you be so sure?"

"Because I may not have a doctor," he said, giving her a chummy smile, "but I have an excellent nurse."

He was sure she knew he referred to the second year of their marriage when he'd broken his leg playing weekend football with friends. She'd done everything for him that first week when he'd been in pain and seriously frustrated by the imposed inactivity. Ill temper had made him impossible to live with, but she'd been patient and nearly saintly—until he'd barked at her for no reason, she'd told him off, and he'd apologized abjectly. She'd suggested a bath to help him relieve his tension, and when he'd reminded her that he couldn't get the bad leg wet, she'd told him she'd take care of everything.

And she had. He'd learned that a broken leg did not preclude lovemaking if both parties were cooperative. He wondered if she remembered that.

She gave him The Look again. She remembered.

"That was when…we were happy," she said, her voice and her manner stiff. "That's all changed."

Before Matt could react to that statement, a tall man in jeans and a leather jacket, a badge pinned to a breast pocket, pushed the curtain aside and stopped at the foot of the bed.

"I'm sorry to bother you," he began to apologize, "but I—" He stopped abruptly, and smiled. Matt recognized him at the same moment and slid off the bed to offer his hand.

"Jim Machado!" he said, wincing a little at the pain any kind of movement seemed to cause. "How are you?" Jim and Matt had met when Matt was covering an accident to which Jim had responded. Jim had been in the game when Matt broke his leg.

"I'm good," he replied, noting the wince and placing a steadying hand on Matt's shoulder. They were about the same height and weight. "But you're not looking too good despite the snazzy tux."

"I'm okay. I just have to remember not to move the arm."

"What brings you home?"

"Rosie's sister, Francie, got married. I gave her away."

Jim turned to Rosie, his eyes going over the functional blue parka over the long, frothy, berry-red dress.

"I was maid of honor," she explained. "Good to see you, Jim."

He smiled at Rosie. "It's been a while. I thought Francie was still about fifteen. You'll have to get arrested once in a while so you can keep me current on what's going on."

Rosie gave him a quick hug. "Yeah, well, you know how there's never enough time to do all the things you want to do."

They all shared a laugh. In the old days, Matt and Rosie, and Jim and his wife, Laurie, met for pizza after the games. Then Matt left Maple Hill and heard that Laurie and Jim had divorced.

Jim grew serious. "The doc told me it's just a flesh wound."

"Yeah."

"I have uniforms checking the spot opposite the inn where the shots would have come from. They've found a spent .22, but the owner of the property says there're always hunters on his place. I'm guessing that's how you got shot—" he grinned "—unless you still fumble the ball like you did in the old days. Then maybe someone is out to get you."

"Funny."

"Matt thinks someone was *aiming* at us," Rosie said.

Jim focused his attention on her, suddenly serious. "Who'd have a reason to do that?"

She shrugged. "No one I can think of. Someone did leave a message on my answering machine, though, warning me not to bring Tolliver Textiles to Maple Hill, but I didn't take it too seriously."

"*Now* you bring up a threat?" Matt asked, his voice raspy with pain. "Why didn't you tell me this before?"

"It wasn't a threat exactly, it—"

"Who was it?" he interrupted.

Jim stopped him with a raised hand. "Let me be the cop, okay?" He turned to Rosie. "Did you recognize the voice?"

"No."

"Was there a direct threat?"

"Not exactly," she said, frowning as she thought back. "It said something like, 'Let them stay in Boston, or you'll wish you had.' Something like that."

"And you didn't save the message?"

"Rosie…" Matt said in a critical tone.

Jim frowned at him. "What's Tolliver Textiles, Rosie?"

"A business we tried to bring to Maple Hill a couple of years ago, but…" She hesitated, glancing at Matt. He looked back at her intrepidly, refusing to look guilty for having left her. "It all fell through, but I've just contacted them again. We're trying to interest them in coming here. We had a lot of trouble with an environmentalist last time, but I don't think this was him. He has a huge voice, and this one was very quiet."

"What's the environmentalist's name?"

"Ben Langlois."

Jim nodded, apparently familiar with the man. "I know him, but it's my understanding that he's changed. Got married and got religion. Matt, how do you know the glint of sunlight wasn't off the chrome on a truck? There *is* a road up there."

Matt shrugged his good shoulder. "If you've ever been picked out by a sniper, you don't forget the moment."

Jim didn't look entirely convinced, but he agreed to check out Langlois.

"Makes more sense than the hunter theory," Matt said. He pointed to Rosie's dress. "Not many deer that color."

Jim in turn pointed to the black and white of Matt's tuxedo jacket and shirt. "They might have mistaken you for a—"

"What?" Matt demanded. "A Holstein? Do you hunt cows now in Maple Hill? In *December?*"

Jim acknowledged that ridiculous suggestion with a smiling nod. "Glad to see you haven't lost your sense of humor. How long are you staying?"

"A couple of days," Matt replied.

"At this point, I'd say this was an accident. But I'll look into it." He reached inside his jacket and extracted a business card. Rosie caught sight of a shoulder holster. "Meanwhile, maybe we can get together for pizza before you go."

"Sounds like a plan."

"Can I drive you home?"

Rosie shook her head. "Thanks, but some friends, Jackie and Hank, brought my car to the parking lot and left the keys at the front desk."

"Okay, then." He put his pad and pencil in his pocket. "I'll be in touch. Take care."

Matt and Rosie left the emergency room and walked down a short corridor to the parking lot. Rosie had a light grip on Matt's good arm. That amused and intrigued him. He was tempted to pretend weakness, just to see what she would do. But on the chance she'd simply let him fall and walk away, he decided against it.

At the exit, he tried to free his good arm to push the heavy glass door open, but she kept a grip on him and did it herself.

"Nice of you to help me," he said as they walked out into the frigid air. A cold wind blew and the snow crunched under their feet as they headed for her silver-blue Chevy Tahoe. "Even though you insist you don't want to be my nurse."

"Basic Christian charity demands that I help you." She aimed the remote at the car to unlock the doors.

"Oh, please," he groaned. "Spare me your charity. I'd rather relive that last month of silence."

In the month before he'd left a year and a half ago, she'd pulled so far away they hadn't even made eye contact.

"Matthew." There was a warning note in her voice as she opened the passenger door. "Let's not do this."

"Let's not do this, let's not do that," he grumbled as he climbed in, then pulled on the seat belt. He had a little difficulty adjusting it one-handed. "Let's not fight. Let's not even speak. Let's just let everything go to hell so you can stay in your little cocoon of pain."

She leaned in to help him, glowering at him even as she held the belt away from his injured arm. She reached over him to snap it into place, her movements all cool efficiency.

He still had to lean back to stop himself from planting a kiss on the side of her neck.

She laid the shoulder belt gently against his shoulder. "Does that hurt?" she asked.

Everything hurt, but the wound was several inches away and unaffected by the belt.

"No, it's fine. I might mention again that you're pretty concerned for a woman who hates even talking to me."

She slammed his door without comment, then came around and climbed in behind the wheel.

"I guess it's time to believe you," he said. "You couldn't have been more clear when you killed our marriage."

"I thought we weren't doing this," she said wearily.

"There was no reason to stay," he went on as though she hadn't spoken. "You'd retreated so far, you weren't there."

She put the car in gear and drove slowly toward the exit. "You're making me wish I wasn't here *now*."

It was pointless to argue, and he was in too much pain, anyway. He laid his head back against the rest and tried to remember what time it had been when the doctor gave him the medication. He'd been told he'd feel relief in half an hour. That had been about fifteen minutes ago.

Great. He had to feel like hell for another fifteen minutes.

Or maybe longer. Hadn't the doctor said it might take a second dose before he felt better?

Rosie drove in silence, her profile set as she concentrated on her driving. His anger dissolved into remorse and he closed his eyes, knowing there was no good way out of the swamp their relationship had become.

If he were to tell her the whole truth about what he'd learned before he'd left, he'd only cause her more grief. Although that seemed to be all he was doing now, anyway.

Still, she had her icons in place—her father, her brother. Together, Matt and Rosie had destroyed their present, and she'd taken all the pleasure out of the prospect of his future. The least he could do was let her have the past.

CHAPTER FIVE

ROSIE HELPED MATT out of the car. She let him go to unlock the door, then tried to take his arm again to help him inside.

"I'm fine," he insisted, moving out of her reach. His face was pale and pinched with pain as he went toward the stairway.

"Do you feel like eating anything?" she asked his back.

"No, thank you," he said stiffly.

"A cup of coffee or tea?"

"No." He stopped at the bottom of the stairs and put a hand on the newel post. His eyes were red-rimmed and weary. "But you should have that brandy."

"I'm going to go pick up Chase. Will you be all right?"

"Sure."

"I'll be back in fifteen minutes."

He didn't respond to that, just made his way up-stairs. She watched him go with a nagging sense of guilt and regret. He'd been right all along. He hadn't left on his own. She was beginning to remember that she'd driven him away because she'd been unable to deal with the enormity of what had happened. And she wasn't sure she was any better able to deal with it now. She turned on her heel and went back to the car.

She drove back to town and Jackie's house on the hill behind the commercial area, thinking that he'd still left. No matter how bad their marriage had become, his abandonment was unforgivable. She had been horrible during those last months, she admitted to herself defensively, but the whole situation had been horrible. He should have understood.

She'd called Chase from the hospital to tell him Matt was going to be fine, but he now shot out of Jackie's house with a barely audible thank-you, and raced to the car.

Rosie hugged Jackie. "Thank you so much for watching him," she said. "I'd have hated to take him to the hospital with me."

"Well, of course. I was happy to help. Thank goodness it was just a flesh wound. What on earth happened?"

"Jim Machado's investigating," Rosie explained, "and thinks it was hunters across the road. He and Matt were friends before Matt left."

Jackie frowned. "There's an ordinance against firing in the direction of town. It's wilderness on that side of the road, but not on the inn's side."

"Had the bullet hit Chase..." Rosie couldn't even finish the thought.

Jackie hooked an arm in hers and walked her to her car. "But it didn't, so don't even think in those terms.

Go home, have a drink, and take good care of Matt. Well...you know what I mean." Jackie squeezed her shoulders apologetically.

Everyone in town knew what had happened to the Erickson family, and to Rosie and Matt's marriage as a result.

"Yes. Thanks, Jackie."

"If I can help any time, in any way, call me."

"I will, thank you. Good night."

Chase asked about Matt over and over in the car, and insisted on seeing him for himself when they got home.

Matt had left his door partially open. With a finger to her lips for silence, Rosie pushed the door wide enough that Chase could see inside. Peering in, too, Rosie could see Matt's dark head against the white pillowcase, his injured arm held closely to him.

Before she could stop Chase, he walked into the room and right up to the bed.

"Hi, Uncle Matt," he whispered loudly.

Matt's head moved on the pillow and he put his good arm out to touch Chase's shoulder. "Hey, buddy. What's up?" His voice was a little groggy, very hoarse.

"I wanted to see if you were okay." Chase took something out of his pocket and put it into Matt's hand. "Here, you can have this. In case you get hungry during the night."

"What is it?" Matt held the object up, but probably couldn't see it in the dark.

"It's an atomic fireball candy. They're really hot. Rachel gave it to me."

"Rachel?"

"Her mom is Jackie. I stayed with her while you went to the hospital."

"Oh, yeah. Well, thanks. If I get hungry, I'll eat it."

"Are you gonna be able to play with me in the morning?"

"We'll see, okay? Maybe we can go for a walk around the lake."

"Okay. Sleep tight."

"You, too. You got a hug for me?"

"Yeah." Chase leaned into Matt, very careful of his bandaged arm.

Matt held him for a moment, then let him go. "Thanks for the candy. See you in the morning."

Chase turned away, looking relieved and happy.

"Why don't you get ready for bed," Rosie said quietly, "and I'm going to see if Uncle Matt needs an extra blanket."

"Okay." He skipped away, all right in his world again now that he'd seen Matt.

Rosie walked into the room and stopped several feet from the bed. "Are you warm enough?" she asked. She noticed that his chest was bare.

"Yes," he said.

She moved closer, suddenly wondering if he had a fever. Her mother always kept the temperature low on the second floor, insisting it was more conducive to sleeping. He should feel cold if he was bare-chested. She put a hand to his forehead.

"Do you feel feverish?" she asked.

"No," he replied. "Just sleepy."

"Want me to get you a shirt?"

"I have a shirt. It just feels better to have nothing resting on the arm, not even fabric."

She had a sudden inspiration. "What if I found you a shirt and cut out the sleeve?"

"Rosie," he said with mild impatience, "that sounds like something a nurse would do, and you don't want to be my nurse, remember? I just want to sleep."

"Fine." Her feelings hurt, she pulled his blankets up anyway, careful not to touch his arm with them. "I thought it sounded like something a…a clever friend would do. But have it your way."

"Friends talk to each other. They're not always angry at each other."

"Oh, shut up!" Why had she ever thought she owed it to him to try to make him comfortable?

"Hey. You're the one who woke *me* up."

"My mistake. Good night."

She closed the door behind her, went to check on Chase and found him waiting to be tucked in.

"He didn't die," Chase said with a wide smile as she secured the blankets around his feet.

"I told you he was going to be fine." She leaned over him to kiss his cheek. "You should believe me because aunts know everything."

Chase giggled and wrapped his arms around her neck. "You told me the capital of Louisiana was New Orleans, and it isn't. It's Baton Rouge."

"I've apologized for that." She tickled him for

bringing that up again. "I didn't know it was for your homework. Next time you ask me a question, tell me it's for homework and I'll look up the answer to be sure. In fact, *you* should look up the answer."

"If you knew everything," he said, "you wouldn't have to look it up. So aunts *don't* know everything."

Chase was beginning to sound a lot like his uncle Matt.

"You need water before I go?" she asked.

"Got some."

"Went to the bathroom?"

"Yep."

"Okay." She hugged him again, then turned off his light. "Good night, sweetie," she said as she went to the door. She left it half-open. "I love you."

"I love you, too."

Those words reassured her as she walked past Matt's room to decide where to sleep. Her mother's room was less orderly than one would expect of a woman who accomplished so much for charity. Her organizational skills suggested nothing out of place in her brain or her surroundings. And yet her room was quite human—lacy undies on the bed, books open on her antique desk, cushions from the window seat on the floor because she'd been collating minutes of a board meeting there.

It would be a pleasant room to sleep in, but Rosie didn't share her mother's preference for a rock-hard mattress.

Francie's room was too chaotic to even consider

sleeping there. It was only half packed to move to her new apartment. The other half was on the bed, in and out of boxes and strewn all over the floor.

Rosie peered into the guest room Aunt Ginger had been using and decided it would be perfect. Ginger had taken most of her things with her, except for a hooded winter coat and a pair of boots she didn't think she'd need in Palm Springs.

The room was pale blue and white, calming if a little unimaginative, and had a wonderful view of the lake.

Now all Rosie needed was something to sleep in, a detail she'd forgotten when she'd brought what she'd needed from the guest house that morning. But she could find something in her mother's things.

She did a check of the house, making sure doors and windows were locked, looked in on her two charges and was happy to see both of them asleep, then invaded the lingerie section of her mother's wardrobe closet.

Sonny Erickson was a lover of dramatic nighties. Everyone always knew what to give her for Christmas or her birthday. She had peignoir sets in every color, nighties in every length, robes galore.

Rosie looked for the midnight-blue slip nightie and sheer cover-up she'd given her last year. The cover-up was randomly dotted with small sequined stars. She found it, the price tags still attached. She cut them off and pulled on the nightie.

She draped the cover-up over a nearby chair, climbed into bed and turned off the light. The events of the day ran through her mind. Francie's wedding, then her and Derek's happy escape in the limousine. Her mother at the reception, gracious and gregarious. She remembered how Sonny had hugged Matt and encouraged him to kidnap her daughter and take her with him to China.

Rosie made the same scornful sound she'd made earlier. Despite her indignation, she had a mental image of her and Matt on a road in the Chinese countryside, far from all the issues that had beset them in Maple Hill. And she wondered if the distance would change anything.

She shook off the thought as memory took over again when her mother's taxi drove away. She'd turned to see why Chase had exclaimed and was surprised to see Matt's hand on the boy's head, pushing him to the snow. Then Matt was lunging toward her, his eyes on something across the road.

Lunging toward her.

She shot upright in bed as she suddenly realized what that meant. If someone had been taking deliberate aim with that shot, they'd been shooting at *her,* then Matt had gotten between her and the bullet. On purpose.

She found herself shaking. It could have been her with a bullet in her arm, or, considering the disparity in their sizes, her head.

But Matt had prevented that with little time to think about what he was doing. He'd operated on instinct without considering the cost to himself.

Her heart thudded. She got out of bed and paced to the window, then back again, enervated by her realization. How stupid was she that this hadn't occurred to her before?

Well, he'd been bleeding and she'd been caught in a time warp, revisiting old pain and horror.

She paced some more. Hadn't Matt exhibited that kind of selflessness eighteen months ago, when she'd treated him cruelly and pushed him away?

A sudden crash from across the hall sent her running toward Matt's room. She found him sitting on the edge of the bed, the lamp from his nightstand on the carpet, light splayed drunkenly across the wall. The clock, which had also fallen, read 1:10 a.m.

She flipped on the overhead light and went to him. His arm was bleeding and he held it with his other hand. She put the lamp back on the table and righted the shade so she could see what she was doing.

"Sorry," he said as she knelt to inspect the bandage. "I rolled over on it in my sleep and woke myself up. I tried to put the light on to see if I'd done any damage, but I managed to dump the lamp instead."

"No harm done." She went back to her room for the bag of bandaging materials the doctor had sent home with her.

He held his hand out for the bag, but she put it out of his reach and dug into it for what she needed. "I'll do it," she said, and forestalled what she was sure would be his next remark with "Yes, I know it sounds like the nurse I've insisted I don't want to be, but you're obviously not coordinated enough to change the bandage yourself."

His eyes roamed her face as she sat beside him. She pretended not to notice. "That was exactly what I was going to say," he said.

"I've always been able to read your mind." She put her supplies aside, then pulled gently at the tape that covered the bandaged wound.

"You only thought you did," he argued quietly. "Half the time you were wrong."

She didn't know if that was true or not, and directed her entire focus to the bandage, preparing to bare the wound and deal with what she would see. She hoped it wouldn't bring back all those old images again.

The wound wasn't as bad as she'd expected, though there was fresh blood. She wiped it away with an alcohol pad, careful not to touch the wound with it. The stitches seemed to be intact, but his rolling onto his arm had probably just caused a spurt of blood.

She applied antibiotic cream, placed a gauze pad over the wound and directed him to hold the pad in place.

He complied and she put tape over it, then leaned back to assess her work.

"Too tight?" she asked.

No. It's fine."

"Good. Excuse me while I go get you some water. It's time for your second pain pill."

MATT'S PAIN seemed to stop while he watched the delicious movement of her slender hips in the snug and silky fabric of her nightgown. Dark blue rippled around her ankles as she padded off in bare feet.

The moment she was out the door, the painful throbbing resumed. Then she was back again with a bottle of water and a pill in a paper cup. He downed it in a single gulp and lay back against the pillow again. He thought he was hallucinating when she climbed onto the bed on his other side. She took the second pillow and forced it gently under his injured arm.

"That should keep you from rolling onto it," she said. "Is it comfortable?"

"Yes, very," he answered. Then he asked, "Are you okay?"

"I'm fine."

"Well, why are you being sweet?"

She looked away, picking up the clock and fussing with the arrangement of things on the bedside table. "I wasn't aware that I was."

"You are. You don't have some *Misery* scenario planned for me, do you?"

She pulled his blankets up. "I used to dream about that. Not in such an ugly, bloodthirsty vein, of course, but I was going to do things to you that were more clever than fatal. Like drive your Miata into the lake."

That notion would have hurt more if he still had the car. "I sold it a year ago."

That seemed to distress her. She'd given it to him one birthday. "Why?"

"You're the one with the inheritance, remember?" he replied. "I needed some new camera equipment and I was lining up gallery shows and needed some production money."

"But you loved that car."

He nodded. "I loved a lot of things I lost."

She tossed her head; he knew that meant she didn't want to talk about it. But it was a dramatic gesture in the dark blue nightgown. Her hair flew around her face and bare shoulders and brought back memories that tortured him.

"You now have a big cash advance, right?" she asked. "You can buy yourself whatever you want."

He nodded. "Yeah. But it seems as I get older, the things I want don't carry a price tag."

She looked suddenly a little off balance. "And the less care you take with what you already have."

He couldn't imagine what she knew about his current life that would have prompted that remark. "Pardon me?"

She folded her arms defensively. The swell of her breasts appeared above the low neckline of her nightgown. "You could have gotten killed today."

He was happy that that possibility seemed to upset her. "I didn't, though."

"But you could have." She heaved a deep sigh and her bottom lip trembled, but she looked him in the eye. "And you did it for me."

He was on fragile ground here, and all he could do

was be honest. He sat up again, the need to sleep suddenly vanished. "I'm sorry if that upsets you."

"Why?" she demanded. "Why are you sorry after all…after everything! Why would you risk your life for me?"

It was entirely possible his taking the bullet was going to have value, after all. He got to his feet. She took a step back.

"I left Maple Hill, but I didn't leave you," he said, "and I stepped in front of the bullet because you're my wife. Protecting you is my job. To be perfectly honest, I thought I'd be able to pull you down before another shot was fired."

"How…how could you leave Maple Hill and not leave me?"

"We don't live together, but we're not divorced," he reminded her. "And you wouldn't even talk to me anymore, so I didn't know what else to do. Again, I left the situation, but I didn't leave *you*. There was no way to work out our problems until you came out of your foxhole."

She frowned. "Foxhole?"

"Like in the military. When you're being shelled, you hide in a foxhole. But there comes a time when you have to climb out of it and fight back. Are you out?"

She put a trembling hand to her heart. "I thought I was, then I saw that blood on you and remembered Dad's blood, my blood…when I lost the baby." She shook her head. "I don't know."

He took two steps to close the gap between them, wrapped his good arm around her and drew her close. He felt the cool, smooth skin of her back under his fingers, caught her rosy, spicy scent, then looked for one solemn moment into her eyes, at the tears brimming there. He wanted to tell her that everything was okay now, but he knew there were things in the past she was going to have to work through before her life could go forward.

"I left eighteen months ago," he said, kissing her damp cheek, "because that was the only way I could think of to help you. But I've got some new ideas. I'm staying until I make them work."

She took a step back, out of his arms. "You have a job."

"I took two weeks' leave. I was going to photograph the Berkshires, but I think I'll stay here, instead."

A tear fell and she firmed her lips. "I appreciate your getting shot for me," she said, "but we're over, Matthew."

"I'm not leaving until we know who shot at you," he insisted, "and when I do leave, it'll be to get my stuff from Sacramento and bring it back here, or to take you with me."

She shook her head. "I can't go through all that again."

"The only way out is the way we came," he said. "The woman I fell in love with had courage to spare."

"That woman's gone."

"She's in a foxhole."

"She's dead!" she snapped at him. "Chase said it. Everybody in our family dies. I'm just still walking around."

That did it for him. A declaration of death was more than he could stand.

He caught a fistful of her hair and drew her back to him. "You are not dead," he said firmly. "Trust me."

He kissed her, wanting to fill her with life, with all the love they used to have for one another, with all the old hopes and dreams.

Aware of his mission, she pushed against him, inadvertently clamping a hand over his wound.

Pain ricocheted through him, filling every corner of his being.

She uttered a little yelp and drew her hand back, then began to weep an apology.

He simply held on to her and took advantage of her open mouth. He didn't understand why it happened, but the pain drove him to be tender. He didn't want her to hurt the way he hurt, physically, emotionally, or in any other way. He wanted her to know only pleasure, love, gentleness.

He felt her ignite, respond, lean into him with the memory of how it used to be.

But agony was imprinted on her, and it seemed she couldn't just shake it off, no matter how much he wanted her to.

She pushed out of his arms, careful to use his left arm for leverage this time. "You can't stay," she said breathlessly.

He'd felt her response. Ben-Hur couldn't drag him away now. "I'm staying."

"There's nothing to be gained—"

"I beg to differ."

She firmed her stance, but her voice was frail. "I don't love you anymore."

"The hell you don't."

Her hand fluttered to her forehead. "Matt, you're wearing me out."

"Then go to bed," he suggested, using his good hand to throw his covers back. "I could use some rest myself. We'll both feel better in the morning."

She opened her mouth to speak, then apparently unable to think of how to respond, turned and gave him those wonderful few seconds of watching her walk away.

He sank into bed, exhausted and in pain, but smiling.

CHAPTER SIX

ROSIE PACKED Chase's lunch and sipped a cup of coffee while he ate breakfast. She wore a classic green suit with a simple but elegant silver Christmas-tree pin on the left shoulder. The stones representing a string of lights on the tree were just glass, but she loved the pin, anyway. Jay had given it to her years ago.

"Keep eating, Chase," she encouraged, keeping a watchful eye on the clock. Her nephew had a tendency to zone out on her and kick his feet in a rhythmic pattern, his attention focused on something imaginary. He made motor sounds rather than eating his pancake and fruit.

"I'm going to fly stuff between islands when I grow up," he said, pouring more syrup onto his plate. "Like medicine and food and stuff people really need."

"That sounds very worthwhile." She added a napkin to the sandwich, apple and candy bar in his lunch.

"There's a place where there are lots of little islands," he said, "and Uncle Matt says I could probably make a lot of money."

"That's true," Rosie felt compelled to say. "But

your job should be about more than making money. You should do something that makes you happy every day."

He looked at her as though he understood. "Yeah. Flying an airplane would make me very happy."

She carried his lunch to the table and placed it on top of his reading book. He dutifully stacked up three bites of pancake on his fork and put the whole thing in his mouth.

"Good morning."

Matt appeared in the doorway. He looked a little bleary-eyed as he smiled at Rosie and then at Chase. "How's everybody?"

"I'm good," Chase replied. "And Aunt Rosie's always good."

"Really." Matt came into the room to sit opposite Chase. "And how do you know that?"

"She says you have to be," he told him, "because the world's going to keep turning, anyway." He leaned toward his uncle, obviously prepared to share a confidence. "That means everybody's got their troubles, so they're not gonna care about yours."

Rosie poured Matt a cup of coffee and put it on the table in front of him, daring him to remark on her philosophy. She imagined he thought she was a case of having to practice what she preached. Although after the episode in his bedroom last night, she was no longer sure what he thought—or even what *she* thought. And Chase had to be at school in fifteen minutes. There was no time to think right now.

"That's absolutely true," Matt said to Chase after a simple thank-you to Rosie for his coffee. "And very wise. But it is nice to help each other along the way."

"Yeah. She said that, too. 'Cause it's not good to think you're the only person in the whole world. 'Cause you're not."

"Right again. You going to school today?"

"Yep. And Aunt Rosie's going to work. She thought you were gonna sleep in."

"No, I thought I'd got to work with her," he said, sipping his coffee. "Take a look around town and see what's going on."

"It's so cool!" Chase said, suddenly more animated than usual. "There's Christmas stuff all over. And Jesus, Mary and Joseph are on the lawn in front of St. Anthony's. They have diamonds on them and everything."

Matt turned to Rosie for an explanation. "Diamonds?"

"Beazie Braga restored them a couple of years ago for Father Chabot," she explained, doing her best to appear unaffected by his presence. "She decorated the wise men's and the angel's clothing with phony stones and trim. They're very beautiful."

"Well. Can't wait to see it. What time do we leave?"

"Five minutes. Want me to come back for you after I drop off Chase?"

"No, I'm ready. I just have to grab my jacket."

"You should eat something."

"I'll get something at the bakery." He pretended sudden alarm. "It is still there, isn't it?"

"It is." She remembered that his favorite pastry was

a buttermilk bar, a glazed doughnut stick with buttermilk in the recipe rather than milk. "And just to add to our temptations, there's a new tea shop with more sinful treats than you can imagine."

He smiled knowingly. "I'll bet you have trouble staying out of there." Her sweet tooth was legendary.

Chase was happy to inform on her. "She likes this special chocolate cake with whipped cream on it."

"It's cream cheese and sour cream," she said, taking Chase's plate away since he was ignoring it, anyway. "And you have to go brush your teeth and comb your hair."

"She won't share it with anybody," Chase added, on his way to do as she'd asked.

Matt agreed. "She was always like that. Very selfish about her sweets."

She made a threatening move toward Chase and he ran off laughing.

"Why don't you stay home and try to recover?" she asked Matt with a calculatedly neutral tone. She sounded as though it didn't matter to her one way or the other—exactly the note she'd been going for.

"I'd just as soon you weren't alone," he said, standing with his coffee cup. He disappeared for a second, then returned with his jacket, still sipping his coffee. "Maybe there's something I can do to make myself useful."

"In a bridal shop?"

"You don't have cupboard doors that stick? Faucets that drip?"

"Occasionally," she replied. "But I have Whitcomb's Wonders for that. And you have a serious injury. Aren't you in pain?"

"I'm better. Pills are working." His eyebrows came together over the rim of his cup. He took a sip and lowered it. "Whitcomb's what?"

"Whitcomb's Wonders. Jackie's husband started the company." She checked her hair in a small mirror in a corner of the kitchen. "They do plumbing, wiring, carpentry, almost any kind of service you can think of." She grinned. "Jackie likes to tease that they've eliminated the need for a husband."

Matt laughed lightly. "Or freed him up for more important work."

She ignored the suggestive remark and went to the row of pegs near the door for her coat. "I think he's making a fortune. He has gardeners, a janitorial crew, furnace repair. I've even heard a rumor about a new security force."

He took the coat from her and held it open. "In Maple Hill?"

She slipped her arms into the sleeves. "Yeah. I'm not sure what they'll be doing, but Prue Hale's husband is training them." Her coat on, she turned to him, buttoning it, and saw his blank look. "Used to be Prue O'Hara, remember? Sister, Paris? Mom's a model and a movie star?"

"Oh, yeah." He smoothed her rumpled collar, then watched her dig in her purse for her keys. "So, you're telling me you have no need for me? Even as a handyman?"

"I've managed without you." She found her keys and shouldered her purse, giving him what she hoped was a distant and superior look.

He looked back and she had the darnedest feeling he saw through her to the troubled, lonely, didn't-know-what-the-hell-she-was-doing woman inside.

"Have you liked it?" he asked seriously.

She wanted to say that she had, but his presence in her mother's kitchen, in the middle of her own bleak and going-nowhere life, made it difficult to lie. She guessed he could see all the memories in her eyes, all the happy times that were coming back now that she knew he'd risked his life for her.

She sighed and admitted grimly, "No, I haven't, not really. But that doesn't mean I'd do anything foolish."

"Like what?" Matt challenged. "Admit that you'd missed me? That you had some part in what went wrong between us? That there might be a place to start again?"

Chase ran toward them, jacket sleeves tied at his throat, flying out behind him.

He was a most welcome diversion. "What kind of plane are you this time?" she asked, opening the door.

"I'm not a plane, I'm Motor Man!" He rolled his eyes at Matt, sharing his tolerance of her inability to distinguish between a plane and a superhero.

Matt followed them out the door and closed it behind him. "Motor Man," he repeated. "I don't think I've heard of him."

Chase climbed into the back of the Chevy Tahoe and buckled himself in. "I made him up. He's this guy whose stomach's really a motor and he can fly anywhere. And he's got guns in his feet, and his fingers are handcuffs, so he can catch bad guys."

"Wow. But how come a motor and not jets or rockets?"

"'Cause when my dad died," Chase said matter-of-factly, "he was fixing this little putt-putt boat motor in the garage. I dragged it out the back to my clubhouse."

"You have a clubhouse?"

"Yeah. The shed behind the garage. And I thought I should do something cool with it to remind me of Dad. So I'm Motor Man."

Matt turned in his seat and reached out a hand to touch Chase's cheek. "That's good. Motor Man. I like it."

"You want to be my sidekick? Usually superheroes have a kid sidekick, but if I'm a kid, I should have an old guy."

Matt pinched the toe of Chase's running shoe before turning around again. "Okay, I'll be your sidekick. What's my name?"

"How about…" Chase was thinking. "Just Matt," he said with sudden excitement. "Motor Man and Matt!"

"Good." Matt nodded, slanting Rosie a grin as she started the car. "Since I'm such an *old* guy I won't have to remember a complicated name."

"What about Buttermilk Boy?"

"Hey," said Matt. "Who asked you?"

WITH CHASE SAFELY deposited at school, Rosie drove to town, a small, busy area centered primarily around an old village green complete with a statue of Maple Hill ancestors Caleb and Elizabeth Drake, who'd defended Maple Hill from the British. Also in place was a contemporary American flag, as well as one from the day of the original thirteen colonies. Two city workers were putting up a Christmas tree near the statue.

"Should we stop at the bakery first?" Matt asked, then added seriously, "We wouldn't want to forget. It's still right down from the *Mirror*?"

"Yes. You'll be in heaven, Buttermilk Boy," she said, driving up a side street and pulling into a parking area behind the stores. "You can get yourself something to eat every hour on the hour. And the tea shop is just a block away from my shop."

"I may just have to move back to Maple Hill for that reason." He climbed out of the car and walked around to open her door while she was still collecting her purse and the tote bag that contained a minor alteration project on a veil. "Who runs the *Mirror* these days?"

"Haley Megrath, Jackie's husband Hank's sister."

"I'll have to check it out someday."

"Why don't you go this morning?"

"Thanks, but I want to keep an eye on you for a while. I'm still concerned about yesterday."

She pointed up at the clear blue of the sky and the bright winter sun. "Maybe you just misinterpreted what you saw. It's hard to believe in the light of day

that anyone would deliberately shoot at us…at me."
She started off toward the backs of the shops, picking
her way carefully through the snow in hiking books
that looked very out of place with her elegant suit and
coat.

Distracted by the flight of a cardinal, crimson
against the bright sky, she slipped on a patch of ice
under the snow. She executed a gracefully balletic
move, arms flung out and legs scrabbling for purchase,
as she tried to regain her balance. He caught her arm
to steady her and held her to his side.

"Want me to take the tote bag?" he asked with a
teasing smile. "It's hard to do justice to a pirouette with
a Maple Hill Library bag in your hand."

She giggled; he couldn't quite believe it. He hadn't
heard that sound from her since before her brother
had been killed. And though they'd been separated for
eighteen months, he had a suspicion she hadn't giggled much in that time, either.

"These boots are usually so dependable," she said,
lifting one to show him their serviceable soles, "that I
forget to be careful. This snow-over-ice stuff gets me
every time."

He tucked her arm in his. "Well, hold on to me and
I'll get you to the shop without injury."

She surprised him by doing as he asked. They
crossed a broad expanse of slick parking lot without incident, then she unlocked a bright red door in the back
of the brick building that housed several other shops.
A narrow sign over the door read, Happily Ever After.

"That's quite a claim," he said, holding the door open as she walked inside.

"Happens for *some* people." She went inside and turned to look at him over her shoulder, a sad expression in her eyes. "It's the luck of the draw, I guess."

"I don't think so," he disputed. "I think you have to *want* to hold a marriage together. Otherwise, there's always a reason to let it go."

They stood in a large storage room filled with dresses and gowns in plastic sleeves. The sad look and the giggle were gone. She was clearly annoyed. "I know you hate it when I repeat this," she said, "but—"

He finished for her. "I'm the one who left, I know. But you'd let the marriage go long before that. And let's stop arguing about that. We're never going to agree. I didn't see much when you fitted me for the tux, so show me what goes on in here."

She began a little stiffly, explaining about the wide variety of dresses, the broad choice of headpieces and the incalculable combinations. She really warmed to her subject as she gestured to a bulletin board covered with photos of the brides she'd dressed. All wore wide smiles and hopeful expressions, and looked very much like candidates for Rosie's happily-ever-after claim.

"We pick out dresses and veils in here," she said, "then they try them on in there." She pointed to the dressing rooms with louvered doors. "Can you imagine Mom and Francie and I closed into a room that size? There was very nearly a murder."

He could understand that. "Your mom's personality takes up a lot of space."

A tidy desk in a corner of the room had neat stacks of paperwork and a pen-and-pencil cup. Tacked to the wall on two sides of it were pictures from magazines, fabric swatches, photographs and several children's drawings. A large, square signature read, CHASE.

The front room of the shop was feminine and welcoming, and appointed with another, more formal desk, several chairs with lavender velvet upholstery and a glass counter containing various wedding accessories. In the display window, a life-size Santa mannequin wore a tuxedo, and Mrs. Santa, a lacy red dress with a fuzzy white hat and muff.

"Very elegant," Matt said, looking around him. The lace curtains were a nice touch. "You were always good at making a place beautiful but still comfortable."

She seemed surprised by the praise. "Thank you. I didn't think you'd noticed."

He shrugged. "If I never said it, I was remiss. That big old barn we bought in the country was turning into quite a showplace. Are you still renting it out?"

"No." She stiffened a little, picking a veiled white hat off one of the chairs and placing it on the counter. "I…didn't want to live there anymore after…after…" She turned to him, wanting some sign that he knew what she meant without her having to say it.

He thought it would be good for her to say it—after our baby died, after everybody died. Best to get it out of her rather than keep it in. But he was no psychologist and she was pleading.

"Yeah, I know," he said.

"I sold it to someone," she went on in a little rush, "who's going to build condos. I didn't want to drive down that road and see the house that represented our dreams...."

He nodded. That was sad, but he could understand the instinct to destroy memories of the good dreams that never came to life.

She stood uncomfortably in the middle of the room for a moment, then crossed to one of the dressing rooms. "If you're serious about helping with some handyman duties," she said, showing him how one of the louvered doors hung by only one hinge, "this could use some work."

"I'll see what I can do. Is the hardware store still down the street?"

"It is." She handed him a bill from the cash register. "And you can get us each a coffee and something from the bakery on your way back. Knock on the door. I don't open for another hour, so I'll be in the back, working on an order."

"Okay. You have a tape measure?"

She shook her head. "I have a dressmaker's measuring tape."

"That'll do." He stood over her while she dug it out of her desk. Then he teased her with a frown. "But if anybody hears I handled a dressmaker's tape, I'll know who told."

The Look, but it was accompanied by a smile. "Relax. It's not going to make you grow breasts or anything."

That was the second time she'd teased him today. And she'd smiled. There might be hope here, after all.

ROSIE WATCHED Matt measure the hinge on the other door, then pretended absorption in her paperwork— bills, mostly—when he looked up to tell her he was leaving. "I'll be ten minutes tops," he said, pulling on his jacket, moving his right arm gingerly.

"Okay. Don't forget my scone."

"I won't. You want to come lock the door after me?"

She handed him her keys. "Better idea. You do it, then let yourself in."

He took the keys from her. "Okay. Be right back."

Rosie tried to occupy herself writing checks, but Matt's face kept getting in the way of the numbers. She was going to throttle Francie when she and Derek got home—not because Rosie hated having Matt here, but because…she didn't.

That was a difficult truth to accept. On top of the fact that he'd taken a bullet for her, it was paralyzing.

And after eighteen months of living on memories of watching him walk out the door with one suitcase and his laptop when she'd been dying inside, she could clearly recall that her grief and anger had driven him away. She just didn't remember why she'd turned away from him instead of toward him when she'd needed him the most.

And their being together now only brought back all the painful memories of the baby they'd made together but never got to see, the brother she'd grown up with but wouldn't get to see grow old, the father she'd loved but whom she'd never been sure loved her.

Love softened everything inside. It opened doors and broke down walls. It left you vulnerable.

She couldn't let herself love again. Not ever.

She'd let Matt stay his two weeks, then make him leave. With Chase between them for most of that time, remaining immune to Matt's charm shouldn't be too difficult.

She sat up a little straighter and focused on the bills with new concentration. The one from Bride With Child Designs—$769.99. Great. Focus decimated with the first invoice.

Happily Ever After had bought a maternity dress from BWCD for a beautiful young woman whose fiancé had tracked her halfway across the country when she'd gotten cold feet and run away. She'd been bright-eyed and apple-cheeked and alight with excitement over her baby and the man she loved.

Rosie had a sudden sharp memory of feeling just that way herself—so in love and so anxious to bring her baby into the world. Then everything had gone bad.

She'd just begun to write a check, when she heard the door to the storage room/office close. She looked up, expecting to see Matt standing there, preparing to tease him about wanting to hide their pastry transgressions from anyone passing by her large windows.

But he wasn't there. She was alone. As she stood up to open the door, wondering if Matt hadn't locked the front and somehow a gust of air had closed it, she heard the very firm click of a lock. She stared at the door dumbly.

"Matt!" she called after a moment's silence. "Matthew, what are you doing?"

She heard subtle movement beyond the door and decided he was teasing her. Withholding her scone or something.

"Okay, you want me to beg? I will. Gladly. I have no pride where pastry is concerned! Please, Matthew! Give me my scone!"

Nothing. Not even the little sounds she'd heard before.

She rapped on the door. "Matt?"

Still nothing.

Honestly, she thought, walking to the back door and turning the lock. If he thought she'd be amused by the theft of her morning pastry, he had another think coming. She was absolutely not...

The door wouldn't give. Thinking she'd left it unlocked when she'd walked in and had only locked it again, she fiddled with it. Whatever direction she turned the lock in the middle of the knob, the door wouldn't open.

And it was only then that she felt a prickling on her scalp, a chilling sense of being in the sight of someone's gun.

She dropped to the ground, her hands trembling, a

metallic taste in her mouth. Then she cursed herself for
an idiot when she remembered there were no windows in the back room. No one could take aim at her
if they wanted to.

But why was she locked inside her own shop?

She stood up again, trying to pull herself together.

She went back to the other door and tried it again.
Still locked. Then she noticed the curious smell and
the smoke billowing up from under the door.

Oh my God! Her store was on fire!

The dresses! They were all back here with her, but
smoke wasn't going to do them any good! Nor, of
course, would the eventual flames.

She realized with a sense of terror mingled with
self-deprecation that she was losing it. For something
to do, she moved all the dresses nearest the smoke to
the rack at the back of the store. By the time she was
finished, the smoke was making her cough, causing her
eyes to burn.

She tried the back door again, and when that still
didn't work, she went to the wall at the side, thinking
that if she pounded on it, someone in the bakery would
hear her.

She did that for about a minute, then realized that
the effort was making her gulp in smoke. Her throat
burned and her eyes teared so much she could barely
see.

She had to sit for a minute. Just a minute.

No. She didn't have a minute.

She dragged her desk chair to the back and lifted it

to throw against the door, but it was too heavy for her to get a good swing. She tried ramming the door with it, but to no avail.

She heard glass breaking in the front of the shop and imagined the fire had grown so hot that it burst the windows.

Her shop! Her orders!

Her life? As smoke billowed around her she considered the possibility that she could lose her life. Even as recently as a few days ago, death might not have held much horror. She'd learned to enjoy bringing about other people's happiness, but there'd been little enough of her own.

Now, though, a little spark of something came to life inside her. It wasn't happiness or emotional resurrection, but rather simple anger that someone else thought they could choose the time and place of her demise.

She heard scraping on the other side of the door, someone fiddling with the lock.

So the fire wasn't taking her fast enough? She looked around desperately for a weapon. Unable to find anything she could use, she braced herself for the door to open, then flung herself with a shrill scream at the burly form in the swirling smoke in the doorway.

She threw him backward and they landed in a tangle on the carpet.

"You rat!" she shrieked, pummeling a sturdy chest. She heard a gasp of pain. "You cowardly—"

Then she realized that her attacker wasn't fighting back, and that there was something startlingly familiar about the position she was in—astride a lean male waist, the body under hers letting her have her way.

"So much for my concern about whether or not you're all right," Matt said wryly.

Rosie closed her eyes, now mortally embarrassed, as well as fearful for her life. Though something about the sight of Matt's face seemed to quiet that fear.

"I'm sorry. I thought you were…whoever did this." She looked up to see several firefighters at work in the rubble of her shop. As the smoke dissipated, she saw that what was left of the curtains hung askew, and a trunk she'd bought at a secondhand store and embellished to look antique and interesting was burned to cinders. A firefighter directed a blast of water at it while another worked on one of her velvet chairs that was aflame. The glass counter was untouched.

"Well, that's a step forward," he said. "I thought you were trying to kill me just because it was me. Want to stop leaning on my arm?"

"Oh, God!" She had one hand planted in the middle of his chest and the other hand holding his bad arm. "Matt, I'm sorry!" She climbed off him and helped him sit up. "Are you bleeding again?"

She started to unbutton his shirt and leaned over him to feel into the sleeve for dampness on the bandage.

One of the firefighters, the chair now extinguished, watched them with interest.

Matt grinned at him. "Danger puts her in a seductive mood," he said.

In spite of his teasing, there was a touchingly relieved look in his eyes when he put a hand to her cheek. "Are *you* all right?"

They sat side by side on the wet carpet in the debris of her shop, and she was surprised to discover that she *was* all right.

"Yes," she replied. "But you… Should we take you back to the ER?"

"No, I'm okay." He got to his feet and reached his good arm down to help her up. "Get your coat and let's get out of here."

Jim Machado walked into the shop as they walked out. "Are you both all right?" he asked, frowning in concern at the broken window and the firefighters at work inside.

"Yes," Matt replied, "but someone locked her in the back room while I was out, and set fire to the front."

Rosie wrapped her arms around herself at the memory of what had happened. Matt's teasing had lightened the mood for a moment, but now she had to face the fact that someone was trying to kill her, or at least do her serious injury. "And the back door wouldn't unlock," she added. "I'll bet they did something to it, too."

The three walked through the small crowd that had gathered in front of the building to the back of Happily Ever After. The sabotage was instantly obvious. Someone had tied nylon cord several times around the doorknob, then tied the end of the cord to a hook she used to hold open the old screen door during deliveries.

"Okay," Jim said as he frowned at the cord and the obviously murderous intent of it. "Definitely not hunters."

CHAPTER SEVEN

MATT GOT RID OF his fear by focusing on his anger. For all the personal problems he had with Rosie, he knew her to be an honest businesswoman, and when she'd worked with her father on community projects and the Industrial Growth Committee, a dedicated servant of the people. She never took advantage of anyone. The very thought that someone wanted to hurt her invoked rage in him.

"What happened, Rosie?" Jim asked.

He took notes while she related the sequence of events after Matt left the shop.

"When I was leaving the hardware store," Matt added to her story, "I heard windows breaking and saw smoke pouring into the street. People were already stopping to look and someone must have called the fire department. They raced in right after I did. What did you find out about Langlois?"

"He wasn't home. His mother lives in Agawam, and she said he and his wife had gone to New York for the weekend. You're sure you don't need to go to the hospital?" Jim asked Rosie. "If you inhaled a lot of smoke…"

She shook her head. "I didn't inhale much. But I'm not sure Matt's okay."

"I'm fine," Matt insisted.

"What happened?" Jim asked.

Matt explained briefly about her attack on his person.

Jim shook his head pityingly. "You were taken down by a girl?"

"A very angry girl," Matt qualified. "I think I get extra credit for that."

Jim laughed. "Okay. You can leave. I'm going to call the state guys to see if we can figure out what happened here. Then I'm going to try Langlois again."

"I'm going to take Rosie to the Breakfast Barn. You want our cell phone numbers so we can keep in touch?"

"Sure." Jim took out his notepad and wrote them down. "I'll let you know what we find out."

"Thanks. Talk to you later."

Rosie looked down at her smoke-smudged suit. "I'm not very presentable to go to breakfast, am I? I'm not sure I'm hungry after what's happened this morning."

"I'll get your coat. No one'll notice your suit. And if all you can eat is a roll, that's fine, too." He rubbed the smoke off her face with his handkerchief. Over her shoulder, he saw a young woman with a camera running from the direction of the *Mirror*'s office.

He retrieved Rosie's coat from the coat rack in the rear of the shop, then hurried her to the parking lot before the reporter noticed them.

"Hate to do that to a fellow newshound," he said to the woman, "but we have a few important things to do, and fast. Before we go to the Breakfast Barn."

In the car, Matt called Information for the number of Whitcomb's Wonders as he drove in the direction of the school.

Rosie blinked from the passenger seat. "What are you doing?"

But he was concentrating on the operator's response and let the system dial the number for him.

"What's Jackie's husband's name?"

"Hank. Why? What are you doing?"

A woman answered and he asked for Hank, who picked up immediately.

Matt introduced himself and explained what had happened at Rosie's shop.

"Jackie told me about your getting shot after the wedding reception," Hank said. "What do you think's going on?"

"I have no idea, but I understand you have a security service. I'd like to hire you to watch Maple Hill Elementary."

When he said the words, Rosie turned in her seat, her eyes horrified. He put a hand to her arm.

"I don't think whoever's doing this would take it out on Rosie's nephew, but then I'm not really sure what we're dealing with. Chase Erickson is in the third grade."

"I know him," Hank said. "He's in my daughter's class."

"I think it'd be good if his routine continued as normally as possible, but I'd appreciate it if you could watch him while he's in school. He's been through a lot. I'd rather he didn't know what was going on."

"Sure. I'll do it myself. He's in school right now?"

"I'm pulling up in front of the building," Matt said. "I'll stay until you can get here."

"I'm on my way."

Matt turned off the phone and pocketed it while he scanned the playground for some sign of Chase. Children ran, jumped, screamed and wrestled in the snow.

"Ten o'clock," Rosie said. "This is the younger kids' recess. He should be out here. He's probably running wild somewhere, being Motor Man. There!"

She pointed to the end of the playground clear of swings, slides and monkey bars. Matt spotted Chase's green parka, hood, sleeves, back flying out behind him as he ran in his superhero persona.

"Do you believe that!" she exclaimed, reaching for her door handle. "He's going to catch pneumonia! And where are his mittens?"

Matt stopped her and pointed. As though on cue, a teacher who was apparently monitoring the playground stopped him and, after a brief exchange, helped him put on the coat. She dug in his pockets and handed him his mittens.

Rosie sank back in her seat and folded her arms, a picture of angry resentment. "Do you really think whoever's after me will go after Chase?"

"No," Matt replied. "Just better safe than sorry,

though. With your friend watching him, we can get serious about trying to figure out what's going on."

A silver midsize car pulled up across the street.

"Is that Hank?" Matt asked Rosie.

She frowned at the car. "I'm not sure. I usually see him in a truck with his company name emblazoned on the side."

A tall, dark-haired man in a brown barn coat and cords stepped out of the car and crossed the street toward them.

Rosie laughed in relief. "That's Hank." She reached for her door handle again, and Matt stopped her a second time.

"Stay inside," he said. "I'll talk to him."

"But—"

"Please. Stay inside."

Matt climbed out of the car and offered his hand to Hank Whitcomb. He liked the man's firm grip and the steady look in his blue eyes.

"This may all be unnecessary," Matt said, "but I want to be sure Chase is safe without having to keep him home."

Hank nodded, turning toward the playground. "He'll never know I'm around."

"How large is your security team?"

"We have ten men. Security's a relatively new avenue for us. The two of you need protection?"

"Not yet," Matt replied. "But if it comes to that, I'll call you. We'll pick up Chase at 3:10. You're okay for that long?"

"We'll have him covered until you pick him up, then we'll be here before you deliver him in the morning."

"That's great." Matt shook hands with him again. "Thank you."

Rosie was silent, her expression pensive as Matt drove to the restaurant. He'd had to assure her several times that Chase would be watched every moment.

"I never thought about *him* being in danger," she said.

"He probably isn't. I just thought it was a good idea to cover all the bases."

"We have to find out in a hurry what's going on or I'll never have a moment's peace. Thank goodness everybody else is gone."

"We're going to work on it," he promised. "Right after we have some breakfast."

All the old streetlights downtown were decorated with evergreen wreaths around the globes, and bright red bows trailing ribbon. Their festive cheer seemed to mock the events of the morning.

"I don't get it," she said as he turned into the restaurant's parking lot and found a spot on the far side. "Langlois was so in our faces last time. I can't believe he'd operate this way."

"Of course you don't get it." He let himself out and walked around to open her door. In the old days she'd been too impatient to keep moving to allow him to perform the small courtesy, but she was weighed down by her thoughts this morning. And no wonder. "It's hard to grasp. I've never known you to have an enemy."

She accepted his hand out, let him close the door for her, then casually caught his good arm as they walked to the door of the restaurant. He'd be happy to have her this distracted all the time.

"Still," she said, "there has to be a reason. It's only logical."

"Is it possible you've hurt someone without being aware of it?"

She thought about that while he opened the door. They were assailed by delicious breakfast smells, and to her surprise, her stomach grumbled in hunger. "I've been racking my brain for something like that, but I can't come up with anything."

There was an empty booth near a window and she headed for it.

He caught her hand to stop her and started for a table in the middle of the floor.

She pulled against him with a puzzled frown. "A booth's more comfortable. You've always preferred a booth."

He pulled insistently the other way. "I don't want you near a window. The table's better."

She went with him. "Oh. You think somebody would try something with all these people around?"

"I don't know," he said honestly, holding a chair out for her. "I have no idea what—or who—we're up against. But there were a lot of people on the street this morning, yet your shop's in shambles, anyway."

"Yes."

As he sat at a right angle to her, he saw her anger

dim and helplessness take over. He regretted his thoughtless choice of words. "On the good side," he tried to joke, "I have the hinge in my coat pocket to fix your dressing-room door."

A tear spilled over and she swiped it away with her fingertips, tossing her head in an effort to regain her composure. She smiled. His joke *was* funny.

"I'm going back this afternoon," she said, "to start cleaning up. Whoever's doing this is not going to win."

"You might have to wait a day or two." He handed her a napkin. "The police will keep the scene secure until they've gone over everything. But as soon as we can get in, I'll help you."

Rita Robidoux appeared with a pot of coffee in one hand, two cups in the other, and menus under her arm. She took one look at Rosie's red-rimmed eyes and demanded of Matt, "What did you say to her?"

He waggled his eyebrows at Rita. "I told her I was running away with you," he said dramatically, "and it broke her heart."

"Oh. Well, get over it, honey," she said, nudging Rosie's shoulder with an elbow. "You'll never be able to keep him with those skinny hips and that innocent face. A man wants a woman of substance, and I'm not talkin' character or bank account, I'm talkin' ballast. And he wants a woman who gets around, you know what I mean?" She waggled her eyebrows the way he had. "He has to know you've got a bad side."

Rosie rolled her eyes. "Yeah, right. You volunteer

at the hospital, and you help out with Sunday school. Just how bad are you?"

Rita sputtered a little. "Well…I…I mean…I *could* be bad if I had time."

Rosie shook her head sadly. "You'd never have enough time. The truth is, you're just a good woman, Rita. I'm sorry."

"You mean I can't have him?"

"No."

Rita turned to Matt. "You're going to let her break us up?"

"If you're not as bad as you claim…"

"I'm wearing black underwear," she offered gamely.

Rosie patted her arm consolingly. "Amateur. I'm not wearing any."

Rita laughed. "Guess I'm out of my league." She poured their coffee. "I'll be right back."

That silly exchange had put a little of the sparkle back in Rosie's eyes. She consulted her menu studiously, then closed it with an air of finality and picked up her coffee cup.

"French toast with blueberries and a side of bacon?" He guessed her order while closing his menu.

She seemed surprised that he remembered her favorite, then apparently decided to rise to the game. "You're having a country omelette with gravy," she said, "hash browns and sourdough toast."

He was pleased and surprised. "Right."

"Did you really take two weeks off?" She sipped

her coffee, then put her cup down and crossed her arms on the table. She was more relaxed suddenly and he'd do anything to help her stay that way.

"I did," he replied. "I was going to spend the extra time shooting snowscapes, but I'll spend it helping you clean and redecorate instead. I wield a mean wallpaper brush."

"I remember. You're also pretty good with a floor sander."

Well. Another inside joke.

When they'd been working on their house, she'd been impatient to use the sander, ignoring his suggestion that she wait until he got home from work and could show her how to use it. Operating it was simple, but holding it firmly so that its power didn't wrest control from the operator was a concept she refused to consider a problem.

He'd walked into the front door to find her staring mournfully at an old buffet they'd bought at an antique shop. The beautiful gray oak finish she'd labored over now had a large, round spot in it where the sander had climbed the furniture and continued working.

"It's harder to control than I thought," she'd explained, her tone repentant. "Go ahead and say it. I never listen. I should have waited. I always have to do it my way."

"Why don't I sand the floor," he'd bargained, so in love with her he didn't have the heart to say "I told you so." "And you can refinish the buffet."

She'd wrapped her arms around his neck. "You

know what happens to husbands who don't behave in a superior way when they have every right to?" she'd asked.

"I give up."

"They're made love to all night long by their very appreciative wives."

He remembered that night as a highlight of their marriage. When he'd been particularly morose in his small apartment in Sacramento and he'd wanted to torture himself, he'd thought about the long, velvet hours of that night and her delicious, deliberate attentions. He'd wallowed in his pain.

Now, with her smiling at him across the table, even considering the strange circumstances, the memory brought pleasure instead.

He wondered if she was remembering, too, but Rita had returned to take their order. By the time Rita walked away, Matt could see in Rosie's eyes that her thoughts were back to the fire.

"I was just remembering," Rosie said, "that Langlois dropped a tree on the Department of Environmental Quality guy's truck two years ago. He claimed it was an accident, and no one was able to prove otherwise. He took the whole committee to court for trying to build on land that should have been protected. I mean, once we discovered the environmental-impact statement had missed a heron rookery, I was on his side."

With the knowledge Matt had acquired later of Hal Erickson's sometimes shady dealings, he wouldn't be surprised if Hal had bought the impact statement. Matt had worked for the newspaper at the time, and while reporting on a shopping center being built on the edge of town by a construction company that was not his father-in-law's, he'd discovered that a considerable sum of money had changed hands.

The developer had paid six figures to Sonic Industries for some nebulous consulting. Matt trailed the consulting firm to a Boston bank account—in Hal Erickson's name.

A short time later several occupants of the building filed a joint suit against their landlord for faulty wiring. Matt could only guess that Hal had arranged for an inspector he'd already paid to pass the project and had kept a hefty sum for himself.

Matt had checked and double-checked his facts, and had been deciding how best to approach Rosie with the information when Jay had his accident, then Hal had killed himself. The whole issue moot at that point, Matt had kept the information to himself.

Now he couldn't help but wonder what other shady maneuverings Hal might have been involved in and, more importantly, who might know about them. Maybe there was someone out there who'd participated in one of Hal's schemes and lost out when he died. But why would he take it out on Rosie?

It didn't make sense.

But then, neither did the two attempts on her life.

"Maybe we should find out if Langlois is home," Rosie said. "Maybe if he got wind of the project, he thinks we intend to use the old spot and that we're out to ruin the rookery, after all. But we have a different spot in mind."

"Have you had any contact with environmentalists over this?"

"No. Nothing's gone that far. And we're trying to keep it quiet until Tolliver comes to talk to us. But you know how it is. Members of the committee have husbands or wives, and no matter how quiet you try to keep it, somebody shares something. Then it's shared again over coffee or a bridge game, and before you know it, everyone's got the wrong idea."

"What other groups do you belong to?"

"Kiwanis and Saint Anne's Circle of the Altar and Rosary Society."

He grinned. "How subversive."

"I know. Hardly groups to inspire hatred or revenge."

Rita brought their breakfasts, refilled their coffee cups, then walked away with a wink at Matt and the promise in a loud whisper that he knew where to find her if he changed his mind about running away with her.

He blew her a kiss.

"Try not to think about this morning while you're eating," he advised Rosie. "Indigestion isn't going to help anything."

She made an exasperated sound. "I feel like I'm living in a movie."

He swapped her the syrup for the pepper shaker. "Then there's big money for us at the end of filming?"

"No, this isn't a Sandra Bullock–Keanu Reeves flick, but one of those where the sound track's horrible and you've never heard of anyone in it."

"An independent film? Sometimes those turn out to be sleeper hits. And the filmmaker usually has a message, so you'll emerge victorious after all."

"Well, that's a relief." She cut a piece of French toast, cooked blueberries on top and sweetened cream cheese oozing out of the middle, and stabbed it with her fork. "I was afraid I was in real danger of getting killed."

"I'd never let that happen." He remained as casual as she sounded.

"How's your arm?"

"Fine."

"I'm sorry I keep hitting it."

He shrugged. "I forgive you. It's probably some unconscious need on your part to hurt me."

She appeared offended by the suggestion. "No, it isn't. It was an accident. Both times." Her angst was replaced by a sudden offhand acceptance when she added, "And you're the one who got in the way of the bullet. You should have just let it hit me and you could be on your way home right—"

She stopped abruptly when he caught her closest wrist and applied a small amount of pressure. A score of recriminations rose to the tip of his tongue, but there was such fear and misery in her eyes that all he said was, "Self-pity isn't going to get you anywhere."

She yanked free of him. "And acting like a Neanderthal isn't going to get you anywhere, either."

"Just be quiet and eat," he advised.

CHAPTER EIGHT

MATT AND ROSIE finished breakfast in silence, then stopped at the cashier on their way out.

"I'll be in the car," Rosie said, taking off in that direction as Matt put a bill on the counter. He caught a fistful of her coat and pulled her back to him.

"Would you stop *doing* that?" she demanded, trying to slap his arm away. She didn't know what had come over him. He'd always had a mind of his own in the old days, but he'd never imposed it on her.

He held on, smiling in the face of the cashier's concerned expression as she rang up their meal. "Stay with me," he said to Rosie.

"I'm just going…" She pointed in the direction of the car.

"Stay—with—me." He enunciated for emphasis, retaining his hold.

She growled her impatience while the woman behind the counter handed Matt his change. He left a generous tip for Rita, then caught Rosie's hand and walked out into the cold morning.

"If you're going to keep grabbing me," she began,

squaring off with him the moment the doors closed behind them, "you can just—"

"I *am* going to keep grabbing you," he interrupted, doing just that as he took her arm and drew her with him to the car, "because you have to start thinking before you act. You're in danger, Rosie. From now on you stay with me at all times, and never do *anything* to make yourself a target."

She raised her head, pleading to heaven. "It's not like there's a sniper waiting behind every bush to pick me off!"

He raised an eyebrow, letting that claim echo between them. "Isn't it?" he asked, opening her door. "I thought I had the wound to prove it."

He was absolutely right; she hated that. She got into the car and he slammed the door after her. He slid behind the wheel.

"You used to wear that same face in the old days," she accused, as angry with herself as she was at him. It was easier to take it out on him. "When you don't understand me, you get angry."

"When I don't understand you," he said, turning the key in the ignition, "I lose you. I've been here before, Rosie."

He backed out of the parking spot and headed for the exit.

When I don't understand you, I lose you.

Memories of her feelings at that time were becoming clearer. Three tragedies in a row had felt like such a personal attack that she'd been at war with the whole world. And—in some little corner of her mind she hadn't completely sedated in the intervening time— she'd stored a vague memory of Matt being the enemy, too.

Now where had she gotten that? She could pull up images of him trying to offer comfort and her pulling away; of him sitting beside her on the window seat in what was going to be the nursery, and her walking away; of him pleading with her to tell him what she thought and felt, and of her taking a certain pleasure in staring back at him blankly and not speaking.

She was appalled now at that memory. She found herself wondering—not how he could have left, but why he'd waited so long.

She could only think that she'd had too many tragedies in a row to reason with sanity. She'd been like a beaten animal, wanting to hurt whomever came near.

Matt drove through town and was some distance into the countryside when she realized he wasn't going home. They passed a pair of cross-country skiers, a whole neighborhood of children sledding down a man-made hill and an older woman wearing an apron over her parka and twining garland on her porch pillar.

"Where are we going?" she asked.

He sighed and gave her a brief, testy glance. "Lan-glois's place."

"I'm not sure he still lives there. He got married, you know."

"If he's moved, we'll find out where he went."

Danbury Road was two miles out of town and into

the woods. The homemade and rather small A-frame was patched together with random pieces of lumber, pressed wood and masonite. Smoke curled from a little metal chimney protruding from one slope of the roof, and someone had added a window box to the structure's single window. There was nothing growing in it at the moment, but it was a cheery note, anyway.

A large yellow dog emerged from a doghouse apparently built to the same plans as the dwelling. He ran toward the car, barking.

Matt pushed open his door. Rosie caught his sleeve. "Be careful of the dog!" she cautioned.

"That's a Lab," he said. "Have you ever met an unfriendly Lab?"

"He's barking at you."

"He's saying hello and letting me know he's in charge." Matt opened her door. "You coming?"

She pretended shock. "You mean I'm actually allowed to get out of the car?"

"If you promise not to mouth off at every opportunity."

She followed him up a set of rickety stairs, marveling that he'd been right about the dog. Now that they approached the house, the animal was more of a reception committee than a security force. He licked Matt's face when Matt leaned down to scratch his ears.

The front door flew open suddenly and Langlois appeared in the doorway. Rosie had always considered him an intimidating presence, though she'd always tried to conceal her fear.

He was taller than Matt and barrel-chested, in a worn but spotless blue-and-gray-flannel shirt and jeans. His pale blue eyes had the scary wildness of a zealot's and his left eye had a puckered scar across the outside edge of it that pulled up that side of his face and made him look even more frightening. Rumor was he'd sustained the injury while trying to help an injured heron.

That would have been a noble goal, but the fact that he'd done it by disabling logging trucks and planting booby traps in the woods to keep loggers and hikers out, albeit deeds no one had been able to prove him guilty of, sullied his cause.

Rosie tried to look as fearless as Matt did when he faced him. She wasn't sure Langlois would recognize Matt, but he did.

"What do *you* want?" he asked belligerently.

"I want to ask you about a threat that was left on Rosie's answering machine," Matt replied. "About a shot that was fired at her yesterday, and a fire that took place in town this morning."

Langlois didn't react for a moment, then he shifted his weight and folded his arms in a defensive gesture. "I don't have a phone or a gun. And where was this fire?"

"Rosie's shop in the Porter Building. She was locked inside and it was partially destroyed."

Rosie had to admire Matt's technique. He was perfectly calm, but gave the impression of fury about to erupt.

Langlois looked him over, probably getting the

same sense of controlled temper. "I don't know any-thing about it," he said finally, firmly. "Any of it."

A plump woman appeared at his elbow, her pink cheeks, freckled nose, and wispy, light brown hair es-caping her bun, bringing conversation to a stop. She seemed so maternal and so wrong for the reclusive, an-tisocial activist.

Langlois placed an arm around her shoulders and drew her close. "Betsy, here, can tell you I've been home all morning. And we were in New York over the weekend. Got back late last night."

"It's true." Betsy leaned into him, wiping her hands on a tea towel. "Ben's been up since seven, chopping wood. I baked all day Friday and used up what we had." She smiled with convincing sincerity. "Nothing like corn bread baked in a woodstove."

"Why would I want to do anything to you, any-way?" Langlois asked, looking at Rosie. "Our squab-ble was two years ago over Tolliver Textiles, and the plans for that plant went down."

"You haven't heard that we're trying to bring it back?" Rosie asked. At Langlois's sudden frown, she added, "Not in the same place."

Betsy patted his stomach, which looked consider-ably rounder than it had two years ago, and said qui-etly, "Remember how we solve these things now."

His frown slowly dissolved as he drew a deep breath. "I'm a peaceful man now," he said, and Rosie noticed his new air of dignity. "We work for nature in a different way."

Betsy pulled a silver chain from the inside of her big sweater. A cross dangled from the end of it. "We pray about it, and we do what we can in a peaceful, loving way. I'm sorry about your shop, but Ben didn't do it."

"I didn't," Ben echoed, then pulled the same kind of chain out of his shirt. He met Matt's gaze defensively, as though daring him to ridicule.

Matt nodded. "All right, then. If you're truly dedicated to peaceful solutions, I'd appreciate it if you hear anything about who might have done this, you'll contact the police. Or me."

Langlois was no friend of the police, but Betsy agreed willingly. "Of course. We don't save God's wild creatures by hurting his children."

The yellow dog walked Matt and Rosie back to the car, and Ben and Betsy watched them drive away.

"Do you believe them?" Rosie asked Matt.

"I'm not sure." He turned the car back toward town. "She's convincing, but with that face she could have bumped off three husbands and no one'd suspect her. On the other hand, if she is being honest, Langlois does look like a man in love. He might have changed for her."

"So that leaves us suspecting my friends in Kiwanis, or the ladies in my church circle?"

"I don't think so. There's someone else out there with reasons we don't know."

That undefined element was more upsetting than being able to put a face on whoever was after her. She recalled how she'd felt only hours ago when she'd realized someone had locked her inside her shop and set it on fire. She'd been frightened, certainly, but anger had predominated.

Now that she had some distance from the incident and couldn't imagine who was doing this, fear was getting a stronger hold. She folded her arms, put her feet up against the dash and contemplated her world.

It wasn't pretty. She was childless, separated from her husband, she'd lost her brother and her father, was left with a mother with whom she had difficulty relating, and the wild little sister who'd driven her crazy but still provided comfort and support was now embarking on a life of her own.

Chase was part of her life, and while that would have been a definite plus at any other time, now that someone was trying to get rid of her, keeping him safe was a terrible worry.

Matt gently slapped the side of her thigh. "Relax," he said. "I'm not going to let anybody hurt you."

Yes, he'd proven that. But neither did she want anyone to hurt him.

"I was just worried about Chase," she said.

"Chase is fine. Hank's on it. You can admit that you're a little worried about yourself."

She hugged her knees and hitched up a shoulder as though it didn't matter. Admitting to one vulnerability would open the door to all the others, and her life was crowded with them. If they escaped her, she might cave in on herself.

"You've assured me that I'm fine," she said. "I'm not worried."

"I'd like to believe you trust me to that degree," he said. They'd reached the outskirts of town and he slowed to the lower speed limit. "But I don't."

She pretended that what he thought didn't matter either. "What can I tell you?"

"Why is it so hard," he demanded, "to tell me what you're feeling? Why can't you admit to me that you're frightened or upset or so deep in grief you don't think you can go on?"

She didn't want to go where this conversation was taking her, so she gave him the look she'd perfected in that time just before he left.

"Fine," he said, pulling off the road and stopping. "Put me off with that look, but the ploy won't work forever. Eventually you're going to have to face what you're feeling or it'll poison you."

She sighed and said with as much firmness as she could muster, "Matthew, I can't go back to that time emotionally and survive. I can't. I'm just trying to inch ahead."

"You won't look behind you," he said gently, "so you can't see that all that stuff is following you. You have to deal with it."

She met his eyes. "Have you?"

"Not completely," he admitted. "My responsibility in the whole thing is tied to how you choose to handle it, and you won't. You're ruining our lives, Rosie."

"Someone's trying to *take* mine before it's ruined. But you *could* save yours by going home."

"I'M STAYING," he told her, seeing the heartbreak in her eyes and unable to force the issue further. "Whoever's after you has to go through me."

She sighed. "I don't want you to die for me, Matthew."

"Nobody's going to die. We'll find out what's going on and stop it."

"Yeah." She did not sound convinced. "I should go back to the shop and assess the damage."

"Okay," he agreed. He knew finally what would cheer up both of them. "But there's something we should do first."

"What's that?"

He pointed to the sign that bracketed the road just ahead of them. CHRISTMAS TREES, it read. "We should get a tree." When they'd been together, buying their Christmas tree and putting it up had been a highlight of their holiday for her.

She sighed wistfully, regretfully. "Mom doesn't like the needles all over the rug. We have a tall artificial one in boxes in the basement."

He thought quickly. "Well, when she comes home, I'll promise to clean up the mess. If she still complains, I'll take the tree down. Or we'll move it to the guest house."

She looked hopeful. "That's silly and a lot of trouble, isn't it?"

"Would you like to do it?"

He caught a glimpse of her smile from years ago. "I would."

"Then let's." He drove down the road, and pulled into the parking area. It was empty, business still slow this first week of December.

"We'll be able to get a twelve-footer," she said, looking around with real interest, "before the banks and businesses grab them all."

This was good. She was coming back. "I know," he said. "That was always your plan."

It took an hour for her to find the perfect tree. He didn't mind trailing after her, holding up one tree after another, keeping it steady as she spread branches, trying to determine how symmetrical it was. For now, she seemed to have forgotten everything else in the simple task of picking out a tree.

The tears had washed off her makeup, and she looked sweet and youthful, like the young woman he'd fallen in love with. The bun she'd started out with this morning had been downgraded to a ponytail after the traumas of the day, and it now swung behind her as she spotted a giant tree on the far corner of the lot and raced toward it.

The tag said it was a twelve-foot white pine. It was lush and pliable, and when she opened it out, she breathed a sigh of satisfaction. "This is it," she said.

Then almost as an afterthought, she asked, "Do *you* like it?"

"Sure," he replied.

"No," she said, stopping him as he reached through the branches for the trunk and began to drag it toward the trailer where a clerk waited. "It's important that you like it, too."

It was? "I like it," he assured her.

"A lot?"

"A lot."

"Okay." She swept a hand in the direction of the trailer.

The clerk helped him tie the tree to the roof of the car.

It protruded over the vehicle at both ends, and that seemed to delight her. "It's been so long since I've had a real tree," she said chattily as they got back into the car. "Chase is going to be so excited."

"Can I interest you in some mistletoe?" the clerk asked with a suggestive smile. "Complimentary on a ten-footer or taller. I carry the most effective stuff around. You can test it first, if you like."

Rosie was clearly indecisive and embarrassed. They'd always hung mistletoe when they were together, and used it with playful frequency.

"Sure," Matt replied, following the clerk back to the trailer. The man disappeared inside, then leaned out of the doorway with a sprig of the green stuff tied with a simple red bow. He winked at Matt. "Use it in good health."

Matt went back to the Chevy Tahoe where Rosie waited and handed her the sprig. "Take good care of that," he said as he climbed in behind the wheel. "It's critical to the full effectiveness of the season."

She turned the stem in her fingers. "Yes," she said with a faint smile. "I remember."

With her spirits somewhat lifted, he hated to take her by Happily Ever After. "You're sure you want to go by the shop before we go home?"

She nodded, her spirits apparently fortified by the purchase of the tree. "Yes. Ignoring the fire and the damage isn't going to erase it."

"We might not be able to get in."

"That's okay. At least I'll have some idea what I'm up against."

Jim Machado was inspecting the front of the building when they arrived. He offered a hand to Rosie so that she could climb over the crime-scene tape. Matt followed.

"No fingerprints." Jim pointed with his pencil to the doorknob. "Obviously someone who watches *CSI*," he said dryly. "The arsonist's been very careful. But the ignition point was that old trunk. It'll be the end of the week before we know what the accelerant was. Maybe that'll tell us something. We should stay out of there to keep the scene clean in case the guys need another look."

"We went to see Ben Langlois," Matt said while Rosie peered through the broken window.

Jim arched an eyebrow. "Why? I told you I was going to check him out, but I've been a little busy here."

"I wanted to see him myself, judge the situation for myself."

Jim frowned at him. "When was the last time you saw me write a news story?"

"Pardon me?"

"I don't write news stories," Jim clarified, "you don't conduct police investigations. Leave this stuff to me, all right?"

"I want Rosie to be safe," Matt said, "and if Langlois did know about the committee, I thought he might be going after her again."

"Which becomes police business. My job. You've already been shot once. You trying for permanent disability pension?"

"Sergeant's stripes have made you bossy," Matt complained.

"They also make me grumpy, so don't cross me, okay?" That threat delivered, Jim asked, "So what did he say?"

"I think he's got a wholesome woman. She insists he was home with her this morning, chopping wood. She says he prays now for conservation issues, instead of fighting the system on them."

"Do we believe him?"

"I don't know," Matt replied in a tone that was a bit jocular. "So we *are* all policemen, are we? Some of us are just getting in your way."

"That's true." Jim seemed to be trying not to smile. "But I've known you to have good instincts."

"Okay, then. We believe him."

Rosie got between them. "Jim, maybe you'd like to come over for pizza when you have the results from the lab."

"I would. I'll bring the wine."

"Okay. When can I get into the store?"

"End of the week. Call me first to make sure it's clear."

"I will." She turned to Matt. "Let's go put up the tree."

Jim looked from one to the other in confusion. "You got a tree already? And you're putting it up? Together?"

"We needed an infusion of cheer," Matt said.

"Then…you're staying?"

"For a while."

Rosie was quiet as they walked back to the car and drove home. He suspected she was wondering where this time together would take them. So was he. It was an issue they should probably address at some point, but there'd be time for that. Right now he was preoccupied with keeping her alive so that she would *have* a future.

CHAPTER NINE

ROSIE FOUND a Christmas-tree stand in the attic and brought down boxes containing all their old ornaments. They'd also been kept, along with some other personal things, in her mother's attic because of the lack of storage room in the guest house.

They put the tree in the stand near the windows in the living room with its view of the lake. She wrapped an old sheet around the base and dug through the boxes until she found a little balsa-wood village Matt had made to go with the electric train she'd given him one Christmas. She wanted to wait for Chase to help them decorate the tree, but she couldn't help dressing up underneath.

Matt had made coffee while she'd fussed with the village, and he came to sit cross-legged on the floor beside her and handed her a steaming cup.

"Wow," he said. "Bedford Falls."

They'd given the village that name because of the classic Christmas movie *It's a Wonderful Life*.

"Do you still have the train?" she asked. This was touchy territory, memories from a time when their love had been deep and their romance hot.

"Of course. I still haven't gotten over the thrill of having it. I have a long mantel in the living room of my apartment. The train can't run there, but I can see it. It reminds me of the difference you made in my life."

She was surprised by that candid claim. She presumed he meant the good difference she'd made in the beginning. He'd had a nightmare childhood, despicable parents—a druggie and an alcoholic, and absolutely no connection to a time that should have been full of innocent fun—athletics, birthday parties, electric trains. He'd once told her he'd always admired a friend's toy trains, so she'd bought him a set the first Christmas after they were married. It reminded her of her father's old train set, which he always brought out at Christmas.

"I knew early on that my life was unusual and a real sinkhole compared to other kids' lives." He frowned as he spoke, but she knew him to be remarkably sane, considering his awful childhood. "I was determined to be as different from my parents as possible. I studied hard, worked hard, and built a normal life. But I didn't know what it was like to love someone until you."

"Please," she said, guilt making her uncomfortable under his praise. "You're not indebted to me for anything."

"That's not true." He made no move to touch her, but she felt his eyes rove over her, embrace her. "When you truly learn to love, you can get past the bad stuff. You know that it's forever, good and bad, high and low, laughter and grief, and though it can get pretty beaten up, love endures."

He'd said before that he wanted to talk about what had happened and try to put it behind them so that each of them could move on. She knew that was a healthy attitude, but it wasn't for her—not yet. Still, she had to admire his openhearted honesty. And she had to admit her responsibility for all that had gone wrong.

"I'm sorry I'm not that generous," she said, her throat constricting. "I'm sorry I hurt you."

He seemed shocked by her admission. He held a hand out to her. She knew it would complicate things if she took it, but her hand seemed to reach for his of its own volition.

"I only wanted to help," he said softly. "Why wouldn't you let me?"

"I don't know." She squeezed his hand. "I don't remember. I don't *want* to remember."

"I loved you anyway."

"I know." She did recall hating that he loved her. Not hating *him,* but his love for her that held on in spite of everything.

He used the hand he held to draw her closer. "I love you now, Rosie."

She understood that she loved him, too, but admitting that would take her back to the baby they'd created together and lost, and all the other awful events of that time. And she simply hadn't the strength. She held on to him, but didn't reply.

"I know." He sighed and smiled. "It's the wrong

moment, and there's too much in our way right now, but we have a little time and distance from what happened, and I think we could work it all out if we tried. If you can remember what you felt and tell me."

She was afraid he was going to want agreement from her, but instead, he picked up his cup and got to his feet. "What box did you say the lights were in?"

She pointed to a carton with the name of a grapefruit grower on the side. "That one."

He looked at his watch. "Are they all entangled?"

"Of course not."

"Good. Then maybe we can string them on the tree before we pick up Chase, and you and he can spend the evening putting on the ornaments. I'll ply you with hot chocolate."

He did precisely that. Chase was ecstatic over the tree and ran upstairs to get a small box from the floor of his closet. In it were ornaments his father had given him, some from his grandmother and Rosie, and several he'd made at school.

But before he put them on, Rosie dug out several strands of garland that were made of plastic beads faceted to make the optimum use of light. When she and Chase had finished placing them on the tree, Matt plugged in the lights just to measure their progress.

"Woooow!" Chase said, leaning into Rosie and wrapping his arms around her waist. "*Look* at it! I like Grandma's tree, but it isn't half as beautiful as that. Uncle Matt, look!"

"Pretty great, huh?" Matt came to stand behind

them, a hand on each of their shoulders. "Your aunt is one of Santa's helpers in disguise, did you know that?"

Chase turned to look at her, his eyes uncertain. He was caught in that place common to eight-year-olds at Christmastime, somewhere between skepticism and belief.

"She doesn't have pointy ears," Chase said finally. "And I always thought she didn't like Christmas." He looked up at her to verify that. "Right? Last year you went to Hawaii 'cause you said you didn't want to be around snow and Christmas trees."

"You did?" Matt seemed to be trying to analyze why she'd done that.

"Yes," she admitted, sure he'd figure it out. "I wanted to escape Christmas. The year before, it had all just happened and I was too numb to know what was going on. But last year, I was sharply aware of everything and wanted no part of the holidays, so Sara and I took off. I thought getting away to some nontraditional Christmas environment would do the trick. But there was still Christmas music everywhere, manger scenes in the church, and excited people buying presents. So the sunshine and the palm trees were out of sync for me and only made me long for home, anyway."

"Well, I'm glad you didn't take off for Hawaii this year," Matt said, "because look at what you'd have missed." He pointed to the living-room window. On the other side of it snow fell in large fluffy flakes.

"Woooow!" Chase exclaimed again. "Maybe we'll have a foot of snow tomorrow!"

Matt shook his head. "The weather report said just a good dusting. No blizzard."

"Bummer."

"I'll get dinner while you two keep decorating."

"No." Chase caught his wrist. "Can't you help us?"

"I can," Matt replied, "but I thought you must be getting hungry."

"I am. But can't we all cook dinner, then we can all decorate? Something easy for dinner like sandwiches or something."

"Excellent solution." Rosie caught Matt's arm and Chase's hand and set off to the kitchen. In the doorway between the dining room and the kitchen, Matt pulled her to a stop. She was confused until he pointed to the mistletoe hanging from the molding above their heads. Before she could think about it or even complain, he kissed her, then went into the kitchen to put on the coffee.

Not that she *would* have complained.

Rosie made leftover meat-loaf sandwiches while Matt stirred canned soup and Chase set the table. While they ate, Matt asked about Chase's day at school, probably anxious to know, Rosie guessed, if he'd detected Hank's presence.

Chase talked about the terrifying aspects of long division, the fun of making "goopy" papier-mâché sculptures, and a girl named Misty who thought she knew everything. "Course, she does," he added. "She's the smartest kid in school. She wants to be president."

"Of the United States?" Matt asked.

"Yeah," Chase replied. "She's gonna put me in charge of the army."

"Wow. That's a big responsibility. 'Cause everybody wants peace instead of war. You know that, don't you?"

Chase nodded. "Yeah. We don't want people to die. Enough of them die already from stuff that isn't bombs and guns." He spoke with surprising conviction, clearly the product of firsthand information. He smiled at Matt. "I'm glad that hunter guy didn't kill you."

Matt nodded. "Me, too."

Rosie had told him about the fire in the shop, but had left out the part about being locked in, and told him they thought it was caused by a wiring problem. She wanted him as free of worry as possible.

They all pitched in on the kitchen cleanup, then went back to decorating the tree. Chase wanted some of his ornaments halfway up the tree, so Rosie got him the kitchen stool and played spotter while he found the perfect positions for a wooden snowman, a plastic dog with an antler headpiece, a glittering glass ball ornament with Santa painted on it. Rosie helped him put a clear ball with a Nativity inside near a yellow light.

While they worked, Matt stood on a ladder he'd hauled in from the garage and placed ornaments near the top of the tree. When Chase had finished with his, he handed others up to Matt, then pleaded for a spot on the ladder. Matt let him climb near the top but remained behind him.

Rosie handed up the jeweled star she and Matt had

bought at a church bazaar and always used as a tree topper. It was free-formed of gold wire and had been beaded randomly so that light glinted off it in irregular winks.

The task completed, Matt pushed the ladder and the kitchen stool aside, then turned off the lights and went to stand behind Chase and Rosie to admire their work.

Rosie couldn't speak. Her heart was so full it ached. For the first time in recent recollection, she felt as though she'd survived what had happened two years ago.

"My dad," Chase said solemnly, "would have liked this tree. Do you think he can see it?"

Matt picked him up with his uninjured arm and sat him astride his hip. "I'm sure he can. And I'll bet he's thinking that not only is this the coolest tree he's ever seen, but that you're turning into the coolest kid."

Chase smiled, then asked, serious again, "What do you think my mom's doing?"

Matt turned to Rosie for help with that question. Explaining a woman who'd run out on her child was more difficult than imagining someone looking down from heaven.

"She's probably still playing in a rock band," she replied, "maybe in some big city, or some friendly little town somewhere. Do you miss her?" He so seldom spoke of her, she couldn't imagine that was true, but he'd brought her up, so something was obviously on his mind.

"No," Chase said with convincing sincerity. "I just

wondered. 'Cause if I am in charge of peace someday, I'd like to know that everybody's happy."

Rosie exchanged another look with Matt, and this time there were tears in her eyes.

Matt turned Chase upside down and held him by his ankles, making Chase laugh hysterically. "Your job," Matt said, "is to make sure there's enough room under the tree for all the presents that are going to have to fit there. What do you think?"

"There's lots of room behind the village," Chase said, still laughing. "Do you think Santa's going to come?"

Matt swung him upright again, earning more heart-felt giggles. "Yes, he will," he replied, setting him on his feet. "If you believe."

"I sorta believe," Chase said frankly. "Sometimes I think it's kid stuff, then other times I'm not sure. So, I don't want to be wrong. I don't want him to skip me 'cause he thinks I don't believe in him."

"Being Santa's helper, Aunt Rosie gets all the news from the North Pole before anyone else does." Matt smoothed Chase's hair. "And you're definitely on his route."

"Oh, boy. I want a bike. Do you think I'll get a bike?"

"When he comes to town, you can ask him for one."

"When's he coming?"

Matt turned to Rosie.

"Um…December tenth, I think," she answered. "Then he'll be around until Christmas Eve."

"What are you gonna ask for?" Chase asked Matt.

"Adults don't get to ask for things. Only kids do. Adults have to get what they want for themselves."

Chase thought about that for a minute, then declared, "Bummer."

"Tell me about it. Do you have homework?"

"No. I got everything done in school. But I'm getting sleepy." He stretched theatrically. "I'm going to bed."

Rosie put a hand to her heart in shock and pretended to faint. Seeing his cue, Matt made a production of catching her.

"Cut it out, you guys," Chase said with a grin. "I want Santa to think I always go to bed on time. There's only a couple of days until he gets here. And if I want to get the bike…"

Matt stood Rosie on her feet.

"That's a very sensible idea," she said. "Matt, do you mind tucking him in? I have to get a few things ready for tomorrow."

MATT WAS HAPPY not to be left alone with her with the Christmas tree like a bright memory of their past right in the middle of the present.

He sat on the edge of Chase's bed while the boy changed his clothes in his private bathroom and brushed his teeth. His room was large, and as interesting as the boy was. His bed was fashioned like a Conestoga wagon. The bare ribs that would have held a canvas covering on the way West gave the occupant of the bed a sort of cozy, protected feeling without blocking the view of bookcase, stuffed animals on every surface, cars and trucks all over the floor, and a neighboring bed piled high with other toys.

Chase ran back into the room, climbed in under the covers, his smile wide. "What would you want if you *could* ask Santa for something?"

"Ah…let's see…" Matt wanted Rosie to love him the way she had when they'd gotten married. He wanted to have back those wonderful few months when she'd been pregnant and they'd looked forward to a future of baby photos, school programs and birthday parties. But that would take God, himself, rather than Santa. "A Nautilus, maybe," he said.

Chase blinked. "You mean, one of the big machines those muscley guys exercise on?" He looked over Matt's chest and shoulders dubiously.

"Yes." Matt pulled the covers up. "And don't look at me as if I couldn't work one. I'm strong. Want to see?" He pretended to push Chase into the mattress.

Chase giggled infectiously. "I wasn't! You already look kinda buff."

"That's better." Matt released him. "I work all the time and I never get a chance to exercise. A Nautilus would help me get a workout at home."

"I think they cost a lot of money. That's probably why you'd ask Santa instead of getting it for yourself, huh?"

"That's right. You need me to look under the bed or in the closet for monsters?"

Chase shook his head. "No. I'm not scared of them

anymore. But you could close the closet door—just in case."

"Right." Matt tucked him in, then did as he asked. "Anything else?"

"No. Thanks, Uncle Matt. I wish you could stay with us all the time." Chase joined his hands behind his head and smiled a little sadly. "There's no other guys around here. And you know how girls are. They're scared to let me do stuff."

Matt commiserated with a smile. "They just want you to be safe, but I know what you mean. You sleep well, and I'll see you in the morning."

"G'night."

Matt returned to the kitchen to find it empty, two cups left out on the counter near the coffeepot. He went into the living room where only the tree was lit and looking wonderfully old-fashioned in the contemporary space.

Rosie stood on the kitchen stool, apparently searching halfway up the tree for the right spot to place the ornament she held in her hand.

He approached her with a teasing remark about the possibility of the tree falling over with one more ornament, but realized as he got close that she was crying.

"Rosie?" he asked, catching the hand with which she balanced herself at the top of the stool. "What is it?"

She turned with the ornament in her hand and he saw that it was a Baby's First Christmas ornament Sara Ross had given them when they'd announced

Rosie's pregnancy at a friends-and-family party. It was a two-inch resin figure of a smiling new baby in a red-and-green-striped Christmas stocking. The baby held a banner with the year on it and the words *baby's first Christmas*.

To his utter and complete surprise, she opened her arms to him, still sobbing. He lifted her off the stool, set her on her feet and wrapped his arms around her.

For the first time since her miscarriage, they wept together over the loss of their baby.

She finally wedged a space between them and held up the ornament. "I thought we should put this on the tree," she said, her voice still contorted with tears but her eyes hopeful. "Though we lost the baby, she'll always be ours. I've spent the last two years wondering how I could live without her, but…that doesn't have to be, does it? I mean, she'll always be with us. Don't you think?"

He swiped at his eyes and swallowed. "I think you and I were always together—even while there were three thousand miles between us. We made her together, loved her together, even though we never got to see her. The three of us will always be part of each other, whatever happens."

"I like to think of her with my dad and my brother," she said.

He felt that pinch of guilt but ignored it. Who was to say how God decided eternal fates? Certainly he knew things they didn't. Hal *could* be in heaven.

"I think hanging it is a very good thing." He helped

her up onto the stool and steadied her while she looked for just the right place. Then he saw a bare spot. "There." He pointed. "Right next to Chase's Nativity."

She placed the ornament, looking happy with the spot. Then she turned to him again and to his complete shock, framed his face in her hands. He saw love in her eyes—probably remembered love, but love for him all the same. He drank it in like a man lost in the desert.

She leaned down to wrap her arms around him. "Oh, Matt," she said wistfully. "We loved each other so much."

"I love you now." He'd said that before, but he gave it more volume this time.

She held him tighter. "I still have trouble feeling anything but hurt and loss."

He lifted her off the stool and into his arms. "We can change that," he said. "Want to try?"

"But, your arm."

"It doesn't hurt. Well?"

He half expected her to refuse. But she leaned her head on his shoulder and relaxed against him. "Yes," she said.

Life and energy streamed through him and he headed for the stairs.

CHAPTER TEN

MATT CARRIED Rosie to his room, the one that she'd grown up in and that had been theirs when they'd come home for family events and holidays. It smelled of the fresh-air fragrance of his after-shave, and the scent of pine that had wafted upstairs.

As he put her on her feet near the bed, she saw the falling snow drifting past the window and thought there'd never been a more bittersweet moment in her life.

And she felt Matt's love restoring her. She found plans for the future taking place in her mind, was grateful now to be in this time and place, despite the threat that loomed somewhere outside.

They stood in each other's arms. She looped hers around his neck as he embraced her. She'd always felt so safe with him, so precious to him. She struggled to remember why she'd let that go.

He crushed her to him. "Don't think about what hurts, Rosie. We can't forget what's happened. It's part of us. But focus on my touch. Remember how much in love we were. How loving each other could make the rest of the world go away."

"I'm somebody different now." She closed her eyes and concentrated on the circling movements of his hand between her shoulder blades, down her spine. "And you're different, too. But you improved. You're even steadier, stronger than before."

She had more to tell him, but he made more words impossible by kissing her—and continuing to kiss her as he gathered up the bottom of her turtleneck. He placed that circling hand against her bare flesh and she sighed in surrender. She raised her arms obligingly, and he pulled the sweater off.

He waited patiently while she unbuttoned his shirt. She pulled it off his shoulders, careful of the dressing over his wound, then he ripped off the T-shirt underneath, forgetting that the arm was touchy. The removal of slacks and jeans left them standing in their underwear in the chilly room.

"This is a moment we should savor," he said, reaching around her to unhook her white lace bra. "But you'll catch pneumonia." The bra tossed aside, he put her in the middle of the bed and removed the matching panties. He shed his briefs in an instant and they scrambled under the covers, settling into each other's arms with an easy familiarity.

She was surprised that she should feel so comfortable, considering all that had happened. But his hands explored her with all the old possessive confidence and she forgot to wonder about it. He'd always been a passionate and tender lover, and she'd always responded eagerly, happily.

"Is your arm okay?" she whispered.

"Everything is great," he replied.

He shaped every curve of her body, traced the length of her legs with apparently fascinated interest. She was already pulsing for him when his hands swept upward again.

MATT HAD DREAMED this a hundred times over the past eighteen months. She'd finally let go of the past, and she wanted him with the same desperation with which he wanted her.

The thought of all she didn't know about her father briefly intruded on the moment, but he resolutely pushed it aside and entered her. He heard her little gasp of satisfaction in his ear, felt her encourage him deeper as she wrapped her legs around him.

He made love to her with the strength and determination that had brought him back to Maple Hill. He gave the task all the longing for her he'd felt in the darkest months of their separation, all the emotions he'd kept alive in his dreams of renewing their life together.

She tightened on him with the intensity of her own response, his name on her lips between little cries of pleasure.

"Matthew! Ah! Matthew!"

His name whispered in the throaty contralto of orgasm drove him to his own. The world seemed to fly apart. Pain, loss, happiness, satisfaction, all exploded in the moment, then resettled inside him, anguish buried, hope on top.

They slept, wrapped in each other's arms.

THREE DAYS PASSED in blissful quiet. They drove Chase to school, did some Christmas shopping, had lunch downtown. In the afternoon of the second day, Jim called to tell them they now had access to the shop.

Rosie called Whitcomb's Wonders's janitorial crew to clean the store, but pulled on old clothes, preparing to supervise. "They don't need you," Matt said, reaching into the closet for a sweater. "Let the professionals handle it. Then we can shop for a bike for Chase."

Rosie stood in an old sweatshirt and mint-green panties and thought about that. He'd have been happy to watch her take until tomorrow to decide. "I like the not-having-to-clean idea," she said finally. "But if Chase has a bike, I won't be able to keep track of him."

"Every kid has a bike." Matt pulled on the sweater and pushed his arms into the sleeves, his injury almost healed. "You just set boundaries on where he can go. If he doesn't comply, you take the bike away. But I can't imagine him giving you that kind of trouble."

She looked worried. "Mom might be upset."

"You can blame it on me." He grinned as he ducked down to look into the mirror and comb his hair. "She always liked me better than you, anyway, so I might get away with it."

She swatted him as she passed him on her way to the closet. He caught her around the waist and wrestled her to the bed while she laughed and struggled.

Then she looked into his eyes with smoky passion in hers and he forgot he'd had other plans for the afternoon.

THAT FRIDAY, Jim Machado called to invite himself to dinner. "I have a report on the fire," he said. "Am I still invited for pizza?"

"Of course."

"Do you like white wine or red? I never know which goes best with pizza."

"How about a blush wine?" Rosie suggested cheerfully. Making love with Matt had made her feel almost optimistic, despite all the old stuff inside her.

"You should be an arbitration attorney," Jim said. "Anything else I can bring?"

"Yes. Could you please bring whoever's after me so I can give him a serious talking-to?"

"Any day now. You can help me with that tonight. What time do you want me?"

"How's six?"

"Great. See you then."

Matt and Rosie picked up Chase after school, passing Hank's truck with a wave, then picked up pizza on the way home. Rosie prepared a salad while Matt and Chase played on the computer. Chase had pleaded to build a snowman, but Matt refused, saying he thought he was getting a cold. But a glance in Rosie's direction told her he didn't want to be outside with the boy when the security lights made them easy targets.

The boy, always happy to be with Matt, cheerfully

ran after him upstairs to the bedrooms where the computer was.

Rosie decided they should eat in the kitchen—it was cozier—and she covered the table with a cloth patterned with moose, bears and pine trees. They'd use the mossy-green stoneware her mother never used. She found hot-pepper flakes, grated fresh Parmesan cheese and tossed the salad.

The doorbell rang ten minutes before six and she went to answer it, expecting to see Jim, but Sara stood there instead. She looked gorgeous in a snug lavender jacket over lavender knit pants, and hiking boots that somehow managed to look chic.

She carried a small brown grocery bag and pushed her way into the hallway with a frown. "What is going *on?*" she demanded, turning to look at her once she was inside. "I had afternoon coffee at the Barn with a friend from the office, and Rita told me Matt had been shot after I left the wedding and that somebody set fire to your shop—when you were in it! What's the matter with you? Don't you have me on speed dial anymore?"

Rosie frowned regretfully for having left her friend out of the loop. Before Matt had arrived, they'd talked on the phone every few days and met for lunch once a week when schedules permitted.

"I'm sorry. It's been pretty hectic around here with the wedding and Matt staying over. Can I take your coat?"

Sara shook her head. "I don't want to intrude. I

just want to know what's happening." She pushed the grocery bag at Rosie. "But if you're not busy, you can explain it to me over a bowl of Chubby Hubby."

Rosie drew her with her toward the kitchen. "We're expecting Jim Machado for dinner. He's been investigating the case. We're just having pizza. Want to stay? We can have the Chubby Hubby for dessert."

"Jim Machado." Sara said the name as though she found it familiar.

"He's a police detective," Rosie said. "Tall, whiskey-brown eyes, quite gorgeous. He's an old friend of Matt's."

"Oh, yeah." Sara grinned. "I don't really know him. We travel in different circles, but I read about him in the paper. He solved a crime while visiting in Boston or something?"

Rosie nodded. "That's him." There'd been a story about that in the *Maple Hill Mirror*. "He's ever alert. And he's single."

Sara decisively unzipped her coat. "Okay, I'll stay. My new plan is supposed to be about going it alone, but frankly it stinks. I'd love to meet somebody new."

Rosie took her coat, admiring the white angora sweater underneath. It molded itself flatteringly to Sara's lovely bosom, an asset she'd had augmented in Boston last year.

"You look so great," Rosie said, appreciating how much the change in physical appearance had done for her friend's morale. "If ever there was a case for what cosmetic surgery can do for a woman in a totally positive way, you're it."

"Thank you, thank you." Sara put her hands on her waist and pretended to flaunt her chest. "It definitely does earn a woman more attention. We're not all born with everything like you."

Rosie rolled her eyes as she went to hang up Sara's jacket. "Everything? My hips are too wide, my nose is weird and my ears and my feet are too big. I have everything, all right—in too great a quantity."

"But you make the whole package look just right." Sara smiled wryly and followed her into the kitchen. "Oh," she observed in an aside as she pointed to the mistletoe. "You must be taking full advantage of this."

She sank onto a stool as Rosie put the ice cream in the freezer. Then she pulled a large bowl of salad out of the refrigerator. "Listen to us talking about our physical assets as though women haven't evolved at all since the fifties. Who cares what we look like, anyway? We're brilliant."

Rosie laughed. "I'm willing to say reasonably clever."

"You, maybe, but I'm brilliant." She paused. "So how's it going with Matt?"

As Rosie considered how to explain the change in her relationship with Matt, Sara must have caught a betraying expression. She gasped. "No!" she said, sliding off the stool and coming to throw her arms around Rosie. "You're getting back together?"

Rosie shook her head. "No, but we're…communicating."

"Communicating," Sara repeated flatly, clearly wanting details.

Rosie had no explanation. "I don't know. Just…"

"Communicating."

"Yes."

"Well, that's hopeful."

"Keep it to yourself, okay?" Rosie asked, thinking how unbelievable the events of the week had been. On one level, her life seemed to be inching toward renewal, yet on another, she'd been threatened with death—twice. "My mother's been away and you know how gossip works. I wouldn't want her to come home to news of a reconciliation when there isn't one."

"Of course. When's she coming home?"

Rosie sighed and opened her hands. "Tomorrow. Providing she and her sisters haven't already killed one another. What is it about women, anyway, particularly those in the same family, that they have such difficulty with each other?"

"Got me. Maybe it's because we don't duke it out like guys do, so stuff just builds up. Anyway, what can I do for you?"

"Want to toss the salad while I preheat the oven?"

"Sure. Who do you want it tossed at?"

Rosie laughed. "Very funny."

Jim arrived right on time with a bottle of white zinfandel and one of champagne. "Wine's tricky," he said, handing the bottles to her. "It's called white zinfandel, but it's pink. And the clerk assured me that champagne goes with everything. But it's sort of beige. Hello."

He spoke to Sara, who took his coat since Rosie held the wine. "Hi," Sara said, offering her free hand. "Sara Ross."

"Sara's an old friend," Rosie told Jim. She noted with a Cupidlike inclination already at work that he looked particularly handsome tonight in his black sweatshirt and jeans. "She heard that weird things have been happening to me, so she came by to check on me. It's all right that she's here, isn't it?"

Jim nodded. "Of course." He shook Sara's hand. "Jim Machado."

Sara, always self-possessed, said with a smile, "Good. 'Cause I was staying, anyway." She went out to the hall to hang up his coat.

Jim narrowed his gaze on Rosie as he followed her into the kitchen. "You're not matchmaking on me, are you?"

"Furthest thing from my mind," she fibbed. "I wasn't expecting Sara, she just dropped by with ice cream, so it seemed rude not to invite her to dinner. Particularly since I wanted the ice cream."

He laughed lightly.

Matt and Chase appeared, Chase claiming to have beaten Matt in three straight games of Nintendo. "Uncle Matt's kinda slow," he told Rosie.

"He cheats," Matt claimed. At Chase's look of indignation, he put a hand over the child's face and pretended to squeeze. "The little brat knows what he's doing."

Jim accepted the corkscrew Rosie handed him and laughed at Matt. "You always were a sore loser."

"That's because whatever team lost when we played football had to buy dinner for the other team. And you guys ate like sultans."

Rosie put the pizza in the oven and Jim opened the wine. Matt poured Chase a glass of milk, then pushed him toward the living room. "Want to watch cartoons until pizza's ready?"

"But you said Jim's a cop," Chase complained, already sporting a milk mustache. "I want to ask him questions about criminals."

Matt nodded. "You can do that after dinner. Right now all we're going to talk about is dull stuff, like what caused the fire."

"That's not dull," Chase challenged.

"Yeah, it is," Matt insisted. "It was just some wiring problem or something."

Jim winked at Chase. "We'll talk later, buddy."

"Okay." Chase took off for the living room, milk sloshing dangerously.

The four adults converged at the table, Matt carrying glasses, and Jim, the wine. Rosie put out a platter of cheese and crackers, and vegetables and dip, then pointed Sara to a stack of napkins on the counter. Sara brought them to the table.

"We've got fingerprints," Jim said as he poured the wine, "off the inside of a latex glove discarded in the Dumpster at the end of the block. But they don't match anyone in our database."

Rosie blinked. "You can get prints off the inside of a latex glove?"

"We're really pretty clever," he said with a grin, then added more seriously, "But I can't take credit. It's the crime-lab guys."

"So can we find out who the prints belong to?" Matt asked.

"The FBI's running it through AFIS."

"Oh, let's see." Sara screwed her eyes shut and thought. "American Force of Inveterate Sneaks?"

Everyone groaned.

"Automated Fingerprint Identification System," Jim replied. "But good try." He focused his attention on Rosie. "I've already checked out the others on the Industrial Growth Committee, but can you think of anyone else in your life who might have a grudge against you for any reason?"

She shook her head.

"Everybody loves her," Sara said. The women sat at a right angle to each other and Sara patted Rosie's hand. "I don't think she has an enemy anywhere except for Ben what's-his-name."

Jim folded his arms and sat back. "Right. I know that. I was rereading the news stories about all that went on that no one seemed able to prove. What about the Department of Environmental Quality guy whose truck got munched? Could he be mad at you?"

Rosie shook her head. "He died of a heart attack last summer. And why would what happened to his truck be my fault?"

"Sometimes people hate other people for reasons we'd never imagine. Let's reexamine your Kiwanis membership and the church group you belong to."

"There's that woman who makes wedding gowns in her home," Sara reminded Rosie, "who got angry at you because you had a better booth that she did at the bridal fair."

Rosie dismissed that with a wave. "That was nothing. Because I do fairs so often, I have a substantial, well-made booth that I decorate with real flowers, and she just…resented that I was there, too."

"Yeah. She told Rosie she should be home tending her shop rather than trying to solicit even more business at bridal fairs."

Jim frowned. "That *could* be something, Rosie. That's just the kind of bad feeling that makes people do things out of all proportion to the offense, but to someone who's already a little warped…"

"She's not warped," Rosie insisted. "She's just had a bad year. Her husband left—"

"And good riddance to bad rubbish," Sara interjected.

"Amen to that," Rosie added.

Matt and Jim exchanged a look. "Let's hear some details," Jim said.

"She has three little kids," Rosie replied, "and one of them's been diagnosed with ADD. She works at home because one of them's still not in school. I'm sure it's a tough row to hoe."

Jim was making notes. "Well, I'm going to check her out, anyway. What's her name?"

Rosie groaned. "She might *really* want to kill me if she thought I sicced the police on her."

Jim made a face. "Would you give me credit for a little discretion, Rosie? And I'd appreciate it if you'd let me decide what's worth investigating. What's her name?"

"Okay, okay. Catherine Merchant. I just don't think she's psychotic." Rosie bristled teasingly. "And if you don't watch your tone, mister, your share of the pizza is going to shrink."

"May I remind you," he asked with a straight face, "that I'm armed?"

Sara laughed. "He's got you there. Good one, Jim."

"Thank you." He grew serious again. "I looked up the Industrial Growth Committee in the city's data-bank," Jim said, "and found out that Adam Bello wasn't involved at its inception, but the other two members of the group were Molly Bowers and Dennis Sorrento."

Rosie nodded. "Right. Dennis is a pharmacist, and Molly runs a nursery. Flowers and stuff."

"Yes. I see that Molly's still in town, but Sorrento has moved to Springfield."

"Right."

"Do you know why?"

"Ah…" She thought hard. "I'm not sure. Maybe he just wanted a bigger sales market. I always used the pharmacy closer to the lake. But Dennis belonged to our church, and I knew him from various community projects. He cared a lot about Maple Hill, and I always admired that."

"He contributes toiletries to the food bank," Matt put in. "I remember doing a profile on him once for the *Mirror*."

"Why isn't he part of the group this time?"

"Health issues. He's in his sixties."

"And did you have a good relationship with Molly?" Jim asked Rosie.

She nodded. "We always had dinner together before meetings. We agreed on most issues. She's a friend of my mother's. She wouldn't do anything to hurt me."

Jim nodded. "Just examining my options. The accelerant for the fire was alcohol."

"And…?"

"Every household's got it. Or anyone can buy it anytime. I was hoping that whatever the accelerant was it was going to be something found only in a pharmacy. Or only in a nursery."

"So it rules out the other members of the committee?" Sara asked.

Jim frowned. "No. It rules *in* everybody. We've widened the field of suspects rather than narrowed it."

CHAPTER ELEVEN

"ON THE OTHER HAND," Jim added, "both Bowers and Sorrento have substantial bank accounts. Bello makes an impressive amount of money at the auto agency, but it's all accounted for. And he and his family left to go skiing the day after your last meeting."

Rosie ignored the business about Adam Bello and focused on Molly and Dennis. "Dennis is a pharmacist, after all," she countered. "And Molly's mother just died. I know she inherited her home—that beautiful old Federal-style three-story on the other side of the lake, which she sold to some New Yorkers who vacation here. And I think there were stocks and bonds."

"Right. But the sale of the house didn't go through."

"What?"

"It didn't go through. The buyer got downsized at work or something, and decided he couldn't afford a five-hundred-thousand-dollar house on the lake, after all. So where *did* all the money in Molly's bank account come from?"

Rosie frowned, nibbling on the inside of her bottom lip. Matt knew she was thinking hard. And the chewing on her lip meant she was getting close to a discovery, or a solution, or—in this case—an element that just didn't make sense.

He'd noticed it, too, and was getting the most unsettling feeling that the situation was going to get a lot worse before it got better.

"Why would there be money involved in this?" she asked Jim. "You're thinking she might have been *paid* to hurt me? Why, for heaven's sake?"

"No." Jim leaned toward her. "Rosie, think. I think the money means that one of those two people accepted cash as part of your committee. Or maybe they did it together. You said Sorrento was seeing someone he wouldn't talk about."

"But—?" She stopped. What Jim was suggesting finally seemed to dawn on her. It was all Matt's worst fears realized that Jim was coming to the same conclusion he'd been considering for a couple of days. "You mean," she asked in a wary whisper, "a *bribe*?"

"That's exactly what I mean."

"But why? *We* invited Tolliver to come to Maple Hill."

"Are you sure?" he asked. "Did *you* do it?"

"No, but I know…"

"How do you know?"

"Because Dennis brought it up at a…meeting." She stopped again, the last word lamely adding to the dying denial of wrongdoing. Her forehead furrowed. "He said he'd gotten wind of Tolliver's desire to move, that they were looking for somewhere more commercially friendly to relocate. And he knew of an acre for sale on the other end of the lake. It's marshy and not good for much of anything else."

Rosie shook her head. "Wait. Why would he have all this money in his account because he accepted a bribe, when this all happened two years ago?"

"The deal didn't go through two years ago, remember? Your father died. The committee fell apart. But it's entirely possible they all decided that giving the money back would attract someone's attention. So the money just sat in Molly's account until a reasonable amount of time went by and they could bring the subject up again. Like now."

"But…why would anyone be targeting me? I'm on Tolliver's side. I think it'd be good for Maple Hill and not a problem for the environment. The rule of thumb when you're building on a wetland is that you make sure the same size wetland is protected somewhere else."

Jim opened his mouth to reply, hesitated, then finally said with a grin, "I don't have a good answer to that question. But I'm working on it."

The oven timer rang and Rosie got up to retrieve the pizza.

"Unless whoever is threatening you isn't Dennis, Molly or whoever took the bribe," Matt said.

Rosie stopped halfway to the stove. "What do you mean?"

"Maybe it's someone who knew about the bribe and for whatever reason doesn't want Tolliver to come to town."

"But why would that be?"

He considered a moment, too, then sighed and shook his head. "Beats me."

Sara looked from one to the other. "You guys are not very good at this. I mean, for a cop and an investigative reporter, you suck at solving a mystery."

"I beg your pardon," Matt said, pretending hurt feelings, "but I'm a photojournalist. Subtle but important difference." Then he smiled and pointed to Jim. "*He* has no excuse."

"Thanks, pal." Jim glowered at him, then turned to Sara. "He takes pictures because he can't read or write." When Matt opened his mouth to defend himself, Jim forestalled him with, "No, comic books don't count."

Chase, apparently having heard the timer, came running into the kitchen.

"Gentlemen, please." Rosie took the pizza out of the oven and placed it on a large cutting board. "Let's behave like adults. Impressionable child, here."

Sara, obviously trying to reestablish peace, patted first Jim's hand then Matt's. "You've done very well, and I'm sure you have several cases under investigation and probably don't have time to give this one your full attention. And you…well…" She smiled at Matt. "I'm sure Rosie's been a considerable distraction now that you're communicating."

"Sara!" Rosie exclaimed, cutting the pizza.

Jim looked puzzled.

Sara leaned closer to whisper, "You know…*communicating*."

"All *right!*" Jim declared, apparently putting his own spin on what the word meant.

Sara sat back as Rosie put the pizza in the middle of the table. "We're in problem-solving mode tonight. Maybe we can help you get beyond communication to actually living together again."

"You just said we weren't any good," Jim reminded her.

"That was at solving a mystery," she said. "This is love. You're probably better at love, aren't you?"

It was a leading and flirtatious question. Sara seemed to be waiting interestedly for Jim's answer.

"Actually, I'm out of practice," he said finally. "I think we should let them handle it on their own."

Sara seemed surprised for a moment, possibly even hurt. Then she smiled around the table, equanimity restored, and pretended disappointment. "And I was so looking forward to helping with a reconciliation. Oh, well."

Chase made up for whatever tension was left from Jim's gentle rebuff of Sara's advance by talking continually. He interrogated Jim about his work, particularly interested in how fast his car was.

"Now that I'm a detective," Jim explained, "I don't do traffic stops or pursuits. But my Crown Victoria has a big engine. I can catch anybody if I want to."

Chase was impressed. "Do you get to shoot criminals?"

"I do my best to catch them without having to shoot them."

After dinner, Sara gave Rosie a hug. "Thanks for dinner. I'm so glad you're okay." Then she hugged Matt. "You take good care of her. And I'm really happy things are looking up for you two." She framed Chase's face in her hands and kissed his cheek. "And you be good, okay?"

She offered her hand to Jim. "It was nice to meet you," she said. "I hope you find a reason to get back into practice again." She didn't have to specify what kind of practice.

He shook her hand. "Thank you. It's nice of you to be concerned."

Rosie walked her to the door, and Matt and Jim hung back at the table. Matt handed Chase the last piece of pizza. "You can have this in front of the television if you're really careful," he said.

Chase took the pizza and announced firmly, "I want to stay with you."

"I have to speak to Jim privately for a few minutes," Matt bargained. "I'll come and get you the minute we're done."

Chase looked from one to the other, making it clear he'd much prefer to be in on their conversation. "Okay. But I don't see why I can't stay. I wouldn't blab."

"I know that. But it's private stuff."

"Private from Aunt Rosie?"

"Go, Chase."

The boy bit off the point of the pizza slice and walked away.

Matt glanced in the direction of the front door,

where Rosie's and Sara's voices could still be heard. "I think all of this may have something to do with Rosie's father," Matt said quietly, quickly, watching the doorway. "Two years ago, I was doing a story on the building of the shopping center and discovered what had to have been a payoff to him from the developer, who later turned out to have allowed the electrician to violate several codes. Then I dug a little deeper and found a few other instances where I'm sure Hal had taken financial 'encouragement.' I think he was the guy you went to if you wanted deals fast-tracked through the system. Obviously, being married to his daughter, I was in a difficult position. I was trying to figure out how to tell her what I knew when he killed himself. I decided to keep what I'd learned to myself, thinking there was little point in upsetting her and the rest of his family when it would serve no purpose." He sighed and ran a hand over his face. "Now I don't know what to think. Maybe Hal was involved in the Tolliver deal the first time around—though that still doesn't explain why someone's targeting Rosie."

Jim frowned. "Unless you were right when you suggested that it's someone who knew about the last deal and doesn't want it on the table again."

A plausible theory, Matt still thought, but he couldn't come up with candidates. "Yeah, but who could it be? And why *don't* they want the deal reborn?"

"Hey, it's *your* theory."

"I know." Matt sighed. "But it obviously has flaws.

Rosie's mother comes to mind, but she'd never hurt her own daughter. And she'd just ridden away in a cab when the shot was fired."

"Of course, Rosie wasn't hurt."

"Because I took the bullet."

Jim nodded. "But would it have missed her had you not gotten in the way?"

"It didn't seem wise to wait and see," Matt said.

"Right. But my point is that both attempts seem questionable. She was locked into her shop, but that all happened in the morning when all the other business-people that share her building are coming to work, and everyone already at work in the area is at the bakery, on the street at a right angle to you. Almost as though the arsonist wanted to attract attention to the fire. I think somebody's trying to scare her, not kill her."

"Either way, I'm not happy."

"I know. I don't blame you," Jim said. "Look, I'll follow the paper trail on Hal's last few deals for the committee and see if I can get any ideas. Maybe the culprit is someone involved in a previous deal who didn't get everything he wanted, so he's taking it out on the committee in the person of its chairwoman. Or on the descendant of the man he thinks stiffed him."

"Maybe." Matt wasn't convinced, but then nothing else made sense, either.

"And we still have evidence that suggests the in-volvement of the other two members of the commit-tee. Maybe, if Hal took a bribe, he was supposed to share the money with them and didn't."

"But still, why take it out on Rosie two years later?"

"The committee's reconvened, remember? If Tolliver comes to town, it's possible that whatever happened last time will surface again." At Matt's doubtful expression, Jim said, "I know. My theory doesn't come together, but I'll keep working on the case until I figure it out. Meanwhile, you guys be careful. I'll keep patrols driving by the house, and we have a foot patrol downtown that'll keep an eye on the shop. We'll be nearby if you need us."

Matt looked up to see Rosie standing in the doorway, her arms folded in a pugnacious attitude.

"What?" Matt asked.

"Nothing." She walked into the kitchen and poured herself a cup of coffee. When she found them still watching her, she added grumpily, "It's just that I managed to forget for a couple of hours that we aren't just friends getting together for a night of pizza and conversation." She smiled apologetically at Jim. "Like Matt and I used to do with you and Laurie. Then I come back in here to see the two of you talking seriously and I'm jolted into reality again."

Jim nodded. "Yeah. Those days are gone. There are times when my reality isn't great, either."

Matt, hating to both Jim and Rosie so glum, was desperate to cheer them up. He was suddenly inspired.

"You know what you forgot, Madame Hostess?" he asked.

The question suggested criticism and she straightened defensively. "What?"

"Sara's ice cream."

She put her cup down and covered her mouth. "Oh, no! I can't believe I *did* that. She brought it and she didn't even get any."

Matt went to the freezer. "That's okay. We can polish it off for her." He added with phony benevolence, "I'm sure she'd want us to enjoy it."

"Point me to the spoons," Jim said.

Rosie indicated the right drawer as she pulled bowls down from the cupboard. "Poor Sara." She and Matt and Jim converged at the table. "She didn't upset you, did she?" Rosie asked Jim as Matt went to the utensils drawer for a scoop. "She's just very…direct. I've often admired that she never feels compelled to hold back. But a lot of people don't get that. I told her only that you were single. She obviously found you interesting. You are dating again, aren't you?"

Jim dismissed her apology, pairing up bowls and spoons. "Of course she didn't upset me. But I think I hurt her feelings. I'm sorry about that. I'm *not* dating. I'm just biding my time."

Rosie hooked an arm in Jim's. "Divorce requires a grieving process. No one knows that better than…we do."

Matt looked up and met her gaze. That was the first time in his recollection that she seemed to understand his grief as well as her own. In that moment of eye contact, he saw real hope for their future. "We're not divorced," he felt compelled to remind her.

"Hey!" Chase ran into the kitchen, then skidded to

a halt. He looked at Matt and accused, "You said you'd come and get me when you were finished!"

Matt met Jim's guilty gaze. "Ah…we're still talking. But we wouldn't leave you out of dessert." He piled the dish high in recompense and handed it to him.

Greed reigned over hurt feelings. Chase took a spoon and began to take off again. Rosie stopped him and pulled out a chair for him. "Sit at the table, sweetie. Grandma will be upset if we get Chubby Hubby all over her sofa."

"Uncle Matt let me take pizza in the living room," he said, already shoveling in ice cream.

Rosie made a face at Matt. "You'll have to deal with my mother."

"I will. She knows I'm not afraid of her."

"I'm not afraid of her, either," Rosie said. She sighed as he handed her a dish of ice cream. Jim had sat down with Chase and answered more questions. "I guess I just don't know where I stand with her, except that I know it isn't where I want to be."

Then apparently deciding that was more deeply into family laundry than she wanted to go with a child and a non-family member in the room, she shook her head and wandered away.

Jim left when he'd finished his ice cream, and Matt and Rosie tucked Chase into bed shortly after that.

"Want to sit in front of the fire and try to relax?" Matt asked. Rosie looked tense and troubled.

"Sure." She gave him only a half smile. "You build the fire and I'll make some tea."

He was closing the fire screen, flames dancing behind it, when she returned with a green teapot on a tray and two matching mugs. He'd given her the matching set one birthday because he always teased her about still playing tea party even though she was a grown woman. She loved matching pieces and any occasion to use them.

"What's the tea set doing *here*?" he asked as she placed the tray on the floor in front of the sofa. "You live in the guest house."

"Yes." She sat down beside the tray, leaning her back against the sofa. "But I moved a few things in with me when I came to stay the week. And I always loved the set, even when I thought I no longer loved you."

He sat on the other side of the tray. "You changing your mind about that?"

She made a helpless gesture with her hands. "My feelings are complicated, especially at a time when everything else is also confused."

He could certainly grant her that.

"And I've been wondering a lot," she said, "about me."

He picked up the tray, put it on the other side of him and closed the gap between them. For a beautiful, intelligent and usually confident woman, she had strange vulnerabilities and insecurities he'd never entirely understood, except to know that they related to her parents, and to her father particularly. The man had seemed to love her very much while still taking great pains not to let it show.

He put an arm around her shoulders. "Well, I wonder about you all the time. What, exactly, are you focused on?"

She punched his chest lightly in reply. "I was thinking about my father. How fathers are supposed to make you feel safe and good about yourself, but mine didn't do that. I mean, I *think* he loved me, but I always felt that he held something back. And I was always wondering what I could do to get it all—the approval, the compliments, the affection he never seemed willing to give. Francie had the same experience. We used to commiserate as kids about never being able to get his total attention." She gave Matt an apologetic pat. "I know your childhood was awful, and it's amazing you survived to become the man you are. But you knew what you were up against. Our father was a pillar of the community, a man loved by everyone, but he never showed love to us. Except Jay—that was obvious."

"Some men have trouble relating to women, even their own daughters. I seem to remember your mom having the same problem with him."

Rosie nodded, frowning. "I know. She always tried so much harder than he did. I don't think it was that he couldn't relate, as much as he didn't really want to. And what could have proven that more completely than when he killed himself because Jay died? He preferred to die with Jay than live with us."

"It's hard to know what was in his head."

She looked up into Matt's face, her eyes remembering. "No, it isn't," she said in a strangled voice. "He clearly had disdain for the rest of his family. His blood all over the porch showed that. He couldn't care less about our futures. He didn't care that he was taking himself away from all those things—my baby, for example—we wanted him to share."

"Rosie." It was impossible to explain that away or find a place to put it so that it didn't keep surfacing and causing her pain. So he simply wrapped her in his arms and held her.

"Intellectually, I know better," she said, snuggling into him, "but I find myself questioning my worth as a human being when the man who gave me life was willing to just remove himself from it without a second thought."

"You're going to have to accept that you'll never understand it, Rosie. And that he left because he didn't have the courage to stay, not because you and your mom and your sister weren't worth staying for."

"He loved Jay more than he loved us."

"If he did, then it's his loss and nothing to do with your worth as a woman. I, on the other hand, consider you priceless."

She looked into his face, then put her arms around his neck and rested her head on his shoulder. "Thank you, Matt," she whispered. "I'm glad you're here."

He rewarded that concession by making love to her in front of the fire while the tea got cold, then carrying her upstairs to their bedroom to tell her again.

ROSIE AWOKE at 3:00 a.m. to the sound of…what? She wasn't sure what had awakened her but sat up abruptly, her ears tuned to the smallest sound. When a hand closed over her mouth and drove her head back to the pillow, her heart stalled in terror. She grabbed the wrist with both hands, intent on pulling it away, and felt a familiar watch with a woven leather band and caught a whiff of a familiar after-shave.

"Lie still!" Matt said very quietly in her ear. He moved silently to lever himself off the bed and move across the carpet to stand behind their door, which was slightly ajar.

That was when she heard the footsteps on the stairs. They were very slow and quiet, as though someone was being deliberately stealthy.

Rosie clutched the blanket under her chin and prayed that Chase would remain asleep. The footsteps advanced slowly, her own heartbeat seeming to slow in pace with them. She felt the need to gasp for air, but didn't dare.

She heard the creak of the top stair as the intruder cleared it. It had always been a giveaway when she'd been a teenager and returned home later than curfew.

Footsteps advanced down the hall, slowly, quietly, closer, closer. She felt Matt's tension like her own as he waited behind the door for the right moment.

She wanted to reach for the phone and dial 911, but even the slightest movement might betray them and Matt needed the full advantage of surprise. Rosie's heartbeat about to strangle her, she saw Matt move like a spirit in the shadows and dart out the door. There was a scream, a shout, the sounds of bumps and crashes.

She flipped on the beside lamp and raced to the door just in time to hear Matt's "Well, damn it, Mom!"

Mom?

CHAPTER TWELVE

IN THE LIGHT spilling from her room into the hallway, Rosie saw Matt in boxers and a T-shirt, reaching down to help her mother up off the carpet. The always elegant woman, now in brown cords and a nubby brown turtleneck, was flat on her back. Her matching beret lay half over her face, and her graying blond hair fanned out over the carpet, as though she'd landed with considerable impact. A train case had spewed various items of makeup all over the carpeting.

Rosie snatched the hat off her mother's face and took her other arm as she wobbled under Matt's efforts to help her up.

"Mother!" Rosie was torn between laughter and cardiac arrest. "What are you doing home? You weren't due until tomorrow."

Sonny stood for a moment, steadying herself, blinked several times and looked around. "I'm not in a parallel universe, am I? I mean, this is my wallpaper, my carpet, my hallway. You look like my daughter and son-in-law, and yet you tried to kill me."

"I did not try to kill you," Matt said calmly. "I mistook you for an intruder."

"In my own home."

"You're a day early, and we've…there's been some… excitement."

"Excitement?"

Rosie didn't want to have to explain, didn't want what was happening to her to pollute the entire family. She wanted her mother to go back to her aunt's and let them work this out. But since that didn't look as though it was going to happen, she went on the defensive to stall for time.

"Why are you home?" she demanded.

"Because your aunts and I had a falling-out!" Sonny replied impatiently. "They band together against me. It happens every time—I don't know why I'm continually surprised. It happens with you and Francie, too. Three is just a bad number where women are concerned."

A score of reasons why other women might ally themselves against Sonny Erickson came to the tip of Rosie's tongue, but Rosie bit back the words.

"So, Aunt Ginger stayed?" Rosie asked.

Her mother nodded. "She's arranged to fly home from there. I'm supposed to send on her coat and boots." She folded her arms and said with the tilt of an angular eyebrow, "I only wish I'd had her boots with me. I'd have kicked her into—"

"Mom." Rosie stopped her mother's violent train of thought. Sonny could use a little time with Langlois's wife, Betsy. "You get ready for bed, I'll make you a cup of tea—"

"Just a minute." Sonny cut her daughter's peaceful scenario short. "Do not try to manage me, Roseanne. I'm not one of your nervous brides. I realize it's the middle of the night, but there has to be a good reason you presumed I was a prowler rather than simply your mother coming home early." Her calm recounting of events took a loud turn when she got to "Matt came out of your room like—"

She stopped suddenly, thought a moment as though making sure of her facts, then pointed to the doorway of Rosie's old room. "Matt came out of that room…and so did *you*."

"Yes," Rosie replied simply.

"You were sleeping together?"

Her mother never left anyone in doubt about what she was thinking.

"Yes, we were."

Sonny looked stunned for a moment, then looked from Matt to Rosie and smiled. "Well, hot damn! I know that's a very *common* expression, but nothing else quite says it. Is that the excitement you were talking about? No, of course it isn't. Why would that make you attack me in my own hallway?"

Matt smiled thinly and excused himself. "I'm going to put some clothes on."

Rosie caught his arm. "You are going to help me explain."

"I am." He patted her hand. "But I'm going to do it with clothes on."

Rosie got down on her hands and knees to pick up her mother's makeup. "I'd help you," Sonny said, "but I'm already beginning to stiffen up from my little World Wrestling experience there."

Rosie handed up a chic brown jacket that had fallen beside the case. "Why don't you put that away and I'll take care of this."

She collected half a dozen lipsticks, lip pencils, eye shadows, two blush compacts and a tube of concealer. Still her mother's feet hadn't moved.

"I'm glad you've resolved your differences," Sonny said with a gentleness Rosie was no longer accustomed to. She'd thought she remembered that tone from her childhood, but she'd been so long without it, she'd convinced herself it was all in her imagination.

Rosie sat back on her heels, a bag of cotton balls in her hand. "We haven't, Mom," she said. "We're just talking."

"You were in the bedroom talking?"

"Mom…"

Her mother studied her for a moment, then, as though unsure what to make of her, shifted her weight. "Okay, okay. I'll go…change into my jammies and robe and meet you in the kitchen. I haven't eaten since Denver, and I'm starved. I can't wait to hear about this *excitement.*"

She disappeared into her bedroom.

When Rosie had picked up everything, she placed

the train case in front of her mother's door and went back into her room for her robe. Matt had pulled on a pair of dark blue sweats. He looked preoccupied, unusually tense.

"What's the matter?" she asked, groping under the bed for her slippers.

"You mean, besides the fact that I just bodychecked your mother?" His reply was tight, curt.

"She's fine." Rosie tried to cajole him with a grin. "She must be more flexible than she appears."

He dismissed her attempt at humor with a dark glance. "I have a plan," he said, spotting one of her slippers across the room and retrieving it for her.

She stepped into it. "What's that?"

"I'm sending you and Chase and your mom to a hotel in Boston and hiring one of Hank's guys to stay with you."

"No," Rosie said simply. Then she thought about it again. "Okay for Mom and Chase, but I'm not going."

He spotted her other slipper under the chair and handed it over, as well. "Don't argue with me," he said.

She stared at him. "Pardon me, but what century do you think you're living in? 'Don't *argue* with me?'" Her voice was high with disbelief as she stepped into her slipper.

"Oh, give it a rest. It's not male supremacy, it's common sense. I'm getting you the hell out of here."

"Pardon me again, but this is happening to *me!* This is *about* me, and you're not going to take it over or fix it for me or take another bullet on my account!"

"Don't tell *me* what I will and will not do." They were now shouting at each other. "I'm sick and tired of being unable to do anything to put our lives back together. And I'm damn well not going to let this continue until you finally *are* hurt or lost to me altogether! You're going to Boston and I'm going to flush this guy out."

"He won't come out for you. He's after *me*."

They stopped shouting when Rosie turned to the door and saw her mother standing there, looking pale and wide-eyed.

"Bullet?" she asked.

MATT PUT a small measure of brandy into the cocoa Sonny made while Rosie explained calmly what had happened, doing her best to lighten up the darkest part of their experiences.

But he'd never known Sonny to swallow a sugar-coated version of anything. "Flesh wound or not, Matt was shot because he shielded *you* from being shot? And I don't care how minimal the smoke damage is, it means there was a fire! And what do you mean, you couldn't get out?"

Matt didn't want to explain about the doorknob being tied, but told her instead that the presumption was that the fire was to attract attention to Rosie's plight.

Sonny was still horrified, just as he'd been from the beginning. He explained his plan to send her and Rosie and Chase to Boston in the care of Hank Whitcomb.

He put the brandy away, then took his place at the table.

"I'm not going to Boston," Rosie told her mother, "but I think it would be a very good idea for you and Chase to go. So far, he doesn't know that the events have been anything other than accidents. Matt hired Hank to watch the school so Chase can still live his life as though nothing is different. But I think if he got to go to Boston with you and Hank, he'd be happy with that. We can tell him it's a trip to the zoo, or a history trip or something."

"But why don't you want to go?" Sonny asked Rosie.

"Because the problem centers around me," Rosie replied. "At least, we think so. Jim's not sure."

"Jim?"

"The police detective. Jim Machado, remember?"

"Oh, yes. A cutie. Can't believe a woman divorced him."

Matt was amused to hear Jim described as a "cutie," but refocused on the conversation, unwilling to be distracted from the issue of getting Rosie out of Maple Hill.

"Anyway," Rosie went on, "I'm not going to let Matt take all the risks so I can be safe."

Matt gave Rosie his best superior glare. "You're under the misapprehension that you've been given a choice."

"I have not been *given* a choice," she replied with the same expression. "A choice is my right as a woman in charge of her own destiny."

"Oh, please. A woman in charge of her own destiny should still appreciate some muscle between her and who or what is trying to harm her. To reject that on the basis of a woman's independence would be foolish."

She leaned toward him and looked into his eyes. "I do appreciate you. I've been dead for two years and now I'm…I'm back, and it's because you're here. Two years ago, I didn't know how to ask for your help, and it finally drove you away. But you came back, open-hearted and forgiving, and that's made me somebody different than I was when our baby…" She swallowed, her voice a little tight. He had to swallow, too. "When everybody died. Well, you're not going to die, too, as long as I draw breath. Finally, Matthew, we're in this together. I'm staying, so you may as well accept it."

It was against his nature to accept defeat, however nobly and beautifully it was forced upon him. "Rosie—"

"Don't argue with me," she quoted him imperiously.

He turned to Sonny for help. There were tears standing in her eyes. He'd seen her cry at Jay's funeral but not at Hal's, and never since.

She tossed her hair, a gesture so reminiscent of Rosie, and turned to her daughter with a stern expression. Rosie straightened her back, ready to square off.

"I think, Rosie, that Matt is right," Sonny said. "It would be a very good idea if Chase went to Boston."

Matt's brain replayed the words and he realized what she'd said. Not only had he not won that round, he'd lost ground.

"Sonny!" he complained. Then went for her soft spot. "Mom," he implored, "I'm trying to keep you all safe."

She put a hand on his forearm and squeezed. "I know you are. But for a woman, a sense of safety doesn't always equate with being out of danger. Sometimes she doesn't want physical safety if it deprives her of the emotional safety and peace of mind of being with the man she loves. Curiously," she added, "I know this because I always wanted it but never had it."

That last remark was startling, and while he felt he had to be sympathetic to it, he didn't want to be distracted from his principal issue. He prepared to speak sharply, but missed his chance. Rosie was already talking.

"Mom," she said, "Chase would need you with him."

"No, he wouldn't. I love him dearly, and he does love me, the little angel, but we don't really relate very well and he'd be fine with Hank Whitcomb. Hank has all those kids of his own and is so good with them."

"Mom!" Rosie looked a little frantic. Matt couldn't help a certain sense of satisfaction. "I want you to be safe."

"I appreciate that, Rosie, but I, too, am a woman in control of her own destiny." Sonny smiled at Matt with the same determination she'd passed on to Rosie. "My daughter won't leave her husband, and I won't leave my daughter. I guess you'll just have to find a way to keep us safe while we're trailing along behind you."

Matt put both hands to his eyes in a vain attempt to block out the sights of the lovely but determined faces of the women in his life. He considered his options in dealing with them, since neither charm nor forcefulness had worked. What was left? Deception?

He was about to give serious thought to some kind of trickery when he felt something poke his shoulder. He lowered his hands to see Chase standing beside him in pajamas patterned with smiley-faced airplanes. He was frowning, his dark hair disheveled.

Matt put an arm around him. "What's the matter, Chase? What are you doing up?"

"I heard everybody talking loud."

Matt looked condemningly at Rosie and Sonny, blaming their argumentative natures for Chase's sleeplessness.

"We were just having a lively discussion," Matt explained. "Everything's all right."

Chase continued to frown, clearly not in agreement with that assessment. "Then how come I have to go to Boston?"

Matt couldn't help the groan. Sonny went to make Chase a cup of cocoa and Rosie simply smiled at him, awaiting his response to the question.

He lifted Chase into his lap and explained in simplest terms that he wanted Chase, Chase's grandmother and aunt to spend a few days in Boston while he was busy finding a bad guy.

"The guy who shot you?" Chase asked. When Matt hesitated, Chase put an arm around his shoulders and said, man to man, "Rickie Smithfield's mom works for the police department and she says it *wasn't* a hunter that shot you. And when Aunt Rosie's store caught fire, somebody did it on purpose."

Matt felt terrible guilt that Chase had known the truth all along, but didn't think he could share the knowledge because the adults in his life had been trying to protect him from what they knew.

"I'm sorry, Chase," he said gravely. "Have you been worried?"

Chase shrugged a bony shoulder. "I knew the guy in that silver car in front of the school was watching out for me. I saw you talk to him one day when I was on the monkey bars."

"You were *upside down!*" Matt exclaimed. "How did you see us?"

Chase seemed surprised by the question. "I was upside down, but I had my eyes open. It was Rachel's dad."

Of course. He had his eyes open.

"But I worry all the time about a lot of stuff, anyway," Chase said. "Even when nothing's really wrong. I wonder if everybody else is going to die, like my dad and Grandpa. Or if they'll just go away, like my mom." He sighed. "This is the most fun it's been—since you came. I wish it could be like this all the time. It's a little bit like when my dad was still here." He smiled apologetically at Rosie and Sonny. "Grandma and Aunt Rosie, you're really nice to me, but Uncle Matt's a *guy*." He focused on Matt again. "And I know you wouldn't let anybody hurt Aunt Rosie."

Matt suddenly conceived a plan. "That's why I wanted you to go to Boston. So you can take care of Aunt Rosie and Grandma for me."

"But I heard you talking," Chase said. "And they don't want to leave you."

Matt nodded. "But sometimes you have to make people do what they don't want to do because it's best for them."

"Like when Aunt Rosie won't let me have a banana shake?"

Sure he was on the brink of success, Matt said with enthusiasm, "Exactly!"

"No," Chase said.

Matt stared at him, afraid he hadn't gotten his point across. "You'll all be safe in Boston. Rachel's dad will take you there."

"But Grandma and Aunt Rosie want to stay with you. I want to stay with you. You let me have a banana shake that time, remember? 'Cause you knew it was one of my favorite things." Chase grinned winningly. "You're one of my other favorite things."

Defeated on all fronts, Matt cast Rosie a look over the boy's head.

"You told me you came here to put our family back together," she said with a wide smile, apparently unaffected by his threats. "You seem to be doing just that. Big-time."

Sonny concurred. "You have only yourself to blame, Matthew."

CHAPTER THIRTEEN

SATURDAY WAS OVERCAST and cold. Rosie looked out the kitchen window to see that the snow in the driveway was rutted and dirty, but the view of the lake from the living room was quite spectacular. The edges were frozen, but in the middle, a little colony of loons paddled around happily.

The starkly beautiful scene reminded her a little of life here at Bloombury Landing. Ice was closing in, but she and her family managed in relative happiness right in the center of what threatened them.

Her mother had made eggs, potatoes and toast for breakfast, then announced that she was driving into town to have her hair done.

"Sonny, I'm sorry, but you can't do that," Matt said. He and Chase were having a second round of toast.

She turned in the doorway, an elegant figure in a dark pink velour robe. "Of course I can," she argued quietly. "I have an appointment."

"Mom." Rosie guessed he used that title to shake that offended-goddess demeanor Sonny always took on when thwarted. "I mean, you can't just take off on your own. Because of what's happened to Rosie, nobody in this house goes anywhere alone." Then he smiled. "Unless, of course, you'd like to have your hair done in Boston."

Sonny made a face at him and came back to the table. "Matthew DeMarco, do not play games with me. I have a standing Saturday-morning appointment at—"

"I don't care," he interrupted calmly, "and I'm not playing." Chase turned to Rosie, wide-eyed. No one spoke to Sonja Erickson that way. "You can't go alone, and I'm waiting for word from Hank Whitcomb."

"We all have cell phones. Can't he call you on yours?"

Matt shook his head. "The answer I'm waiting for is a person, not a call. Now that you're home, I've asked Hank for a couple of security people, one to keep an eye on the house and one to accompany you about your daily routine. Can you switch your appointment to sometime this afternoon?"

Shocked by that suggestion, Sonny looked to Rosie for support. Rosie shook her head, refusing to intercede.

"Matt, you're obviously not familiar with the etiquette involved in hair appointments," Sonny said.

He replied amenably, "I confess I'm not."

"Well…" She seemed prepared to explain. "This time slot has been set aside for me for years. My hairdresser comes in just to do my hair, she has no other appointments on Saturday, but she accommodates me because we've built a good rapport over the years, and I've brought her several other standing appointments who tip her very well, as do I. I can't switch my appointment to this afternoon because Aurelia will not be there this afternoon." She glanced at her watch. "She's on her way now from her home in the country just to do my hair."

"Call and explain that you're indisposed," he said, intrepidly staring down her displeasure, "and promise her she'll get her large tip, anyway. Then try to reschedule your appointment. That's the best I can do, Sonny."

Her mother frowned at him. "You don't understand, Matthew. Tomorrow I have to stand up in front of hundreds of my friends and neighbors and give the welcoming speech at our community Christmas dinner. I cannot do it in this hair."

She sailed out of the room, her chin in the air.

"Whoa, Uncle Matt," Chase said under his breath. "That was pretty scary."

Matt expelled a breath. "You're telling me."

"But we have to keep her safe, too, right?"

"Right."

Rosie patted Matt's arm. "Well done, sweetheart," she said. "And when she comes back to tear you apart because she *couldn't* switch her appointment, I'll call nine one one."

Matt gave her an affectionately indulgent look. "Thank you. Hopefully our backup from Hank will have arrived by then."

Sonny was back in five minutes with a frown threatened by a reluctant smile. "To think I once scolded Rosie for letting you get away. There's nothing available until Tuesday."

"Is that bad?"

Rosie put a hand over her face at the pathetic innocence of that question. Then she asked her mother, "Why don't I wash and fix it for you." Sonny's obsession over her hair was frivolous, but then, she'd refused to leave Rosie's side and go to Boston. Rosie often suspected that her mother's dedication to seemingly unnecessary rituals gave her something she could take charge of when she controlled so little else in her life. "I always do my own."

Her mother appeared to consider Rosie's offer, looking over Rosie's hair. She'd washed it and blow-dried it after her shower this morning and it was looking its best.

Sonny finally shook her head. "No, you have the great Erickson hair. She flipped a hand at her tied-back, gray-blond ponytail. "I have the Chamberlain hair, thin and uncooperative."

Warming to her subject, Rosie pushed back her chair. "Come on, Mom, you've been having your hair done for so long, you're completely unaware that there are a million products out there to make thin hair appear thick and to bring uncooperative hair into order."

"That's right," Matt said to Sonny. "And most of them are in her bathroom, except for the three-inch-by-three-inch spot where my shaver is."

Rosie punched his arm—the left one—then led her mother upstairs.

"I'll never forgive you," Sonny called several moments later from the shower, where Rosie had sent her to shampoo, "if it just lies there like a dead mop or sticks out like a broom."

"It'll be beautiful," Rosie promised. "You'll want me to do it every week from now on. And you won't have to tip me."

Her mother made a doubtful sound. "You're sure conditioner's okay?" she called from the other side of the shower door. "My hair's so limp anyway…"

"Use the conditioner," Rosie replied. "I've got some great mousse to give it body."

"You'd better be right about this whole thing."

Half an hour later, Rosie had dried her mother's hair, applied mousse, set it in medium-size rollers she'd stopped using ten years ago, and ran the blow-dryer gently over Sonny's bulbous head.

Sonny sat on the edge of the bed in Rosie's old room, patiently still under her daughter's ministrations.

"I'd forgotten about the dinner," Rosie said. "Matt's just doing his best to make sure we're protected."

Sonny sighed. "I know that. My father was that way. Of course, with four girls who'd been indulged and who'd attracted a lot of attention, he had to be."

"I'm sorry you had a falling-out with Aunt Ginger."

"Oh, it's nothing. I told her I advised Camille Malone to ignore the book deal, and she accused me of trying to sabotage her work. I told her that encouraging celebrities to dish about people who'd trusted them was not a life's work, it was glorified gossip that did more harm than good. And Aunt Sukie always sides with Ginger because she's afraid of her."

Rosie patted her shoulder. "Good for you that you're not."

There was a pause in the conversation, only the hum of the blow-dryer filling the room.

"You did a lovely job with Francie's wedding," Sonny said. Rosie stopped working for a moment, shocked by the praise. Her mother usually dispensed it sparingly, if at all. "And you were right about the hat you picked out for her. It was perfect. It softened that…that…wild look she goes for."

Rosie relaxed, suddenly in more familiar territory. She moved the dryer over the rollers. "Well, we got lucky with the eyebrow ring. Nothing bad happened, none of the blood and guts you were worried about."

Sonny laughed.

Again Rosie stopped working. She unfastened a roller to test for dryness just for something to do so her mother wouldn't suspect she was shocking her. She seemed to be almost having…fun.

"How's it look?" her mother asked.

"Great," Rosie replied. "Not quite dry, but we're on our way. You're going to be gorgeous tomorrow even without a trip to the hairdresser."

"Rosie?" There was a suddenly serious note in her voice.

"Yes?"

"I'm…sorry I wasn't much help when you lost the baby."

Rosie turned off the blow-dryer, now sure she'd crossed into a different dimension. Her mother had never mentioned the baby after she'd visited Rosie in the hospital.

Rosie sat beside her, feeling a door open between them. All this time, she'd thought only solid wall stood there. She didn't want to talk about the baby, *never* wanted to talk about the baby, but she couldn't let this opportunity go.

"You were dealing with the death of your firstborn," Rosie replied, putting an arm around her shoulders, "and your husband. I didn't expect you to minister to *me*."

That wasn't precisely true. She understood that her mother's grief was enormous, but Rosie had been so alone in her own grief, because she couldn't share it with Matt, that she'd have loved even one word of comfort or understanding from her mother. She hadn't received it, but she hadn't expected it, either.

Sonny turned to Rosie, her eyes glazed with grief. But Rosie saw them looking into her own as though searching for something. What? Support? Understanding?

"What is it?" Rosie asked gently. She'd waited most of her life for her mother to need her.

Sonny took her hand. "Matt's given you a lot of

strength, hasn't he?" she asked. "He came home because Francie needed him, but you have to know his primary reason was to get you back."

Rosie did know, and the knowledge that his love for her had endured all she'd put him through humbled her.

"I do feel stronger." She squeezed her mother's hand. "You can tell me whatever's on your mind."

Sonny opened her mouth to begin, but didn't seem to be able to find the words.

"It's all right, Mom," she encouraged. "I know you weren't happy with Dad. I know he was as skimpy with his love for you as he was with Francie and me. But life goes on, you know. I figure he's the one who missed out."

Her mother drew a breath and held Rosie's hand in her two. Then she said finally, "Rosie, *you're* my first-born."

You're my firstborn. Rosie heard the words but couldn't make them compute. Jay had been born first, four years before she came along.

"Jay…"

"Jay was your father's child with Aunt Charlotte," Sonny finished.

Rosie had never known her mother's sister Charlotte, had only heard stories of the brilliant and beautiful young cellist who'd captivated audiences all over the world. She'd died on her way to a performance in Rome when her taxi was involved in a traffic accident.

All Rosie could think to say was, "I don't understand."

Sonny nodded and they turned to face each other on the edge of the bed. Rosie looked into her mother's face. It was youthful without the carefully applied makeup and with her hair in rollers. It was like having a conversation with a stranger.

"Your father and I had been married almost a year, and Charlotte came to visit between tours." She shook her head, smiling fondly. "We all prided ourselves on our good looks, but Charlotte was the prettiest and the sweetest. Your father was captivated, I guess, by her beauty and her stories of all those foreign capitals and meeting dignitaries and celebrities the rest of us just read about. And she said she was blinded by his confidence and his stability when her life was terrifying bouts of stage fright interrupted by chaos and continuous travel."

Rosie tried desperately to seize control of facts, to fight her way out of this sudden cloud of confusion. "Your sister Charlotte was Jay's mother." She had to say it simply for it to sink in.

"Yes," Sonny admitted.

"So Daddy…cheated on you with your sister."

That reply came with a little more reluctance. "Yes."

"And…you talked to her about it? She said she was blinded by—"

"Yes. She called and asked me to meet her in New York three months later, and she told me she was pregnant with Hal's baby."

"Oh, Mom," Rosie said breathlessly.

Sonny patted her hand. "You know, those things

aren't quite as horrible as you fear. Somehow, you get your balance and deal."

"But…"

"I didn't understand that right away, though. I was angry with her and furious with your father. She cried and pleaded with me not to hate her, but I walked away from her without another word. Then I left your father and went home to Beverly Hills, intent on going back to school."

Rosie sat in shocked silence, listening to her mother tell her story as though she was reading a piece of fiction.

"Then…Charlotte was in the accident in Rome when she was eight months pregnant, but the baby lived. Jay…lived."

"Oh my God. Did *Jay* know?"

"No. No one knew. Your grandparents and your other aunts knew she was pregnant, but they didn't know the baby was Hal's. She told them the father was someone in an orchestra. I called your father to tell him what had happened, and he told me he was going to claim the baby and asked if I'd go with him." She spread her hands helplessly. "It was the first time he'd ever needed me, so I went. Of course, I fell in love with Jay the minute I saw him, and knew I owed Charlotte for the way I'd refused to forgive her."

"Mom, she made love with her sister's husband!"

"I know. It's a terrible betrayal, but you can't live your life storing those up. So your father and I made a deal that I'd raise the baby as my child and no one would ever know what happened."

"Then…" Rosie couldn't equate her mother's generosity with the way she'd seen her father treat her. "He should have *adored* you for doing that."

Sonny shrugged and smiled sadly. "I think the truth is that you love who you love, and circumstances may require that you love someone else, but your heart will always belong to its own choice. Your father gave me a comfortable life, two more children…"

"And emotional neglect." Rosie sighed as one of her life's big mysteries suddenly became clear. "No wonder he loved Jay best." She squeezed her mother's hand. "Because he was Charlotte's, and he loved her best."

She wrapped her arms around her mother and cried for all she'd been through. Sonny held on to her and wept, too.

They finally drew apart, and her mother said with a sniff, "The first few years after that were good. We had you, then Francie, and Jay was growing into a handsome, talented boy."

Rosie remembered absently snatches of happy memories, of times when her mother had been cheerful and fun. She hadn't imagined them.

"Then, I'm not sure what happened," her mother said. "Maybe your father got tired of pretending, or maybe it was because we came back to Maple Hill to take over your grandfather's company and times were tough. There wasn't enough money to meet payroll and I asked my parents for a loan without consulting your father. He accused me of having no respect for his dignity as a man, to which I replied that Jay was proof he had no respect for my dignity as a woman. It all went downhill from there. I was angry that he was less interested in how we survived than that his dignity remain intact, and he was hurt that I threw Charlotte in his face, though that was the one and only time. That's the point at which we both stopped pretending."

"I'm so sorry, Mom."

Sonny drew a breath and shook her head. "I should have left, and I'm sure he'd have let me go, but he'd have wanted to keep Jay, and despite the circumstances of his birth, he was *my* child. So I stayed." She patted Rosie's cheek, her eyes filled with sorrow. "Was it horrible for you?"

"Well...not horrible," Rosie replied, knowing she had to be honest, "but Francie and I always did feel like second-class citizens where Dad was concerned. And we knew you were, too. We knew you loved us, but we thought you didn't like us very much. And we thought that might be because Dad didn't."

"Oh, good Lord, no." Sonny hugged her fiercely again. "It was all too complicated and upsetting to explain. I'd been very spoiled as a girl, and when I married your father, I thought I'd found everything. He was handsome and charming and ambitious. So when my dream didn't work out quite the way I'd planned, I was angry at the world. And when we were having tough financial times, I went to work for the bank, remember, and I suffered from the working woman's agonies—so little energy left for her family. And without a husband's loving support, it's even worse. So I toughened up to be able to cope." She sniffed and swiped at her eyes. "I'm sorry, Rosie. I know things were difficult for you and Francie."

"I understand about toughening up to cope." Rosie reached to her bedside table for the box of tissues and held it out to her mother. "I did the same thing to Matt when we lost our baby."

Sonny heaved a big sigh and wrapped Rosie in a hug. "I love you, Rosie."

Rosie thought she'd died and gone to heaven.

MATT LOOKED into an open cupboard, trying to decide what to do about lunch, since Sonny's hair crisis seemed to be turning into an all-morning event and he hadn't seen her or Rosie in a couple of hours. There was a firm rap on the door.

He answered it and looked questioningly at the two men who stood there. Both were casually dressed.

"Matt DeMarco?" one of them asked. The taller of the two.

"Yes."

"I'm Gideon Hale. This is Bob Berger. Hank sent us."

Relieved, Matt shook hands. They looked like a security team should. Hale was tall and big with a friendly smile, but an air of competence. Berger was older, shorter and squarely built, and looked as though nothing would rock him.

"Thanks for coming. You may have to sit and do nothing for a couple of days."

"Right. Hank explained," Gideon said.

"Then you know we're not sure if the threat still exists."

"Yes. We're prepared either way." Gideon handed him a pager. "We'll just be parked in the trees off the driveway. Call if you need us. We're in two cars, so we can split up if you need one of us to follow you and one to watch the house."

"I appreciate that."

They walked away and Matt closed the door. Reinforcements were in place. Now all they had to do was see if Jim's investigation of Sorrento and Bowers turned up anything that might enlighten them.

"Uncle Matt!"

"Yeah?"

Chase stopped at the foot of the stairs, then spotting Matt in the foyer, ran to him, his forehead creased. "Something's wrong with Aunt Rosie and Grandma."

They'd been quiet too long; he should have gone upstairs to check on them. He loped off in that direction, Matt following. "What do you mean?" he asked as he went. "Wrong how?"

"They're crying!" Chase said, colliding with him when he stopped suddenly.

Oh, no. He hated crying. He ran up the stairs, hoping this didn't have to do with the missed hair appointment.

"Where are they?"

"In your room."

Matt hurried down the hall and stopped in the doorway to the terra-cotta-colored room. Rosie and Sonny sat on the edge of the far side of the bed, arms wrapped around each other, heads together. They were crying, but the sound was interspersed with words and light laughter.

Something major had to have happened to bring about *that* degree of intimacy. Matt braced himself and walked into the room. Chase, smart boy, stayed in the doorway.

"Are you two all right?" he asked. "Chase said—"

Before he could finish, Rosie had leaped off the bed and into his arms. She had a stranglehold on his neck.

"What happened?" he asked, stroking her spine.

"It's…" she sobbed, "a long…story!"

Matt looked at Sonny for an explanation. She appeared more miserable than he'd ever seen her—and in rollers, to boot. He didn't know what to do for her except offer his free shoulder for comfort.

He was completely surprised when she stood and leaned into him. She wrapped an arm around him, the other around Rosie, and they all stood together in a weeping, anguished knot.

Chase came up beside him. "What's wrong?" he asked in a stage whisper.

"I don't know," Matt replied. "They just need somebody to hold them."

Chase put an arm around Sonny's waist, leaned into Rosie and did his best to help.

CHAPTER FOURTEEN

MATT WARMED SOUP on the stove with Chase sitting on the counter beside him, sneakered feet kicking back and forth.

"Is that that hungry-mushroom stuff Grandma gets from the deli?" Chase asked, his tone suggesting he wasn't pleased.

"It's called Hungarian mushroom," Matt corrected, "and you can have a grilled-cheese sandwich if you'd rather."

Chase looked relieved. "Yeah! When are they coming down?"

"They're combing Grandma's hair. You know how women are."

Chase rolled his eyes.

Matt laughed and pinched Chase's knee. He probably *did* know how women were, poor kid. They were his only company at home.

"Aunt Rosie told you what they were crying about when you sent me to wash my hands?"

"Yes." So Hal had had shady dealings on more than the business front. That didn't entirely surprise him. "But it's kind of complicated."

"When I become Motor Man, I understand everything. Even grown-up stuff."

Matt handed him a cracker from the bowl at his elbow, ashamed that he was using food to sidestep an issue he couldn't discuss. "Mostly, they were just feeling sad. Christmas is a happy time, but it makes you miss the way things used to be."

"Not for me." Chase swung his legs with more energy. That seemed to be a power source for his smile. "The way things used to be, my mom was gone and I really missed my dad. Grandma was grumpy, Aunt Francie yelled a lot, and I didn't see much of Aunt Rosie. But now you're here and Aunt Rosie's in the house and I like that. This is a *good* Christmas! Except for the killer, of course. And Jim's gonna find him."

"He's not a killer," Matt corrected quickly. "He's just somebody threatening what we want out of our lives."

"Yeah." Any fear Matt had that Chase was worried about the "killer" was erased the next moment when he asked, "Can we go see Santa tomorrow?"

"Yes, I think so. We'll have to see what the ladies have planned."

"Ta-daaaa!" Rosie announced, pulling her mother by the hand into the middle of the kitchen and gesturing grandly. "Behold Sonja Erickson, welcoming speaker at the community Christmas dinner."

Matt couldn't quite believe the transformation. Sonny's hair didn't have the slick perfection of her usual style, but he liked this much better. It was curlier and less severe, the wave that was usually her signature feature now softened and flipped up, taking years off her face and softening her aristocratic features. Rosie had given her light, fluffy bangs and done her makeup in a way that was more natural than Sonny usually did herself.

To his astonishment, Sonny was blushing.

Chase leaped off the counter and stared up at her. "You look beautiful, Grandma!"

"I second that, Sonny," Matt said. "You look like a girl again."

She laughed at that, hugged Chase, then crossed to see what Matt had in the pot.

"Found it in the freezer," he said.

"Wonderful! I'll get bowls."

Rosie moved close to snatch a cracker and bumped him with her hip. She looked very self-satisfied. "Am I good or what?"

"You're good," he granted her with a significant glance.

She reached up to the utensil rack for a ladle.

He took it from her. "Chase wants a grilled cheese."

She took the ladle back, adopting an air of superiority. "You're doing so well with lunch, you make it. I'm sure there'll be celebrities calling me any moment, wanting to fly me to exotic locations to do their hair."

"Until then, would you…?"

"The men will fall in love with me and the women will simply envy my skill and my style."

"Uh-huh. Cheese, Rosie."

She spread her arms, overtaken by her success with

her mother. "There's no time for cheese," she said. "I'm Super Salon Woman!"

Chase took her hand. "I'm Motor Man!"

Sonny placed a small stack of bowls on the counter beside the stove and watched Rosie and Chase turn in a circle, holding hands. "What's with them?" she asked.

"I think your head has gone to her head," he replied.

She primped. "Well, I am rather gorgeous."

"Yes, you are," he agreed, wondering how she'd been able to keep the secret about Jay to herself all those years. "And strong and good and generally a remarkable woman. Jay loved you very much."

"And I loved him. That's what it comes down to, isn't it? Not how much money or power there is, but who was loved."

He had to agree.

As Rosie and Chase continued their impromptu dance, he handed Sonny the spoon. "You stir the soup. Something tells me I'd better make Chase's sandwich."

AFTER LUNCH, Rosie headed for the attic.

"What are you looking for?" Sonny asked.

"Dad's electric trains," she replied. "I thought it'd be fun to put them under the tree."

Sonny handed her the plastic step stool from the kitchen. "The electric trains are in my closet. Way up on the top. The last time we had them out, your father thought they were rusting in the attic, so he put them away in our room. You'd better take this. Chase, I'm going to make cookies—you want to help?"

"Um…" Obviously torn between the search for electric trains and the possibility of cookies, he vacillated for a moment. The food won. "Okay."

Chase followed his grandmother into the kitchen as Rosie and Matt headed upstairs.

"Doesn't this strike you as weird?" Rosie asked. "Our Christmas preparations, my mother telling me about Jay, Chase having a great time—all right in the middle of some bizarre plot to hurt me or scare me."

"Yes, it does." He took the stool from her. "It's very weird. But that's easy enough to put up with. It's Christmas, your mom seems more relaxed than I've ever seen her—maybe because she was able to tell you about Jay—and we have a bike stashed for Chase that's going to send him over the moon. More good stuff than bad, I'd say."

Her mother's room was in its customary disarray. For all the refinements Rosie's father had brought to the house since the family had taken up permanent residence, the storage issue was not one of them.

Rosie opened a narrow closet just like the one in her own room and pointed Matt to the upper shelf. Even on a stool, she wouldn't be able to reach it.

"Mom's been pleading for a walk-in closet for years," Rosie told him as he climbed up. "In fact, we all have, but there was always something else that needed the money."

"I'll bet Hank's got somebody who could…do it for you." That claim was interrupted by a grunt. "The long, flat narrow box? Like the kind that goes under a bed?"

"I think so. I haven't seen it in a couple of years, but I think it had blue flowers on it."

"This must be it. Can you balance it just until I get down?"

"Sure." She reached up as Matt lowered the box toward her. She was doing beautifully, anticipating the sight of the train inside, when a spider disturbed from his dark sanctuary skidded across the box toward her.

She screamed and flung the box upward. Matt made a grab for it, but the box was too big to catch in one hand. It fell on one of its corners on the carpet, making a crashing sound as the cars inside collided with each other, dislodging the lid.

Some of the contents spilled out onto her mother's white carpet—an engine, a caboose, several lengths of track.

And a whole lot of money.

Rosie blinked, and when the mound of green didn't disappear, she stared at it in disbelief. Matt, still on top of the ladder, swore artfully.

Rosie got down on her knees to study the bundles of bills bound together—twenties, fifties, hundreds.

Matt came to kneel beside her. The bottom of the box had been upended in the fall. He pulled it up now, revealing the rest of the train.

And a whole lot *more* money.

Rosie gasped, both hands over her mouth. "What is it?" she asked stupidly.

"Ah..." He seemed to be thinking. She guessed what he didn't seem to want to say. Only yesterday, she wouldn't have suspected her father of dishonesty, and she'd have defended his devotion to Maple Hill, if not to his family. But her mother's revelation this morning had taught her that she hadn't known the man at all, much less understood him. "I'd say…it *looks* like someone's ill-gotten gains," he said finally.

"What happened up here?" Sonny's voice asked from the doorway. "I heard something crash…holy sh—" Sonny covered her mouth and bit back the word. Her eyes above her hand were wide with astonishment.

"Rosie," she said, walking slowly into the room, her shocked gaze riveted on the pile of train pieces and cash. "Tell me that's your nest egg."

Rosie sat her mother on a small chair nearby. "Mom, I live in the guest house."

"But…you s-store some of your things here."

"Not my cash. Which consists of about twenty-six dollars. So—this isn't yours?"

Her mother looked a little like her old self as she replied, "When have you known me to save cash? I'd have invested that in Manolo Blahniks."

Matt frowned at Rosie.

"Shoes," she explained. "Then…it's Dad's?"

Sonny shook her head, still staring at the disorderly pile. "I have no idea. I've never seen it before, and I…I can't imagine where he would have gotten it."

Rosie was reluctant to think about it. She picked up one of the train cars and inspected it for rust. She couldn't find any. She checked over the engine, the caboose. So, her father had put the train away in his closet—where he could keep an eye on it—because he claimed it was rusting in the attic. But the attic was warm and dry. Still—philanderer was one thing, but thief quite another.

"How much is there?" her mother asked.

Rosie looked at Matt. "I haven't counted obviously, but eyeballing it, I'd say upward of a hundred thousand dollars."

Sonny stared at him. After a moment, she said, "He wouldn't have *stolen* money."

"No," he said.

Rosie heard something in his tone she didn't like. She tried to read his expression, but he looked away, focusing on pulling the pieces of the train from the pile and putting them on the bed. Then he put the money back in the box and replaced it where they'd found it.

"We have to call the police," Sonny said.

He nodded. "I agree. I'll ask Jim to come over."

"Could this have something to do with what's been happening to Rosie?"

"It might. If Hal did put that money there, he did it two years ago, and the whole Tolliver deal we're considering as a motive happened at that time."

It struck her like a Mack truck. Jim had suggested it yesterday. Someone on the committee may have taken a bribe for the Tolliver deal. It had been her father!

She sat down on the window seat and stared at Matt. He was still avoiding her eyes. And she'd noticed him and Jim in urgent conversation in the kitchen last night when she'd returned from seeing Sara out. "You think this money is the bribe Jim was talking about?" she asked.

He sank onto the edge of the bed, his expression carefully unrevealing. "I'm not certain," he said simply.

"You know something," she insisted quietly. "You may as well tell us what it is."

MATT WOULD HAVE BEEN happy to be shot in the shoulder again if it meant he wouldn't have to answer her question. He'd kept the truth to himself two years ago and lost her, anyway. He hated the thought that revealing it now might have the same result.

She'd learned some truths about her father this morning, but Matt was sure that taking the man even farther down in her estimation wasn't going to help his own fragile relationship with her.

But he knew that he wasn't leaving her again, and if he was staying, he had to tell her the truth.

"I think it *is* a bribe for the Tolliver deal," he said, meeting her gaze. "I think this is the money Jim talked about last night. It was paid to him to get a clean environmental-impact statement. But Langlois protested the findings, then your father died before the whole thing could be resolved."

"But…why would you leap to that conclusion?" She'd listened calmly enough, but now she was annoyed by the suggestion. "What possible reason—"

"Because he did it before," Matt interrupted. "When the mall was built."

She stared at him, momentarily silenced, while Sonny gasped quietly, "What?"

"How do you know that?" Rosie demanded.

"Before I left," he explained, "I was doing a story on new developments in town and sort of backed into some incriminating information. I was looking over the budget for the building of the mall and found a substantial charge for consulting fees paid to Sonic Industries. Your father deposited the same amount in a Boston bank. My guess is he bought off an inspector, because later a group of tenants sued over faulty wiring. He seemed to know who to pay off to speed things along."

"But another company built the mall. Why would he make things easy for a competitor?"

"Because he made a good chunk of money without any of the aggravations of having to conform to codes and laws himself. And he didn't have to pay taxes on it."

Sonny and Rosie stared at him. Each looked as though she'd had all she could deal with for one day. "I found similar evidence on two other sites. Payoffs to inspectors in those cases." He wrapped it up simply. "It's logical to assume that he did it over and over."

Sonny shook her head. "I can't believe it. I mean, he used to have a lot of trouble with cash flow, then suddenly things were easier. I thought he'd just... worked it out."

Technically, Matt thought, he had.

"And you knew all this," Rosie asked, "*before* you left me?"

"Yes," he replied. "I discovered it shortly before Jay's accident. Then when your father died, there seemed little point in upsetting all of you further."

"But…" Sonny closed her eyes, then opened them again, obviously thinking it would change the reality of what she'd just learned. "Why would he keep all that cash? I mean, why not an automatic transfer, or the Boston account, or…anything less incriminating!"

"Cash is more easily handled and distributed," Matt said. "And he might have had to share this and didn't want to write a check and create a paper trail someone could follow."

"Distributed?" Sonny asked. "Do you mean he was supposed to share with someone who thinks Rosie kept the money? Or that the company he was bringing in wants their money back?"

Matt shook his head. "No. If that was the case, I don't think they would have waited two years. And maybe there's new management because the old one was suspect. Whoever's in power now may not know what went on here."

Sonny bit her lip. "True," she said.

Rosie seemed to have nothing to say, but simply watched him with accusation in her eyes.

"I think it's someone on the committee who did something questionable," he said to Sonny. "Or maybe helped Hal do something questionable." Rosie wasn't going to make him feel guilty for wanting to protect her from further pain. "Or someone affected by the action taken by the committee, and they don't want the whole thing coming up again."

"How can it get more confusing the more we discover?" Sonny asked no one in particular.

"Grand*maaa!* The cookies are burning!" Chase's voice could be heard from downstairs.

"Good Lord! I forgot all about them!" Sonny got to her feet and hurried to the door. She stopped to look back. "You'll call your friend Jim?"

Matt nodded.

"Okay. And don't forget the train. First and foremost, it's Christmas and we're together. All the rest of this will be sorted out. You coming, Rosie?"

"I'll be right down," Rosie promised.

Sonny hurried off.

Rosie confronted Matt the moment her mother was out of sight. "Whatever made you think you could keep that from me?"

He stopped to expel a breath. "I kept it from you before your father died because I didn't think you'd believe me. You were so into trying to get his approval, trying to believe he was the man you wanted him to be. When he died, all those horrible things happened at once and I couldn't hurt you again."

She stood and took several agitated paces away from him. "Is there anybody in this house who hasn't lied to me?" she demanded. "How dare you learn something like that and not tell me!"

"It seemed best at the time."

"For whom? I suppose it helped validate your reason for leaving! Put a noble spin on walking away."

Remembering how it had been between them at that time, he lost his battle to remain calm. "Oh, poor *you,* Rosie! Lied to by your mother and me because we wanted to spare you, and lied to by your father because—well, it appears he just lied to everybody. I can only imagine how horrible that time was for you, but I *wanted* to help you through it. I *wanted* to share your grief with you, but you preferred to hole up with it. By the time I left, we weren't communicating at all, and I couldn't see digging your hole any deeper by adding what I knew about your father. He was always more important to you than I was, anyway."

She reacted to that with a start, as though he'd struck her. "That isn't true."

"Yes, it is. You're offended because I didn't tell you the truth? Well, here's some for you. For some selfish reasons of his own, he was always stingy with his affection for you and Francie and your mom, yet you were always trying to prove to him that you were worth it. I, on the other hand, tried hard to give you everything in my power, financially, emotionally, every way I could think of, but in the end it all came down to what your father thought. *He* was a crook, and you're mad at *me* because I protected you from that knowledge."

Her anger was overtaken by sadness. "I wanted him to think I was wonderful. All my friends' fathers—"

"Well, I'm sorry," Matt interrupted, planting himself firmly in her path as she paced back to the window. "That was your childhood. It's time to get over it. We get who we get in our lives and we do the best we can. Ultimately, it's all about what we do, not what anybody *thinks* about what we do—even parents. This is your life now, and *I* always thought you were wonderful. Can't that be what matters most now?"

She put both hands to her face suddenly, overwhelmed, he imagined, with the shocking events of the day. If he was honest with himself, he couldn't blame her. His parents had been far worse than hers, but then, he'd had the luxury of never connecting with them and therefore never caring.

"Okay, forget that question," he said, packing up the train in an empty basket on her mother's window seat. "I'm sorry you've had such a difficult time. We'll have that out when this is all over. Meanwhile, like your mother said, it's Christmas, and Chase is having a great time in spite of everything."

She took the basket from him, her gaze unyielding. "I think I had a right to know the truth."

"Maybe you did," he granted without remorse. "I may very well have been wrong. But if I was, it was out of love, not out of an intention to hurt you further."

He reached into his pocket for his cell phone. "Go help your mother save the cookies. I'll call Jim."

"Do you know anything else you're going to tell him that you don't want me to hear?"

"No."

She gave him one last, lingering look, then she walked away, the electric train that may very well have ruined their effort to get back together swinging in a basket from her hand.

He dialed Jim Machado. Then he paged Hale and Berger to let them know Jim was coming.

Jim arrived within ten minutes and stared with Matt in wonderment at the contents of the box.

"You have no idea where this is from?" he asked.

"No. My mother-in-law never saw it before. I'm thinking it might be the bribe from Tolliver. I'll bet he was paid for a phony environmental-impact statement, or maybe one for which no environmental-impact study was even done. Someone's afraid if the whole thing comes up again, he or she's going to get caught. But the truck driver who might have been bought off is dead."

Jim nodded consideringly. "Okay. So who is it?"

"I have no idea. I'll let you figure that out."

Jim gave him a dry glance. "Thanks."

"Anything new on Bowers and Sorrento?"

"I'm waiting for a fax on some information I'm tracking down on Bowers. I can't seem to find Sorrento. I'll know more later today. Meanwhile, I'll take the money into custody and lock it up. Can I invite myself to dinner again if I bring it and let you know what I discover?"

"What are you bringing?"

"Chinese?"

"Okay. Works for me."

CHAPTER FIFTEEN

JIM ARRIVED at dinnertime with what appeared to be one of everything from the Chinese restaurant.

"Even though they've seen me before," Jim said of the security team near the driveway, "they inspected the bags. And I think they might have kept the fried shrimp. Oh, no. Here they are." He pulled them out of the bag that contained sauces, sesame seeds and tea bags, and put them in the middle of the table with all the other take-out boxes.

"Jim, you didn't get to meet my mother when you were here earlier," Rosie said, stopping Sonny after she'd put plates around the table. "We were busy trying to save a batch of cookies. Sonja Erickson, Jim Machado."

Sonny shook his hand. "Hello," she said. "I believe you once stopped me for speeding."

"Uh-oh."

"I was late for a hair appointment." She smiled. "Men just don't seem to get the significance of hair appointments. As I recall, you told me I should consider my head more important to me than my hair."

Jim's eyes went over her new do. "Seems both are looking beautiful right now."

Rosie placed a steaming teapot in the middle of the table and put several tea bags inside. She did everything without once looking in Matt's direction. "Let that steep for a couple of minutes," she advised. "Jim, is there chicken chow yuk?"

He inspected several cartons, then found the dish and handed it across the table. Sonny began circulating the other boxes and there was a few minutes of quiet while everyone heaped up plates. Chase's consisted primarily of fried shrimp and egg rolls.

"Chase, you have to have some vegetables," Sonny said, handing him a carton of vegetables with flat noodles.

He looked into the box and made a face. "I don't like the stuff that's all saucy."

Matt passed him a carton. "Try the Mongolian beef. It has vegetables in it and it's hot."

"Cool." Chase put a dollop on his plate and passed the carton to Jim.

"I found out," Jim said, "why Molly Bowers has so much money in her savings account." Everyone looked up. "Apparently one of the things she inherited with her mother's house was a Chippendale table she sold at auction in Boston for two hundred eighty thousand dollars. She also sold a whole lot of Tiffany stuff."

Sonny put her fork down. "My goodness," she said with quiet respect.

Jim nodded. "Made herself a small fortune. Legitimately."

"Well, darn," Rosie teased.

"And…something else interesting." He hesitated, then asked Chase if he would get him the cell phone he'd left in the pocket of his jacket. "I think your aunt Rosie put it in the closet in the hallway."

Chase hurried off to oblige. The moment he was out of earshot, Jim spoke quickly.

"Tolliver made a two-hundred-thousand-dollar payment for consulting fees two years ago. All comfortably nonspecific."

Rosie frowned and put both hands in her lap. "Did you count what was in the box we gave you?"

"Seventy-eight thousand five hundred dollars. One of the bundles of fifties had been ripped open and a few bills were missing."

Rosie turned to Matt. "So if my father was the payee, that's a lot of money missing."

"Say he had an accomplice besides the Department of Environmental Quality guy, or someone found out what he was doing and had to be paid to keep quiet, he might have had to split the money. So if he did, that's twenty-one thousand five hundred missing from a hundred thousand dollars. So…twenty thousand dollars for the phony impact statement and fifteen hundred dollars just for pocket change?"

Chase shot back into the room with Jim's cell phone. Jim made a production of checking messages. Finding none, he put the phone in his pants' pocket.

"My bet's on Sorrento," he said, pulling the box of egg rolls toward him. "He disappeared right after the fire at Rosie's shop. And nothing's happened to Rosie since. My guess is he's lying low, probably aware that we've narrowed the search to him. I went to his place in Springfield this morning, and his house is closed up tight as a drum. No car in the garage. Pharmacy's being run by a sub. Even the woman who runs the gift-shop part of it says he left suddenly on Wednesday, but she doesn't know where."

"Gone…forever?" Rosie asked.

"He's gone until I catch him," Jim corrected. "You should still be very careful. We're not sure of anything. Oh," he added. "Except Catherine Merchant. She's been in Montpelier with her sister since Thanksgiving."

Rosie nodded, pleased. "Good."

"The community Christmas dinner is tomorrow night," Sonny said. "And I *have* to be there."

"And I'm going to see Santa tomorrow!" Chase announced. "Uncle Matt said it was okay."

At Jim's frown, Matt assured him, "I've got hired muscle to follow us around. And nobody's leaving my sight."

"Okay. I know the department will have a considerable presence at the dinner because they bought a bank of tickets. And if there's any trouble, nobody likes to mix it up like an off-duty cop."

"I'm not going to the dinner," Rosie said with a glance in Matt's direction. "Chase can't come. It's an adult function with wine and dancing. You can go with Mom, and one of Hank's guys can stay with us."

"That won't work," Sonny put in quickly. "I volunteered you to be Santa's helper. The city's giving awards for service to members of the community, and Santa will need someone to help him distribute awards."

"Mom!" Rosie said.

"Well, I'm sorry. I thought you'd be pleased. You told me you regretted leaving town for Christmas last year. I thought you'd be happy to be involved in such a festive event." She grinned. "And you'll get to show off your legs. It's a skimpy little costume."

"Oh, God."

"Who's Santa?" Matt asked.

"Hank," Sonny replied. "Jackie volunteered him."

Rosie did not want to go anywhere with Matt, particularly somewhere where he'd feel obliged to stay with her every moment because of the implied danger of the crowd. At least with Hank there—the backbone of his own security team—she'd be allowed some respite from Matt's presence.

If she was fair, and she acknowledged that perhaps she was not, she could believe that he'd kept her father's shady dealings from her out of concern for her peace of mind at an awful time. But she still hated that he'd done it. That probably didn't make sense, but nothing in her life had made sense for some time now.

"Then who's going to stay with Chase? The security guys?"

"No," Matt said. "We don't want them distracted by baby-sitting. What about Sara?"

That was a good idea, but Rosie hated to admit that to him. "I'll check. She might have planned to go to the dinner."

"Why don't you give her a call right now so we'll know where we are."

With a glare at her mother for having caused this little tempest, Rosie went to the wall phone and stabbed out Sara's number.

"Hi, Rosie," Sara answered.

Caller ID, Rosie thought, made sneak attacks virtually impossible. "Hi. Are you going to the community dinner tomorrow night?"

"I thought about it," Sara said, sounding unenthusiastic, "but I'd be going only for the food. I've worked for most of those people at one time or another, and I'm not anxious to break bread with them."

To Rosie's recollection, Sara had never been fired, but she'd never been particularly happy in any of her jobs.

"Why?" Sara asked, her enthusiasm up a notch. "You want to do something together?"

"No, I can't. My mother volunteered me to help with the distribution of awards at the dinner. We need someone to watch Chase. Would you be afraid to do that?"

There was a moment's pause. "Why would I be afraid?" she asked finally. "Has he taken a suddenly monstrous turn or something? Am I likely to be tied up and locked in a closet?"

Rosie laughed. Then she winked at Chase, who listened interestedly to her half of the conversation. "No, he's the same sweet genius he's always been, but you will be in my place, sort of. Filling my shoes. And that hasn't been a very safe place to be lately."

"Has something new happened?"

"No, nothing," Rosie assured her quickly. "Life's been pretty quiet here, but nothing is absolutely certain. There'll be a guard on the house the whole time you're here."

"Is he cute?"

"Yes, but he's married. Sara, please be serious. I don't want you to feel obligated. In fact, I'd just as soon stay…"

"I'm seriously happy to do it for you," Sara said. "What time do you want me?"

Rosie covered the mouthpiece. "What time do we want her?" she asked her mother.

"Six o'clock," Sonny replied. "Dinner's at seven, but we need some prep time."

She passed on the details to Sara, who promised to be there. "Mission accomplished," Rosie told her companions as she hung up the phone. "But you owe me big for this, Mom."

Sonny reached over to pat her hand. "I owe you big for a lot of things, Rosie."

Jim wanted to help clean up, but Sonny sent him on his way with a doggie bag and a hug. "It was lovely of you to bring dinner," she said. Then she handed him another bag. "Would you give this to the guys watching the house?"

"Sure."

Matt walked him to the door.

"Do I detect a little testiness between you two to-night?" Sonny asked Rosie as she began to scrape plates.

Rosie collected glasses on a tray and carried them to the dishwasher. "Yes, you did. And how can you be surprised?" she replied aggressively. "He knew all that about Dad and kept it to himself."

Sonny frowned at her. "To protect your feelings."

"He should have told me."

"So you could find a way to make that his fault, too?"

Rosie put the last glass in the dishwasher, then turned to her mother in hurt surprise. "What?"

"Rosie, you're not mad that he didn't tell you. You're mad that you loved your father, and he was a first-class rat. You hate that you wanted his approval. Are you thinking that if Matt had told you the truth, you'd have felt differently about him?"

Rosie hated being understood when she didn't understand herself. "It's hard to tell how I'd feel when I didn't have all the information."

"That was an ugly time of your life, Rosie. You weren't dealing well with the information you had. None of us was. Your brother had died, your father killed himself over it, and that caused you to lose your baby. How could anyone be expected to deal with more? Sweetheart, you have no right to be angry that Matt didn't tell you."

But she was filled with anger.

She put it on hold while she helped Chase get ready for bed and listened to the list of things he intended to ask Santa for.

"A bike," he said, holding up his index finger. "One of those really cool Firepower bikes with flames on the seat." Matt, she realized, had been right when he'd picked it out. "A puppy, now that Grandma's not so upset about messes, and a Nautilus."

Rosie touched a fingertip against the third digit he held up. "A Nautilus? You mean the weight-and-exercise machine?"

"Yeah."

"Okay. But what are you going to do with that? I think it takes a pretty big guy to—"

"It's not for me," he said with a wide smile. "It's for Uncle Matt. Wouldn't it be cool if Santa brought it? I asked Uncle Matt if he could ask Santa for something, what it would be. And that's what he told me."

"But…he's going to China."

"To take pictures, and then he's coming back." Chase leaned on an elbow on his pillow and said casually, "I wish he could live here. I wish we could all live here."

"You and I *do* live here," she reminded him. "Well, I'm just across the backyard."

"Yeah, but that's not the same. I like you being here for breakfast and making my lunch, and all of us getting in the car together when I go to school. It's like Rachel's family."

THE MAN UNDER THE MISTLETOE

She wanted to caution him against longing for other people's families, but remembered that she'd done the same thing.

Instead, she urged Chase to lie down and pulled up his blankets. "I'm sure Santa will be very happy with you," she praised, "because you were thinking of someone else when you made your list."

"Uncle Matt's always doing nice things for me. I wanted Santa to bring him something nice."

"Maybe when we go out to see Santa tomorrow," she said, "we can buy something for Uncle Matt. You know, in case Santa is busy with all the kids on his list and doesn't get to your uncle."

Chase seemed in agreement with that while still confident that Santa would come through. Then he asked worriedly, "But how will we do that? Uncle Matt told Jim he wasn't going to let any of us out of his sight."

True. That did pose a problem. "I know," she said finally. "While we're walking through the store, you keep your eyes open for a present, but don't say anything. And when we come home, we'll order it online. It'll be delivered here and he'll never know it's for him."

Chase wrapped his arms around her neck and hugged. "You're tricky, Aunt Rosie."

She hugged him back, tucked him in again, checked that his closet door was closed and turned out the light. She left his door half open.

She went to the guest bedroom her aunt Ginger had

used, intending to have a long soak in the bathtub and hope no one would come looking for her. She'd always felt guilty about being angry about her father's cool lack of interest, but tonight she thought she had the right.

Matt had already commandeered the tub, however. She pushed open the door to see a pair of long, muscular legs visible from knee to ankle, and feet crossed on the ridge of the tub. Mussy wet hair crowned a scrubbed face out of which stuck a lit cheroot. Powerful shoulders protruded from the water and muscular arms rested on the sides of the tub.

"Hi," he said lazily, the cigar clamped in a corner of his mouth. "Did you want a bath?"

"I can wait until you're finished," she said, turning to leave.

"Or you can climb in with me and save time."

"Thanks, but I'd prefer a nonsmoking tub. When did you start smoking cigars, anyway?"

"Took it up when I was in Yugoslavia. Haven't had one since, but Jim's always favored them and had a couple in his car. He thought I looked like I needed one."

There was an oddly relaxed, surprisingly sexy dynamic at work here. That struck her as odd, since the day had been so traumatic on several fronts and they were angry with each other. He never seemed to stay angry, though, an argument strategy she didn't understand.

"Because I'm such a trial to you, I suppose?" she asked.

"You're very insightful." He made it sound like a compliment rather than the criticism it really was.

She sat on the edge of the tub, suddenly needing to make him understand her point of view. "You're a journalist," she said, looking into his eyes so that hers weren't tempted to wander over the underwater treasures. "What if someone didn't give you the whole truth? How would you do your job?"

"It wasn't your job, Rosie," he said from his reclining position. "It was your life, and at that point in time, it was falling apart."

"And it's never occurred to you," she heard herself say, "that I should have known the truth about him? That if I'd been warned about my father, maybe I *wouldn't* have lost our baby when I found him dead?"

Those words were a complete surprise to her. She almost wished she could hear them again, so that she could be sure she'd said them. She'd had no idea she'd harbored that thought.

Matt sat up, reaching a wet hand for her, his eyes roving her face in empathy. "Rosie."

She tried to pull away. She could feel all the old anguish, guilt and regret bubbling up, and she'd crumble if it surfaced.

"No." He tightened his grip on her. "Rosie, tell me what you're thinking." He tried to pull himself to his feet one-handed, but she broke away and he fell backward with a splash.

She ran through his room, heading for the door to the hallway, but she could hear her mother and Chase out there, probably at the linen closet, talking about Christmas.

She couldn't open the door. She was dragging in air in deep, noisy gulps and she didn't want to have to explain.

That hesitation was all Matt needed to overtake her. He'd pulled on his jeans, but was bare-chested when he caught her hand and drew her back to the bed.

"We're going to have this out," he insisted, pushing her until she sat on the edge of the mattress. "I should have made you talk to me two years ago and maybe we'd still be together. But I thought you were in such pain that I had to be gentle with you. So I let you beat *me* up emotionally, but that didn't seem to help. In the end there was still nothing left of our relationship to save."

She gave one final yank. "Then why do you keep trying?"

"Because I know you're still in there, damn it!" He sat beside her, held her by the shoulders and gave her a little shake. "Come on, Rosie! Tell me how much it hurt! Tell me how horrible it was to lose Jay, then to find your father in a puddle of blood! Tell me that falling down the steps and losing our baby was a little like dying yourself! I know what it felt like. It was *my* baby, too!"

It was that claim that did it. "You had no idea!" She screamed at him like a madwoman. "You wanted to talk! You wanted to make love! But there were no words to express the viciousness of the pain or the magnitude of the loss! How could you have *thought* we could talk about it?"

"What other tools do we have to share what hurts us?" he asked, obviously surprised by her response. "We hold each other, which you wouldn't do, or we talk about how it feels, which you also wouldn't do. Do we have such a Mars-Venus reversal here that I have to explain it to you?"

She remembered clearly how she'd hated him then—almost as much as she'd hated herself.

She stared at him for a moment while that thought blinked in her head like a faulty neon light. *Hated herself. Hated herself. Hated herself?*

"Rosie, don't close up," he pleaded, taking hold of her arm. "What? Tell me what you're thinking."

The truth rose in her like bile, burning the back of her throat, threatening to make her sick. She felt cold and dreaded what admitting the truth would do to her. It was all so bad already that saying it aloud, giving it credibility, would only be worse. But it was gnawing at her, trying to eat its way out.

She looked into his eyes and his dark gaze had a curiously steadying effect. It didn't diminish her pain, but it made it possible to actually speak the words.

"I hated you," she said.

He took that without flinching, though she saw a deeper darkness in his eyes, felt a small jolt in the hands that held her arms.

"I know. I guess…I just couldn't understand why."

The agony of it burst inside her like so much poi-

son moving through her body. "Because…" Her voice
was tight and breathless. Even swallowing hurt. "Because you didn't have to bear any of the…blame."

He stared at her. "What blame?"

"I lost our baby," she whispered, the words ripping
out of her. "I wasn't tough enough. I…I…"

"No!" Matt shook her again. "What are you talking about? No! You didn't do it. You found your father
dead, which would have been enough to upset anyone
to that degree whether you'd known about his crooked
dealings ahead of time or not. You fell! Who wouldn't
be disoriented by that horror and lose their balance?"
He firmed his grip on her, followed her eyes with his
when she looked away. "No one blames you for losing the baby."

"*I* do."

"Well, then it's for no good reason," he said. His
voice gentled when he added, "And if you'd told me
how you felt, I could have reassured you that I didn't
hold you responsible. I could have told you how much
the loss hurt me, too, and we could have helped each
other."

Matt felt as though he could die of her anguish. On
some level, just before he'd left, he'd known her
behavior was pain-driven. But he hadn't suspected to
what extent she'd tortured herself.

"It hurt so much," she admitted, putting her hands
on his arms and holding on. "And I could see how hurt
and disappointed you were. I couldn't share because
I couldn't bear your pain, too."

He closed his eyes and shook his head. "Rosie, if you'd shared mine, I'd have taken yours. You wouldn't have had to bear it alone. I was disappointed because we'd never be able to see the person we'd created, not disappointed in you."

She put both hands over her face and leaned into him, deep sobs bursting out of her. He enveloped her in his arms. He held her for what felt like ages, experiencing every sob as though it had come from him. What a gnarled and ugly misunderstanding had kept them apart for so long.

He finally lay back with her, covering them with the other side of the coverlet.

She held tightly to him, quiet at last. "I'm sorry." Her breath puffed against his chin.

"Stop apologizing," he said, rubbing her back. "No one blames you. Go to sleep."

"I dream about her sometimes."

"I do, too. I figure it's her way of keeping in touch with us."

"That's a nice thought," she said on a sigh. The next moment, she was asleep.

CHAPTER SIXTEEN

GIDEON HALE AND Bob Berger might have been Se-
cret-Service trained, Matt thought, for the vigilant protection they provided without intruding into the
family's shopping expedition. Every time he turned
around, one of them was in view, but Matt felt fairly
sure that Rosie, Sonny and Chase had completely forgotten that Hank's men had come along. Hank, himself, had gone to watch the house in their absence.

Rosie was cheerful this morning, if a little sleepy-
eyed. Matt had run a bath for her when she'd awakened with a start at 2:00 a.m. She'd pulled off her
clothes, then wrapped her arms around him and invited
him to join her. It was dawn before they went to sleep
again.

Matt stood with Chase at the end of a very long line
of children at the Danvers Department Store, waiting
to talk to Santa. Gideon followed the women, who'd
gone off to shop, and Berger was several feet away
from the column of naughties-and-nices and their parents.

Santa sat several yards ahead of them on a throne-like chair festooned with garlands of poinsettias, gift-wrapped boxes on the floor all around him.

"What do you think's in those presents?" Chase wanted to know.

"Toys," Matt replied simply as a little boy vacated Santa's lap and a little girl in a red coat went to take his place. Matt and Chase inched up one spot in line.

Chase leaned out to look over the boxes. "None of those look like a bike," he said worriedly.

"I don't think he usually wraps a bike." Matt silently praised himself for his capabilities in fiction. Fine thing for a journalist. "It's too big. He'd probably just put it under the tree with a bow on it. So he can't set it out with the other toys, 'cause it wouldn't be a surprise."

"Oh. That's probably what he'd do with a Nautilus, too."

"Probably." Hmm.

"Uncle Matt! Come on!" Matt came out of his thoughts as Chase tugged on his arm. "It's almost my turn!" Chase said excitedly.

"You remember your list?" Matt asked.

"Yeah. Just three things."

"You want to tell them to me to make sure you don't forget?"

Chase gave him a look that reminded Matt of the one Rosie often gave him. "I won't forget," he said. Then he asked quickly, "If you ask for a puppy, do you have to tell him what kind or what color?"

A puppy? "I don't think so. I think Santa asks your parents about it."

"He does? You mean, you've *talked* to him?"

Now, that was dangerous thinking. "Well...I'm just your uncle, Chase."

"Oh. Yeah." He looked a little shaken by that thought for a moment, then he laughed in embarrassment. "I forgot."

Matt worried about that for the two minutes Chase spent on Santa's lap. Matt couldn't hear their conversation, but Santa seemed taken with Chase and asked him questions. They even laughed together. At one point, Chase pointed at Matt. Santa gave him a wave. Matt felt weirdly blessed.

Chase jumped off the dais and ran to Matt, his eyes glowing. "All taken care of," he said with supreme confidence.

As they went off, trailed by Berger, to meet up with Rosie and Sonny, Matt was feeling good about the bike but worried about the puppy.

The annual Christmas frenzy was picking up. Shoppers abounded today, slogging through the now-dirty snow, picking their way toward the shops in boots and serious winter gear.

Matt, Chase, Rosie and Sonny had lunch at the Perk Avenue Tea Room, and Rosie insisted on asking Gideon and Berger to join them. Matt was sure they'd refuse, but he didn't try to tell her that.

She returned, frowning. "Gideon says they can't concentrate on us if they're eating with us."

"They're very good at what they do."

"But they're going to go hungry."

"They won't. Your mom sent them breakfast this morning."

Sonny looked bright and cheerful today, the relaxation in her manner obvious. Matt imagined that sharing the secret about Jay had to have eased her mind, though what she'd learned about her husband yesterday must have shocked her. Still, she seemed to be coping.

Rosie seemed happy, too, if still a little uncertain when she looked into his eyes. After lunch, the women shopped for Sonny's sisters, Matt and Chase occupying themselves with a small tree on the jewelry counter. It was hung with brooches, earrings and bracelets as ornaments.

Matt spotted a particularly pretty bracelet made up of linked gold stars with small diamond centers. Rosie had always had a fascination with celestial motifs.

"Aunt Rosie loves stars," Chase whispered, as if reading his mind.

He checked the price tag. It was considerable, but thanks to his advance, he could make the purchase.

"Can we buy it?" Chase asked eagerly. "I have two dollars left."

"Yes, we can." Matt handed the clerk the bracelet and his credit card.

Chase dug out his money. Matt pushed his hand back to his pocket. "If you'll wrap it, then I won't have to pay for wrapping, and that'll be *your* part."

"Okay. I can get some from Grandma."

Matt had just stashed the purchase in his pocket

when Rosie and Sonny appeared, Gideon right behind them.

"What do you say to mochas all around before we go home?" Rosie suggested. She turned to grin at Gideon. "It won't distract you to have a mocha, will it? You can drink it from ten feet behind me."

He smiled at her, then sent Matt a look that suggested he knew what she could put him through. "Sixteen-ounce, double shot, no whipped cream," he said.

"All right!"

Fifteen minutes later Matt was driving home, Gideon and Berger trailing them.

"What the…?" Matt exclaimed, stopping abruptly halfway up the driveway at the sight of several cars bunched together in the middle, one of them a police unit with rotating lights.

Matt could see several uniformed officers, Jim Machado and Hank Whitcomb. They all seemed to be clustered around a central figure he couldn't see.

Rosie strained forward. "Someone must have tried to get past Hank," she speculated worriedly.

Sonny wrapped her arms around Chase.

Gideon and his companion braked to a stop behind them and ran out to flank the car just as Matt pushed his door open, intent on finding out what was going on.

Gideon pushed him back in. "Stay inside," he ordered. "I've got this covered." He closed the door and responded with a wave when Hank spotted him and beckoned him closer.

Matt bristled with exasperation.

Rosie put a hand on his arm.

He was momentarily distracted from his annoyance by her touch. "You hired him to protect us," she reminded him, "and that includes you."

"No, I hired him to protect *you*."

She patted him placatingly. "Oh, relax. Now you know how I feel. It robs your power, but it's for your own good."

He wanted to tell her that it wasn't the same thing at all, but she was still touching him.

Then he sensed movement in the group ahead and turned to look just as the small crowd parted. He saw a wildly gesticulating young woman, a head shorter than the men gathered around her.

"Oh, God," he said, pushing his door open despite Gideon. It was Jenny Morrow. Rosie tried to grab his arm, but he kept going.

"Matt!" Jenny exclaimed as he hurried toward her.

"Jenny, what are you doing here?" he demanded, opening his arms as she ran toward him. Jim grabbed her, but Matt waved him off. "It's okay. We work together in Sacramento."

"Thank goodness!" Jenny breathed, wrapping her arms around him. She was trembling. "What's going on? Did the dragon arrange this elaborate security setup so you wouldn't stray?"

He opened his mouth to reply, but noticed Rosie standing beside him, her eyes fixed on the young woman in his arms. Her eyes moved slowly from Jenny to his face, temper so hot in them he was sure he'd have blisters.

"You were supposed to stay in the car." It annoyed the hell out of him that she was putting the wrong spin on this—just when they'd almost found a common ground again.

"She hit me with the door handle," Berger complained, his voice a little high. "Then she walked over me to follow you. Maybe we need another team to protect *me*."

"Dragon?" Rosie asked, her voice dripping with the auditory equivalent of The Look.

"Everybody, hold it!" Jim shouted, interrupting the argument. "This young lady says she's a friend of yours, Matt. Can you verify that for us?"

Matt replied with a single nod. "She's Jennifer Morrow, reporter for the *Sacramento Sentinel*. We work together."

"And why is she here?"

Matt couldn't answer that. "Why are you here, Jenny?" he asked.

She seemed reluctant to reply with everyone staring at her, then she looked into Rosie's pugnacious expression and replied with a squaring of her shoulders, "I came to see if you were all right," she said to Matt.

He was puzzled. "Why would I not be all right?"

She indicated the collection of police and bodyguards around them with a sweep of her hand. "I think it's pretty obvious that you aren't!"

"Do *you* have something to do with that?" Hank asked her.

Jim frowned at him. "Who's the cop here?"

"Sorry," Hank replied. "Just seemed like the next logical question."

Jim sighed. "Okay, Miss Morrow. How did you know Matt and his wife were in trouble?"

"His wife?" Jenny looked into Rosie's eyes and said candidly, "I thought you were his ex."

Matt saw something change in the depths of Rosie's eyes. He couldn't analyze what it meant. "Ex-dragon," she replied, "but current wife."

Jenny turned her attention to Jim. "When Matt left Sacramento," she explained with a sigh, "he said he was spending two days here, then he was going to this place in the Berkshires to take photographs. I called and he wasn't there. His cell phone didn't answer. I was worried."

"Why didn't you just call here?" Jim asked. "Certainly a reporter could have found the number."

"I'm used to taking action. And he forgot to leave a roll of film we need for a year-end roundup edition."

"I handed it to Shorty before I left," Matt said. "Did he forget?"

"I guess so. He claims he doesn't have it."

"I'll call him."

Hank ran a hand over his face. "I'm sorry," he said to Jim, then to Matt. "She came racing up the driveway. When I tried to question her, she got testy. Then she got physical. I thought she meant trouble."

"She's always trouble," Matt assured him with a grin. "Just not the kind you're worried about."

"*You* grabbed *me!*" she growled at Hank. "All I did was drive up the road. Don't friends visit other friends in Massachusetts?"

"Jenny, please be quiet," Matt said, yanking her back when she would have continued to rail at Hank. "Can we just apologize for the disturbance and everybody go back to what they were doing before Jenny showed up?"

The uniformed officers waited for an okay from Jim, then got back into their vehicle.

"Somebody will be back at six," Hank said, "to keep an eye on Sara and Chase. I'm sorry, Miss Morrow."

"Forget it," she said, folding her arms. "I just hope you're as tough on *real* intruders."

Matt took Jenny back to the car, Rosie and Gideon following. He introduced her briefly to Sonny and Chase, who moved over to make room for her in the back seat.

"You have a *child?*" Jenny asked Matt before climbing in.

"He's my nephew. By marriage. Sonny is my mother-in-law."

"Oh. Hi, Chase." She tossed her purse in first, then slipped in. "Hello, Sonny. I'm sorry about the fuss."

"That's all right," Sonny replied. "But what *was* it all about? Berger wouldn't let us leave the car."

Jenny explained on the brief ride to the house. "So

we needed the film and I was worried. I mean, I've known Matt as a tortured soul for a year and a half, and I was sure coming back wouldn't be good for him."

As Matt parked, Rosie turned to peer into the back seat. "I suppose you're thinking you *are* good for him?"

The suggestion was clear.

"I've been a good friend," Jenny replied, never one to walk around a challenge. "He seemed to need one."

Rosie gave Matt a dark look and hurried into the house.

His patience with everyone in his life at the snapping point, Matt forced himself to remain calm while he helped Jenny and Sonny out of the back. Chase raced up to the door and held it open for them.

"Grandma, can I borrow some wrapping paper?" he asked.

"Sure. Can I get you some coffee, Miss Morrow?"

"Please," Jenny replied. "I'll call the airline right now to change my return flight to tomorrow."

She pointed Jenny to a chair. "Let's have our coffee first. Chase, you entertain Jenny, and I'll put the coffee on and get you some gift wrap." She glanced at her watch. "We're all due at a community dinner in a little over two hours, so you'll excuse us if we have some things to do."

"Of course." Jenny turned apologetically to Matt. "I'm sorry. I really was worried."

Matt appreciated her concern, though it couldn't have come at a worse time.

"The dragon's very beautiful," she said, falling into a chair that matched the ivy-patterned sofa.

Chase sat near her and taking seriously his grandmother's request that he entertain their guest, launched into a recounting of his visit with Santa.

Matt walked upstairs to the bedroom he shared with Rosie and heard the shower running in the adjoining bathroom. The door was closed. He pushed it open.

Rosie stood on the bath mat wearing nothing but the glossy mass of dark hair she'd pulled out of its clip. It was damp, and beads of water covered her cheeks, her shoulders and the tops of her breasts. She held a new bar of soap she must have forgotten when she climbed into the shower.

Her eyes were huge and angry. No. Huge and hurt. He had to look twice to be sure.

"What?" she asked stiffly.

"I wanted to explain about Jenny," he said.

She opened the shower door. Water rushed beyond it, steaming the small area. "No need," she said. "We were…apart. And she's very pretty. I'm sure…"

"You're sure what?" He grabbed her arm and held her back. He reached in to turn off the water and pushed the shower door closed. Silence ticked heavily. "That I'd be unfaithful to you the moment I was out of sight? That my grief wasn't genuine and therefore I'd behave like a bachelor instead of a married man who'd just lost his baby?"

ROSIE WAS a hairbreadth from a good scream. Certain Matt had been in some kind of danger, she'd evaded the bodyguard to run to his side, only to see a beautiful young woman race into his arms. As his arms opened to welcome her.

Well, of course, she thought stupidly. What had ever made her think that in the year and a half they'd been apart he hadn't found comfort with someone else? He was handsome, clever, protective. What woman wouldn't run to a man with those qualities?

"We work together, that's all," he said. "She's a friend. Never a lover. I've always been loyal to you even though you wanted no part of me."

"That must be why you told her I was a dragon," she retorted.

Rosie shivered, her damp flesh reacting to the cool air. He ripped her terry robe off the hook and wrapped it around her.

"She came up with that on her own. I told her you were more like a turtle, hiding away in its shell, waiting for a more amenable world. Well, it's not coming, Rosie! This is it. Your father wasn't loving, your brother died, we lost our baby, and we're left with each other. That's what we have to work with."

"I understand what we have," she said. "But... Jenny—" her voice underscored the name "—came three thousand miles to find you. That's quite an effort."

"She cares about me. I care about her."

"Do you want her?" she asked.

He dropped his hands from Rosie and took two steps away before he came up to a wall. He spun around. "Did you hear *anything* I've said?" he demanded.

"Feeling a sense of loyalty to me isn't the same as love for me. If you want me back just to comfort me because our baby died…"

He looked as though he could commit mayhem. Nothing in their history had ever suggested violence in him, but he seemed about to explode.

He pulled the bathroom door open. "If I don't leave now," he said, his voice quiet with the effort to control it, "I'll do something we'll both regret. I'll be downstairs at six."

He slammed the door behind him, and a moment later she heard the car leave, then the engine of a second car. Gideon, she guessed, racing to catch up with Matt as he drove off in exasperation.

She wept through a fifteen-minute shower, angry at him for appealing to other women, at herself for acting like a shrew when they'd finally had a chance to come together.

She'd dried her hair and was putting on makeup when she heard a rap on the bathroom door. Hoping it was Matt, she pulled it open.

It was Jenny.

If there was anyone in the world she *didn't* want to talk to now, it was her. But she couldn't blame her for loving Matt at a time when Rosie had taken all her pain out on him.

"Matt left," Rosie said, hoping to discourage conversation.

Jenny smiled thinly. "I noticed that. He went *through* the front door instead of opening it. I guess that meant you'd quarreled about something."

Rosie went back to her makeup, but left the door open. "We're always quarreling."

Stepping inside the door, Jenny asked, "Did he tell you I was too hyper for him and he's too laid-back for me? That we were never lovers?"

"The last part, yes, he told me, but is it true?" Rosie smoothed foundation over her face, glad she wasn't wielding a mascara wand. Her fingers were too unsteady.

"Married for years," Jenny said judiciously, "and you still don't trust him?" Then she softened her pose and added, "I've never seen him look at another woman, and being smart and handsome, he does get a lot of attention."

Rosie stopped to look at Jenny. She was so pretty, with the light of a quick wit in her eyes. Men, though, could make even a smart woman take wild chances. "But you came all this way. Just for friendship?"

Jenny sighed and folded her arms, leaning against the door. "He's just so special and you really have no idea how lucky you are."

It was hard, Rosie decided, to dislike a woman bent on assuring you that what you were afraid you'd lost was really yours after all.

"I pictured you as mean and selfish," Jenny said. "Judging by the fact that he's still here, I can only assume I was wrong and apologize."

Rosie felt a terrible pang at the thought of him working alone in a big city, mourning the loss of his baby and his marriage. She had to make that up to him.

"Do you have an evening dress?" she asked Jenny.

"Ah…no. I hadn't intended to party while I was here."

"Do you want to come with us to the community Christmas dinner?"

Jenny studied her suspiciously. "You *want* me to?"

"I can lend you a dress. I'm a little taller, but we're about the same size." When Jenny continued to stare at her, she added, "Maple Hill has lots of eligible young men. And many of them will be there tonight."

"I'm going home tomorrow."

"All the more reason to enjoy tonight."

Jenny smiled again. "This isn't some wicked plan to dump me in the lake when nobody's looking, is it?"

"No, it isn't. But there is a certain danger involved."

"Yes. Your mom told me about what's happened to you. But she said Matt has bodyguards all over the place. I'd love to come. Sounds like a story. But Matt's already annoyed at me for coming."

"He gets over things quickly. Let's find you a dress."

CHAPTER SEVENTEEN

MATT WAS SURE he'd sustained brain damage from prolonged exposure to Rosie. That was the only thing that could account for her and Jenny coming down the stairs together at just before six, Jenny in a gorgeous red dress that clung to every fulsome inch of her anatomy, and Rosie in a flirty little black thing that glittered and moved like midnight surf around her knees.

Sonny had come down earlier in a festive red wool suit.

"Are those the dresses Prue designed?" Sonny asked. "You both look beautiful!"

"Yes, they are." Rosie did a quick turn, encouraging Jenny to do the same. "Jenny's joining us," Rosie said, leading her to the kitchen where Sara was putting chicken strips on a baking sheet for her and Chase's dinner. Rosie introduced Jenny.

Sara put a hand to her heart at the sight of them. "Please. Leave *one* single man for me."

"Not to worry," Jenny said just as Matt answered a knock at the door. "I'm going home tomorrow."

A tall young man with dark brown hair and hazel eyes stood in the doorway. He was squarely built and smiling.

"I'm Fox Hitchman," he said, shaking Matt's hand. "I'm replacing Berger tonight. He's staying to watch the house. Gideon says we'd better get moving if we're going to make it on time."

"Then again," Jenny said, staring after him when he went back outside, "maybe one more day wouldn't hurt."

Chase stood at the door for hugs, then Sara closed and locked it as the group took off.

The dinner was held in the high-school auditorium, which had been cleared of folding chairs and replaced with tables set with green linens and red-and-green-checked napkins. Garland interwoven with beaded twigs served as table runners, and an old cathedral chair from the drama department's prop room stood empty on the stage, waiting for Santa to occupy it.

Rosie made an effort several times to get Matt alone, but there was always someone or something requiring his attention—old friends who hadn't realized he was back; Jim reminding him to be careful. He wasn't sure he was eager to know what was on Rosie's mind, anyway.

FOX AND GIDEON CLOSED in behind Rosie and Jenny. "This crowd's making me nervous," Gideon said with a frown. "You ladies stay close, just in case."

Rosie found it hard to take the threat seriously. It

was so good to be among friends. For so long, there'd been little pleasure in it, not because the people of Maple Hill weren't wonderful, but because she'd been so preoccupied with her own losses she'd been unable to enjoy anything.

Now, it was as though a breeze had run through her life and blown away the bad residue of the past and found a corner to tuck in the good memories.

She watched her mother laughing with a nice-looking older man Jackie had introduced her to, and thought how much the last few days had changed her. She *did* remember this warm and smiling woman from her childhood, before the effort to keep her husband's secret had made her unapproachable.

Rosie realized this was an odd time to reassess her life, when even the next moment was a mystery. But she was truly happy for the first time in two years, and that seemed to inspire a reevaluation of her position, the creation of a plan to stretch this moment into her future.

Jenny expressed a desire to dance, and Fox looked doubtfully at Gideon.

"Go ahead," Gideon said after a moment. "But don't forget what you're doing."

Matt was at Rosie's side at dinner, but their table was crowded with friends, and discussing personal matters was out of the question. Gideon and Fox retreated to positions in a corner where they could observe without distraction.

Then Sonny moved to the microphone and asked

for attention. Rosie thought she'd never seen her mother look lovelier. After a few moments, conversation stopped and everyone turned to the podium.

"Welcome," she said, "to the annual Maple Hill Community Christmas Dinner. The Revolutionary Dames are so happy you've all chosen to join us. This year the money raised will be donated to the food bank."

There was applause.

"We take this opportunity," she continued, "to wish all of you a happy holiday season, to thank you for being our friends and neighbors, and we ask Father Chabot of St. Anthony's to say grace so that God knows how grateful we are for his bounty and for each other. Father Chabot?"

The cheerful, rotund pastor of the Catholic church stepped to the microphone to bless the food, those who'd prepared it, and those partaking of it.

Then the volunteer staff began serving the food, and conversation returned to a happy roar.

Hank and Jackie sat at Matt, Rosie and Jenny's table, along with Haley Megrath and her lawyer husband, Bart, and Sonny and the gentleman she'd kept company with all evening.

"This is Jim's father, Toby Machado," Sonny said, introducing her companion.

Toby, smiling and gracious, had owned a restaurant in Fairhaven, in southeastern Massachusetts, as Rosie recalled. Of Portuguese extraction, he was dark featured and handsome.

Rosie asked him about the restaurant business.

"I loved owning a restaurant," he replied. "The regulars make it like dining with family all the time. But when my chef of seventeen years made plans to leave and start his own place, I offered to sell him mine instead. He took me up on it, so I retired this summer and bought a small property on the Cape."

"He came to spend Christmas with Jim," Sonny said. "Isn't that nice? Just like we have our family back for the holidays."

"I'm just a visitor," Jenny piped up. "But I love Maple Hill. I can see why you all want to be here." She toasted Matt with her wineglass.

He raised his, and Rosie touched it with her own before he could put it to his mouth. He hesitated, obviously analyzing what she'd meant by that gesture. She drank to try to show him what she couldn't say in front of everyone.

Before he could drink, too, Carol Walford, chair of the event, approached to tell Rosie and Hank they were needed backstage to prepare for the awards part of the program. The tall, elegant woman with jet-black hair and no smile moved on.

"I'll walk you," Matt said, excusing himself to their companions.

Gideon intercepted them when they were halfway to the door that led to the backstage area. "I've got her," he said, pointing Matt back toward the table. "You stay and enjoy your dinner."

Matt shook his head. "Thanks, but I need a moment

with her. Then I'll count on you to watch out for her backstage."

Gideon smiled. "Okay. Have your moment. I'll keep a discreet distance."

As THEY REACHED the door, Matt pushed it open and ushered her into the dimly lit area. They were in a narrow corridor that went upstairs to the stage in one direction, and toward the back entrance to the auditorium in the other. They were alone, though they could hear voices through the curtain at the top of the stairs, discussing the awards.

Gideon waited by the closed door.

To Matt's surprise, Rosie caught his hands and led him into the shadows near the stairs. "You wanted to talk to me?" she asked.

"You've looked like you had something to say all evening," he returned. He leaned a shoulder against the balusters, struggling to appear unaffected by her nearness when her curves in the glittering dress were driving him to distraction. "It better not be your blessings for Jenny and me."

"It isn't," she said quickly. "She and I talked this afternoon, and she told me you've been a good friend to her and that's all. And it still makes me crazy."

"Good." He wanted to relent, but not too soon. There was a little pride involved. Just a little. "I'm happy to know I've made you a fraction as crazy as you've made me."

She pursed her lips impatiently. "I was trying to tell

you that I'd have understood if you had had a relationship with her. I know I was awful. I think I was still being Hal Erickson's daughter—needing validation, praise, support—instead of being your wife, who already had all those things from you. I'm sorry."

He stared at her, his spine melted by that admission. But fear rose in her eyes when emotion slowed his reply.

"When we got here," she went on, quickly, urgently, "I realized I was happy." He'd folded his arms and she placed her hands on them. "You gave me that. You came back full of forgiveness and hope and the wit I've missed so much while you've been gone, and I finally understand how much that means to me, and how much I want to be with you again."

"Rosie, please!" Carol said authoritatively from the top of the stairs. She must have returned from the other side of the stage.

Rosie's shoulders sagged at the lack of time to explain. "I'll see you after the show," she whispered, and turned to go up the stairs.

"Wait," Matt said. She stopped on the second stair. She turned to face him, her features lighted by an old-fashioned wall sconce. She looked ingenuously hopeful. "Come back here."

"We're ready to start!" Carol snapped at him.

His eyes never left Rosie as he swept her off the stair. "So are we," he said. "Give her a minute." Then he kissed her so that she would never doubt his feelings again.

"I haven't understood you," he said quietly, raising

his head to look into her eyes. "I haven't known what to do for you, but I've never stopped loving you—ever. What I want most in the world at this moment is to be your husband."

JOY EFFERVESCED in Rosie like shaken champagne. She threw her arms around him as the cork exploded and spewed happiness everywhere.

"That's one thing you won't have to ask Santa for," she said.

He kissed her again and lifted her onto the stair. "Go," he said. "I'll see you after the show. Gideon will be back here every minute, and I'll be right in front."

She went down a step to hug him again, then hurried and ran up the steps.

A frowning Carol handed her a red costume with a skimpy skirt trimmed in something white and fuzzy, white tights and a pair of fuzz-trimmed boots. She pointed her to a door that led to a dressing room the size of her mother's closet. And with less light.

Great, Rosie thought, changing into the costume. *I get the love of my life back at the same moment that I completely lose my dignity.*

When she left the changing room, Carol was giving Gideon grief about being where he didn't belong.

"He's with me," Rosie said, drawing him with her toward the wings where Hank waited, changed into his Santa costume.

"Well," Carol grumbled, "aren't *we* the little princess."

Rosie laughed with Gideon, then Hank took her hand and led her onstage.

Santa earned an enthusiastic round of applause, but Rosie, in her thigh-skimming skirt, received wolf whistles, cheers, even a shouted proposal.

Matt, sitting at the table in the front, blew her a kiss. She was so happy she'd have burst into song, completely confident she'd sound like Barbra Streisand.

But Santa was telling the audience how a Maple Hill mayor from the turn of the nineteenth century had created the award to honor citizens of Maple Hill who'd worked hard for their community.

Rosie went to a table holding four trophies and picked one up as Santa explained that the first award winner was a woman who had done more for Maple Hill than any three people combined. He went on with a list of accomplishments, and soon it was clear to everyone that Jackie Whitcomb was being honored.

Jackie hugged Santa, then Rosie. She gave a brief acceptance speech, then the next award winner was announced.

Rosie distributed the next three trophies, then took a bow with Santa and walked offstage. As the group congratulated themselves on a job well done and hurried back to the party, Rosie ran back to the small dressing area to change her clothes and find Matt.

She'd just stepped inside and was about to close the door when she realized she was not alone. Panic seized her when she saw Dennis Sorrento pressed into a corner, gesturing with a gun for her to close the door. He must have gotten in when Carol was harassing Gideon.

Gideon, she knew, stood just yards away, but Dennis wasn't visible to him from that vantage point.

"Close it!" Dennis mouthed, gesturing with the gun. He had dark circles under his eyes and looked vaguely unhinged.

She hesitated, considering her options. She did not want to be closed in the small space with the man who'd shot at her, then tried to burn down her shop, but if she called Gideon, *he* might be shot. He *was* her bodyguard, but he was her friend Prue's husband, and she knew what they'd both been through to get back together again—much as she and Matt had. She couldn't jeopardize their future for her own.

She was about to close the door when it was yanked out of her hands and she was flung out into the hall. Matt caught her and held her while Gideon faced down the gun.

"I saw her hesitate," Gideon said quietly to Dennis. "Come on now. You know you're not going to shoot me. We worked Career Day together at the high school in September. We served Thanksgiving dinner at the homeless shelter."

Dennis sank to the floor of the small room, still holding the gun on Gideon. "I just came to…talk," he said. His voice was high and unsteady. "I have to talk…to Rosie."

"I'm not going to let her near you until you put the gun down," Gideon said.

"No. I want to talk first."

"No. The gun first."

"I'll talk to him," Rosie said, Dennis's desperation scraping at her. She remembered feeling just the way he looked. She didn't know what had brought him to this, but she could empathize with the agony.

"No way." Matt pulled her back when she would have gone to Gideon.

"Rosie!" Dennis shouted for her.

"Put the gun down," Gideon said again, "and you can talk to her."

There was a moment of silence, then Gideon took a step into the room. Dennis handed him the gun and began to weep.

Matt freed her and she walked around Gideon to stand just inside the door. Matt remained nearby, but it was clear Dennis was no longer a threat to anyone.

"Dennis, why did you shoot at me?" Rosie asked gently.

Dennis put both hands to his face and began to sob. "I didn't shoot at you," he said. "I took the money, but I didn't shoot at you."

"What money?" she asked, sinking to her knees to talk to him. It was difficult to believe this was the same man who'd served so competently on the Industrial Growth Committee, who worked generously for the church, who'd been known to extend credit to many older customers of his drugstore who couldn't afford their medications.

He continued to weep.

"What money, Dennis?" Jim asked. Someone had apparently found him in the crowd and brought him backstage.

"Was it bribery money to bring in Tolliver?" Rosie asked.

Dennis nodded, both arms hanging limply on his drawn-up knees. "Your father made the deal with the president of the company before any of us even knew they wanted to relocate. He told me only that they wanted out of Boston, and sent me to talk to them about locating a plant in Maple Hill. What I didn't know then was that the owner of the land was a friend of Tolliver's president. He'd found a nesting pair of herons way back in the reeds and knew he'd need a clean environmental-impact statement to be able to sell the land to the plant. And your father knew how to move anything through.

"When I brought the idea back to the committee, he let me take the credit. That should have made me suspicious," he said with a sniff. He ground the heels of his hands into his eyes. "He was smart and savvy but he was seldom generous."

"How did you find out what he'd done?" Rosie prodded.

"One night," Dennis went on, his voice raspy, "when your father and I were the last to leave a com-mittee meeting, I was in front and saw someone break-ing into your father's car. I shouted for the guy to stop and wrestled with him for the briefcase I thought he was taking out of the car. As we fought over it, it opened and several bundles of money fell out."

Jim handed him a glass of water. He drank, choked, and handed it back with a polite thank-you. "Your father pulled me off the guy and had to explain about the bribe. Tolliver had promised to pay off the moment we got a yes vote from the committee—which we had that night. The guy was putting the briefcase *in*. Hal told me he'd give me half if I kept quiet, that he'd already paid for the environmental-impact statement. He said no one would ever know. I'd be able to remodel the soda fountain, maybe even open another store in Springfield if I cooperated."

The tension drained out of him with a sigh. His legs straightened and his arms fell limply.

"I'd never been dishonest," he said, seemingly still surprised he'd changed. "But I had a high-maintenance girlfriend. That was my first attempt to be bad." He laughed mirthlessly. Before that, my life was so… everyday. Nothing new, nothing…fun. Just loneliness. Until her. I didn't want to lose her."

"So you agreed?" Jim asked.

Dennis nodded. "I took a hundred thousand dollars." He sighed heavily, and then his composure fled as quickly as it had come. He now looked tortured. "Then I changed my mind, and told Hal we had to give the money back."

Rosie shook her head in confusion. "But I was at all those meetings," she said. "I always left with my father."

"Not this time," Dennis corrected. "You and Matt had gone to Springfield to buy baby furniture. You had car trouble and had to stay overnight."

She gasped, remembering that night.

Matt took Rosie's arm. "Let me do this," he said. "Go wait with your mom and I'll—"

"Her mom's right here," Sonny said from the doorway. She moved into the room to kneel beside Rosie. "We have to know, Matt. Go on, Dennis. What happened when you told him?"

Dennis shook his head, seeing something invisible to the rest of them. "He was furious at first, then he seemed to have a change of heart, said we should talk about it, and that he had a busy two days ahead, but if I wanted to meet him the next afternoon, we'd go fishing and talk about how to return the money so no one found out."

He smiled thinly at Rosie. "He and Jay and I went fishing all the time, remember? We'd go out to the middle of the lake, make a pot of coffee, and just sit quietly till we got a nibble."

She nodded.

"I was happy, relieved…" He looked up, his expression filled with self-pity. "And very, very stupid.

"My girlfriend and I had a fight about giving the money back, because she had big plans for it, so I was late getting back to the store, late getting all the prescriptions out, and late meeting Hal at the boat. I pulled into your driveway and ran around to the dock just in time to see Hal standing at the end of it, watching the boat motoring out to the middle of the lake. I didn't know until later that Jay had gotten home early and taken it. Then it exploded."

Sonny put both hands over her mouth, and Rosie sat back on her heels in horror, putting the scenario together before Dennis even said the words.

"At first I thought it was Hal's plan to get rid of me. That when I was late arriving, something must have distracted him and Jay got home and took out the boat without his knowledge, unaware that someone had rigged the boat to kill *me*. I imagined Hal was going to get into the boat with me, then jump out just before it blew and claim he'd been thrown or something. I thought Hal committed suicide afterward," Dennis said grimly, "because, however inadvertently, he'd killed Jay."

Rosie was afraid she'd die if that was the truth—that her father had killed her brother, and she was going to have to get her mother through this, explain it to Francie, find a way to live with the knowledge herself.

Matt got down between them, to put an arm around each of them.

"But you don't think that's what happened?" Jim asked.

Dennis shook his head. "No. Hal never saw me that night. I raced home and found my girlfriend packing my things. It was clear she thought I wasn't coming home. She was shocked to see me walk into the kitchen. I made her tell me what happened and told her I was calling the police. She suggested we make a deal. She wouldn't tell anyone I'd taken a bribe and failed everyone's faith in me if we kept the money and I said nothing about the accident."

"Dennis!" Rosie gasped.

"I know, I know." He covered his face. "But I was a Eucharistic minister at church, I'd served the city and my customers well with never a suggestion of impropriety. At that moment—when everything was going to hell around me—protecting that image, possibly for myself rather than for the community, seemed all important."

"So you stayed with her," Sonny asked tearfully, "after she killed my son?"

"No. I left her all the money and moved to Springfield. She knew I'd never tell, and I was sure she wouldn't. We had too much to lose. But I couldn't be with her anymore."

Rosie frowned at that. "So when the whole Tolliver business came up again, you wanted to stop it because you were afraid that when we contacted Tolliver again, it was likely to come up at some point that a bribe had already been paid two years ago and nothing had come of it?"

"No," he denied quickly. "I didn't care. I'll be relieved to go to jail and get it all out in the open. My conscience got the better of my need to protect my reputation." He was quiet a moment, then he said sadly, "I think *she* did it."

"Who is *she?*" Jim asked, helping Dennis to his feet.

Rosie was afraid they'd lost him. He'd retreated somewhere where the scenario was playing itself over in his mind and he was watching his own behavior with sad disapproval.

"Dennis," Jim prompted.

"She didn't like any of the things I liked," he said, smiling as he thought about that, his eyes unfocused. "She loved to go to the theater in Boston, to have dinner at Quincy Market. She loved weekend trips to the Jersey shore, skiing vacations and summers on Long Island. I always wanted to stay home to…" As he went on, explaining his love of the simple things, a horrible, terrifying truth was coming home to Rosie. She knew someone who loved Boston, the Jersey shore and Long Island. Someone who'd served in the army and could fire a rifle.

She turned to Matt and said on a panicky breath, "It's Sara!"

"What?"

"She was having an affair she wouldn't talk about two years ago, except to tell me that it was with an older man. She wanted to protect his reputation, so she wouldn't tell me his name. She said they always met out of town and went to wonderful places. Matt! It's Sara!"

"Oh my God."

"What?" Jim demanded. "Sara Ross?"

"Sara Ross," Dennis repeated, shaking his head, his eyes still unfocused. "I just called her and told her I was going to tell Rosie. She said…she was going to have to protect herself, but she can't anymore. 'Cause now you know."

"Stay with your mom, Rosie," Matt said, pushing his way through the small crowd collected in the doorway. He stopped in the hallway to use his cell phone.

Rosie caught his arm. "No, I'm coming with you!"

"Wait!" Jim ordered, turning Dennis over to an off-duty officer there for the dinner. "What are you talking about? I'm going to pick her up. What is it with you two that you think you're part of the police force?"

"You don't understand," Matt said urgently. "She's baby-sitting Chase! She knows Dennis was going to tell Rosie, and she has our nephew!" He listened an extra few seconds to his cell phone, then snapped it closed. "And Berger isn't answering." Matt left Jim in his wake as he ran for the door, Rosie right behind him.

"Whoa!" Gideon and Fox stopped them at the door to the parking lot. "Berger just called me," Gideon said. "The baby-sitter's on her way to the airport with Chase."

"How did she get by him?"

"She didn't," Gideon replied. "He's got a bullet in his leg, but he's following her. I know I can't stop you from going, but you're riding with us. Get in the back. Jim'll be right behind us."

"She wouldn't hurt him," Rosie said to Matt, trying to convince herself. "She's my friend. She wouldn't hurt him."

Matt said nothing, but she knew what he was thinking. *She killed your brother. Why would she stop at Chase if it meant she could get away?*

"The boat thing was an accident," she said. "She hadn't *meant* to kill Jay."

Right, was the mental reply. *She'd meant to kill your father and Dennis.*

Matt put a hand over hers, which was knotted in her lap. "Hank's right behind her. We'll get there in time."

"What if she gets away?" she asked, feeling as though she was going to dissolve, be rubbed out by her own fear. "How will we know where to find him? What about Christmas? What about his bike?"

That was a ridiculous concern under the circumstances, and she knew it. But it seemed important to her as she thought about sweet little Chase being kidnapped and used as a shield by a frenzied woman intent on escape at all costs. How many times had he told her that this Christmas was the most fun he'd ever had?

Gideon had Berger on the car's radio phone. They were half a mile from the airport when he said he was right behind her and she was turning into the parking lot. "I'll follow, but I'm not going to be very fast. Incidentally, she shot me with an Anschutz she got out of her car. I'll bet it's the same rifle Matt was shot with."

"We're less than a minute behind you," Gideon said. "And the police are right behind us."

The Maple Hill Airport was a small strip that could accommodate only private and commuter planes. There were two regular flights to Boston a week.

"There's no flight scheduled for Boston today," Matt said as Fox burned rubber into the parking lot. "When I flew in, it had to be on a Monday or Thursday."

"She doesn't fly a plane, does she, Rosie?" Gideon asked.

"Not to my knowledge. But then, it's clear I didn't really know her at all."

Matt was out of the car before it stopped.

"Damn it, Matt!" Gideon shouted after him, hurrying to follow.

Fox, turning off the engine, stopped Rosie from rushing after them. "You stay with me, Mrs. De-Marco," he said firmly. "There's no way I'm explaining to the boss that I let you get shot."

She yanked on her arm. "I'm going after my nephew!"

He was there to catch her hand as she pushed open her door. "We're going, but you're staying behind me. Or I'll put you in the trunk."

She wasted a precious moment trying to assess whether or not he meant that. Then he opened the trunk with the remote.

"Fine," she said. "I'll stay behind you."

CHAPTER EIGHTEEN

MATT AND GIDEON searched the hangars and found a pilot in the second to the last shelter working a rag over the nose of his little Cessna. Matt knew they had her. Who would be polishing a plane at eleven o'clock at night in the middle of December?

The squarely built man in coveralls looked oddly nervous for the casual job he performed.

"Evening," Matt said conversationally. "Taking off tonight?"

The man sent him a stiff smile. "Going home for Christmas."

"At this hour?"

"Just got off work."

Gideon, pretending interest in the airplane, looked it over.

"You taking passengers?" Matt asked.

The man's eyes registered a reaction. "No. No, just me." Then he angled his body and pointed toward the plane.

Matt nodded and made the same gesture to tell Gideon silently that their quarry was inside. Gideon nodded, pointing to himself, then to the back of the airplane.

Praying that he'd interpreted all that sign language correctly, Matt said, "Come on out, Sara. We've got you," as Gideon walked quietly around the plane.

The door opened and Sara leaped down, holding a gun. She held it on Matt and the pilot, then pointed it at Chase, now visible in the cockpit.

He looked frightened but calm.

"I knew you'd come," he said to Matt.

Matt winked at him, his heart in his throat. "Just stay very quiet," he advised. Then he turned his attention to Sara. "Dennis told us all about it. You know you can't escape. Even if you get away from here, you'll have to keep eluding the police. How long can you do that?"

"I've spent my whole life eluding boredom," she said, unnaturally calm as Jim came up beside him and several police cars, lights rotating, pulled up to the hangar. "What's a little more running?"

"Then, if you're determined to run, let Chase go."

She sighed as though boredom had caught up with her. "Men have always underestimated me. Do I look that stupid? I know Chase is going to get me safely out of here as well as I know that your bodyguard came with you. Where is he? Somewhere behind me? You might remind him that I have a gun on Chase."

Gideon, just where she thought he was, checked her proximity to the boy and put his gun down on the concrete.

"Thank you," she said cheerfully. "And fortunately for us, Mr. Baker here was working on his plane, and I persuaded him to fly us off somewhere exciting." She'd taken several steps in front of the door as she spoke, less concerned about Chase than she was about the growing group inside the hangar. Her smile grew a little tight.

Gideon inched closer at the same moment that she took a backward step toward the door. She pointed the gun at him. "Don't," she warned.

Matt saw Chase get on his knees on the seat and wondered what he was up to.

"You know about filing a flight plan and all that?" Matt said, trying to prevent her from going all the way back to the door. He had to keep her out of the plane. "I mean, Mr. Baker's going to have to do that before you can leave."

Now she looked impatient. "No, he won't," she said. "I'm sure not filing one is against somebody's regulations, but it's done all the time. You're not going to have any idea where I've gone."

"Sara, no!" Rosie pleaded, running up to Matt, trying to get past him to Sara. "Where's Chase?"

Matt pulled her back. "He's inside the plane. He's fine."

"I'm taking him with me," Sara said. "He'll have a good time."

"Sara, how can you do this?" Rosie pleaded. Sara stepped out of Gideon's reach again, moving toward Rosie, the gun now aimed at her.

"Oh, come on, Rosie," she said. "You're always such a Goody Two-shoes. I can do it because I've committed a crime for which I don't want to spend a lifetime in prison. God, didn't living with your father teach you anything?" She studied her a moment, then shook her head. "No, I guess not. I remember you telling me you knew he didn't like you, but you never understood why. Don't you get it still? You're good and he wasn't. It's as simple as that. And I'm a lot like he was. You're not very good at identifying bad people."

"I know you killed Jay," Rosie said. "I just don't know how."

Sara threatened Gideon with another look. "I am sorry about that. I never wanted to hurt you. At the time, all I wanted was to keep the money. I'd already scheduled my boob job and I wasn't giving it up for anybody. I'd have missed all of you with those shots the day of the wedding if Matt hadn't tried to protect you. I had no intention of hitting you. And I never intended the fire to hurt you. There were too many people around. I knew someone would notice."

"Nice of you," Rosie said. "But what about the boat?"

"Yes. Well. I was going for your father and Dennis. Dennis told me he was giving the money back and talking to Hal about it. You'll be horrified to know there's a Web site with clear instructions on how to make a hundred different bombs from easily acquired stuff. It didn't cost me anything, just the nineteen ninety-five for membership to the Web site. With a tennis ball and matches, I made a bomb and planted it in the recessed propane stove. When Jay and Dennis and your dad went fishing, they always went out to the middle of the lake and put on the coffee. I was sure they'd do that. Unfortunately, Jay was just as predictable by himself."

Rosie gasped. "Please, Sara—"

Sara shook her head. "You're not going to make me feel guilty for wanting to keep the money. It got me a lot of the things I've always wanted. I've worked every clerical job in town. You wouldn't believe what employers want of your time and effort for minimum wage! Well, I don't have to do that anymore. I'm not plain old flat-chested Sara." She gave Jim a quick, sad look. "I guess I didn't impress Detective Machado, but that's okay. I'm going to Europe to see if their men have livelier imaginations than American men."

Chase, still kneeling on the seat, stared at Matt, obviously trying to tell him something.

Matt returned a firm look that he hoped told the boy to be still.

But Chase silently insisted, his small hands on the door making an almost imperceptible movement with it.

Matt finally understood.

"Let Rosie have a word with Chase," Matt said, knowing that would drive Sara back to the door.

"Don't be ridic—" Sara began, and as she turned, the gun aimed at Chase to urge him back inside, the boy swung the door and hit her squarely in the head. She fell with a startled little gasp. Gideon caught her and pinned her to the concrete.

Matt stepped over them to pull Chase out of the plane. The boy's body was shaking.

"You did well, Motor Man," Matt praised, holding him tightly. "Are you okay?"

"Yeah. Just kinda scared. But I remembered that when Berger wouldn't let Aunt Rosie out of the car when she wanted to follow you, she hit him with the door."

Rosie had come to wrap her arms around them and Matt opened his to encompass her. "I'm not sure if you set a good or a bad example," he teased.

"He's safe," she said, squeezing both of them. "That's all I care about. Are you sure you're all right, Chase?"

"Yeah. I'm okay. But something weird happened to Sara. I was watching TV while she was on the phone, then she got my jacket and said we had to leave. I told her Berger was watching us so nothing bad would happen, but when he got out of the car and asked where she was going, she shot him!"

"He's going to be fine," Matt assured him. "He followed you here so he could let us know where she was taking you. Gideon called an ambulance and Berger's probably on his way to the hospital right now."

Chase leaned into him sleepily. "Can we go home?"

"How about if I send you home with Aunt Rosie, and I'll come as soon as I can?"

Chase sighed and wrapped his arms around Matt's neck. "I'll just wait for you."

Jim overheard and beckoned a uniformed officer, who'd just put Sara in a patrol car. "Officer Page will take you home," he said. "With so many of us here who were right on the spot we can do tonight's paperwork, and you can file your reports tomorrow."

He ruffled Chase's hair. "Good work, buddy. Someday you're going to make a great cop."

Sonny, Jenny and Toby Machado were waiting for Matt, Rosie and Chase when they got home. Sonny greeted them with tears barely held in check.

"Thank God you're all safe." She hugged Chase tightly, then took Rosie in her arms. "What a completely bizarre and hideous day!" she exclaimed. "But all's well that ends well. Come and sit by the fire. Jenny made cocoa and coffee."

Rosie held on to her an extra moment. "Are *you* okay, Mom? I know this was a hard day for you."

Sonny pulled her toward the fire. "I'm operating on a new principle. "For so long my world was backward—or, I thought it was the world, but it was just your father. He did what served him alone, and that can never turn out well. But because my life was tied to his, that was my experience.

"In spite of all the ugly things that have happened to us, we're all still here. Now I'm starting fresh, just like you and Matt are. It's Christmas. Everything's new and anything's possible."

Toby approached and looped an arm through hers.

"I, personally, live for a good breakfast. And I understand the Downtown Business Club is serving one tomorrow morning to celebrate late-night openings from now until Christmas. Will you all be my guests?"

They agreed on time and place, then Sonny walked Toby to his car. Jenny appeared with a tray of steaming cups, which she placed on the coffee table, then disappeared again. Matt, Rosie and Chase sat close together on the sofa in front of the fire.

"I was sure glad to see you, Uncle Matt," Chase said. He had both arms wrapped around one of Matt's and leaned his head against him. "I wish you didn't have to go to China."

Matt kissed the top of his head. "I was thinking," he said, "that we'd all go to China."

Chase sat up abruptly. "What do you mean?"

"I mean you, me, Aunt Rosie."

Rosie sat up, too, wondering what he was suggesting. "He has school." He couldn't be thinking what had begun to cross her mind ever since she'd been taking care of Chase, could he?

"We can get him out of it if we make sure he does his assignments," he argued. "And how many third-grade kids get to see China?"

Chase's eyes grew huge. "You *mean* it?"

"Yeah. What do you think?" Matt asked Rosie. "Francie would run the store for you, wouldn't she? We wouldn't go until after the holidays."

She was supposed to talk to Tolliver Textiles after the holidays, but because of what they'd learned, Tolliver was going to discuss the matter with their board and take legal action against the former president, so the project might be delayed. She smiled as she warmed to the idea. She couldn't be separated from him for two months, even if he was coming back to her. And she didn't want to be separated from Chase, either.

"I like it," she said, trying to read Matt's face.

"Me, too," Chase seconded. "But do you think Grandma will let me go?"

"I'm going to talk to her about that," Matt said.

Sonny returned to the room. "Talk to me about what?"

Matt explained the plan, meeting all her questions with solutions.

"I think it's a brilliant idea," Sonny said finally. "I've been thinking about a Caribbean cruise, and that sounds like the perfect time."

"You mean, cruise alone?" Rosie asked with a frown.

Sonny shook her head. "It's a seniors' cruise, actually. Addy and Adam Fortin are going. And so is Toby. They've been friends since Jim moved here."

"Really."

Rosie couldn't believe it when her mother blushed. "Well, I've only just met him, but I enjoyed his company and I think it'll be fun to get to know him better. And all my other friends, as well. Francie and Derek can house-sit for me. It's going to take her weeks to move the rest of her room out, anyway. Well—" she blew them a kiss "—put the lights out when you go up. And make sure the fire's out."

They sat together for another half hour, then Matt smothered the fire while Rosie took their dishes into the kitchen. Matt carried Chase, who couldn't keep his eyes open anymore, to his bedroom, and Rosie tucked him in.

In their bedroom, they turned into each other's arms. Rosie held Matt tightly, then leaned back to look into his face. "Are you thinking we should…adopt Chase?" she asked.

"I do," he replied. "I just wasn't sure if you were ready to talk about that yet."

"I am. I think it's a wonderful idea." She hugged him again, her world such a different place from the one she'd inhabited only a week ago. "He so enjoys being with us. And I think Mom would appreciate having her life back. She loves him, but she should have time to rediscover herself."

"Okay." He kissed her soundly. "You talk to your mom and we'll work it out."

"Do you want to try for another baby?" she asked breathlessly. She'd once been so sure the time would never come when she'd want to try again. Yet here it was, and she was full of hope.

"I would like that more than anything," he replied with such sincerity it brought tears to her eyes.

"It's agreed, then. We give each other Chase for Christmas. And whatever little DeMarco happens along."

FRIENDS CAME and went during Sonny's December twenty-third open house—Jim with matching MHPD sweatshirts for Matt, Rosie and Chase. His father brought blueberry cheesecake he'd had shipped from the restaurant in Fairhaven. Hank and Jackie and their children came, along with Gideon and Prue, Bob Berger—using a cane—and Fox Hitchman, who told them he'd been e-mailing Jenny, and she was coming back to Maple Hill for a week in the spring.

Francie and Derek arrived home from their honeymoon three days early and had brought back tropical shirts for everyone. They were happy to move into Bloombury Landing while everyone was away.

Chase was excited about being adopted, and Matt and Rosie hired Bart Megrath to handle it for them. Sonny, afraid Chase would think she'd somehow given him away, had tried to explain last night that he needed young parents.

He'd nodded sagely. "I know, Grandma," then he'd added with the diplomacy for which he was becoming famous, "I won't give you away as a grandma if you don't give me away as a grandson."

On Christmas Day, Matt wheeled into the living room the bike Chase had been watching for days. Chase was beside himself.

Matt pointed to the bag attached to the back of the bike. "Look in there," he said.

Chase dug into the pouch and removed a Polaroid photo and studied it closely. "What is it?" he asked.

Then looked up with a shocked smile. "Is it a *puppy?* I've never seen one that small."

"It's a yellow Labrador retriever. She's only five days old." Matt went to look over his shoulder. "She can't leave her mother yet, but when we get back from China, she'll be old enough to come home with us."

"Wow!" Chase could barely contain his excitement. He jumped up and town. "A bike *and* a puppy! I didn't know I'd been *that* good."

Then he grinned and pointed to the bow on his handlebars. "That's just what you said!" he told Matt. "Santa would just put a bow on it 'cause he couldn't wrap it."

Sonny took Matt's arm. "Come with me. Santa left one of your gifts in the garage, so you have to go to it."

Everyone trooped out to the garage, where a giant box was affixed with a big blue bow. "Nautilus" was printed on the box in large letters. Matt was shocked.

"Chase told me you wanted it," Rosie explained. "And if you're going to spend a lot of time at home, writing the story to go with your China pictures, you're going to need exercise. But it's from Mom because she didn't know what to get you, and I have something else for you."

Matt hugged Sonny, then Rosie. "Well, thanks for the team effort. I'm flattered that you picked up on that and went to so much trouble, and I'm delighted, even though it suggests I'm getting paunchy."

Rosie put an arm around him as they walked back

to the living room. "No, it doesn't," she disputed. "Just think of it as a preventative measure."

"I had other ideas for exercise," he whispered in her ear.

She laughed. "And we'll certainly implement those, as well. Let's see what else we've got for you under the tree."

"No, your present first." He reached under the tree for the little white box. "Chase and I found something special."

"Stars!" she exclaimed after she'd opened the gift, handing the bracelet to Matt to help her put it on. "It's beautiful! It must have cost your entire advance!"

He wanted to tell her it represented how he felt when they were together, but he didn't think he could say the words without choking up. She must have read the look in his eyes because, pulling Chase in with her, she leaned into Matt and said, her own eyes brimming with love, "Thank you. Both of you! I love it."

Sonny caught Chase's hand. "You want to help me in the kitchen?" she asked, winking at him.

He rolled his eyes at Matt as he let his grandma lead him away. "That means you guys are gonna kiss or something. But the mistletoe's way over there." He pointed.

Rosie touched the clip that held her ponytail in place. It sported a small red bow and a sprig of mistletoe. "I carry my own," she said.

The moment Sonny and Chase were out of sight, Rosie took a small silver box from the mantel and handed it to Matt.

Mystified, he removed the red bow from around it and opened it. Inside was a plastic stick with a bright pink patch visible in a tiny window. He leaned closer to read the small letters.

Rosie couldn't wait. "It's my EPT—early pregnancy test," she said. Her eyes looked just like the stars at her wrist. "We're pregnant!"

HARLEQUIN *Super*ROMANCE

COUNT ON A COP

Forgotten Son by Linda Warren
Superromance #1250
On sale January 2005

Texas Ranger Elijah Coltrane is the forgotten son—the one his father never acknowledged. Eli's half brothers have been trying to get close to him for years, but Eli has stubbornly resisted. That is, until he meets Caroline Whitten, the woman who changes his mind about what it means to be part of a family.

By the author of A *Baby by Christmas* (Superromance #1167).

The Chosen Child by Brenda Mott
Superromance #1257
On sale February 2005

Nikki's sister survived the horrible accident caused by a hit-and-run driver, but the baby she was carrying for Nikki and her husband wasn't so lucky. The baby had been a last hope for the childless couple. Devastated, Nikki and Cody struggle to get past their tragedy. If only Cody could give up his all-consuming vendetta to find the drunk responsible—and make him pay.

Available wherever Harlequin books are sold.

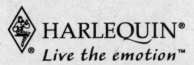

HARLEQUIN®
Live the emotion™

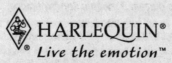

If you enjoyed what you just read,
then we've got an offer you can't resist!

Take 2 bestselling
love stories FREE!

Plus get a FREE surprise gift!

Clip this page and mail it to Harlequin Reader Service®

IN U.S.A.	IN CANADA
3010 Walden Ave.	P.O. Box 609
P.O. Box 1867	Fort Erie, Ontario
Buffalo, N.Y. 14240-1867	L2A 5X3

YES! Please send me 2 free Harlequin Superromance® novels and my free surprise gift. After receiving them, if I don't wish to receive anymore, I can return the shipping statement marked cancel. If I don't cancel, I will receive 6 brand-new novels every month, before they're available in stores. In the U.S.A., bill me at the bargain price of $4.69 plus 25¢ shipping and handling per book and applicable sales tax, if any*. In Canada, bill me at the bargain price of $5.24 plus 25¢ shipping and handling per book and applicable taxes**. That's the complete price, and a savings of at least 10% off the cover prices—what a great deal! I understand that accepting the 2 free books and gift places me under no obligation ever to buy any books. I can always return a shipment and cancel at any time. Even if I never buy another book from Harlequin, the 2 free books and gift are mine to keep forever.

135 HDN DZ7W
336 HDN DZ7X

Name	(PLEASE PRINT)	
Address	Apt.#	
City	State/Prov.	Zip/Postal Code

Not valid to current Harlequin Superromance® subscribers.

Want to try two free books from another series?
Call 1-800-873-8635 or visit www.morefreebooks.com.

* Terms and prices subject to change without notice. Sales tax applicable in N.Y.
** Canadian residents will be charged applicable provincial taxes and GST.
 All orders subject to approval. Offer limited to one per household.
 ® are registered trademarks owned and used by the trademark owner and or its licensee.

SUP04R   ©2004 Harlequin Enterprises Limited